# CLAN NOVEL:
# TOREADOR
## STEWART WIECK

|  |  |
|---|---|
| author | stewart wieck |
| cover artist | john van fleet |
| series editors | john h. steele and |
|  | stewart wieck |
| copyeditor | anna branscome |
| graphic designer | kathleen ryan |
| art director | richard thomas |

White Wolf Publishing
735 Park North Boulevard, Suite 128
Clarkston, GA 30021
www.white-wolf.com

First Edition: February 1999

10 9 8 7 6 5 4 3 2 1

Printed in Canada.

*Love and thanks to my parents*
*—my own Medici—*
*for never failing to encourage*
*my artistic aspirations.*

# TOREADOR

# part one:
# Leopold

Leopold sat with Michelle draped across his lap. They were both naked, though the cold of his workshop basement did not affect Leopold's body as it did hers. Though unconscious, Michelle reacted to the chill. The nipples of her small breasts were pointed and ripples of goose bumps appeared and disappeared across her long legs and up the small of her back to her slender neck.

He'd bitten her inner thigh, where the femoral artery began its descent down the length of her leg. She had feigned her passion at first, but she was slightly startled when he bit. He swallowed several mouthfuls of blood very quickly then, and her excitement became more authentic. Light-headed almost instantly, Michelle must have imagined Leopold very talented and eager to please.

After those first few mouthfuls of blood, though, Leopold was only interested in satiating himself. He fed infrequently because he felt awkward luring women to his basement for what he knew they assumed was sex despite the excuse of modeling for him. They always laughed at that, and then took it back a little when they saw that he really did have a workshop in the basement, but then laughed again when he asked that they take their clothes off.

It was even harder with men, because the man he might desire as a model wasn't necessarily gay, so rarely did he get them to his basement willingly. With them, it took some careful convincing, Kindred-style.

Like some of the girls—or perhaps they were women already, Leopold found that he was already losing the ability to guess the age of a human—Michelle simply took her clothes off and came at Leopold. So many of them just wanted a place to stay for a night. They were willing to work for the roof over their head, but the only work they knew was sex, and Leopold imagined they'd rather have it over sooner than later.

As he did with all the potential models he brought home, Leopold had picked up Michelle along Ponce before nearing his Piedmont Avenue home. Those that seemed disinclined to join him could always be nudged a bit. Leopold knew few of the potentially awesome powers possessed by some Kindred beyond this one, but he had no trouble convincing most mortals that he was harmless and friendly.

Michelle came along without such need to exert himself. She was a pretty girl who had obviously been on the streets just long enough to know how to use her good looks, but not long enough to understand that her good looks wouldn't last. There was something in that tarnished beauty that fit Leopold's mood.

When she sought his sexual attention immediately, Leopold regretted the lost opportunity to sculpt his vision of her, but he was not interested in imposing his will over another mortal that night. He accepted her desire and hopefully did something toward fulfilling it as well. At least she would have a safe roof this night.

He laughed a little at his idea of a safe house. He was keeping her safe by his standards, but Leopold doubted Michelle would characterize a place where she lost a couple of pints of blood to a fanged monster as safe.

Then he sobered and swallowed his laughter. Could this be what Kindred meant when they spoke of losing their humanity? Leopold had felt the Beast—that part of him that exulted when he stalked and killed and lost control of himself—but it was a simple matter to keep it at bay if he let his conscience be his guide.

But where had his conscience led him tonight? Laughter over draining the life blood from a world-weary soul like Michelle? Yes, he needed that fluid to live, but when had it become comical? Where was the sense of violation? Tragedy?

He knew there were many Kindred who regretted the loss of what they considered to be the human parts of themselves. Not the superficial losses, like breathing, or even the psychological ones like sunlight. But the essential qualities that defined humanity. The capacity to love, to dream, to empathize.

There were also plenty of Kindred who did not regret the loss, particulary the vile members of the Sabbat—those murderous and heinous vampires who cared little for Kindred other than themselves and to whom Kine were cattle indeed. Kindred of the Sabbat, and some of the Camarilla too, seemed to toss away carelessly a vital portion of themselves. Perhaps they considered such sentiments as mercy or love as the vestigial organs of mortal existence, but Leopold could not fathom the profound impact of such loss.

But perhaps he was on that very road.

Leopold inspected the wound he'd opened on Michelle's inner thigh. The ragged gash were he'd bitten her was right along the line molded in the skin by the elastic of her skimpy bikini underwear. That made him feel oddly queasy. Regardless, his work couldn't be left undone and especially when he could undo some of the harm, so he wet his tongue in his mouth and tentatively extended it toward the wound. As he licked it, tasting the blood of the injury once more, the rent skin mended. So well, in fact, that the traces of the elastic line were gone too.

Then Leopold regarded Michelle herself. She was paler now, and prettier for it. The ruddiness of the strains she placed upon her body with hard living and low-grade drugs was somewhat washed away. Her almost luminescent skin made her starved body diaphanous and the bruises from frequent injections less evident.

Hers was a beauty he could still capture and preserve. Many Kindred, especially Toreador, might think to cup their hands around her flame through the Embrace, transforming her into a Kindred as well. Leopold didn't wish to have such thoughts himself, and he was pleased that such ideas were still secondary to his first impulse: to immortalize her in stone.

Leopold gave this more thought as he continued to sit cross-legged on the floor with her body supported by his bare lap. Though he was tempted, it was too close to dawn, so even a *bozzetto* would be rushed and ill serve the purpose of sparking his memory later.

With one of his slender fingers, Leopold wiped a few strands of dirty hair from her face and gazed at her. He suddenly felt silly for all the attention he gave her. She was pretty, yes, but he was never one for pets, and on some level he needed to ingrain the reality of his still relatively new station in life: he was Kindred, a being that could only be considered superior to mortals.

With that, he stroked her hair again, but this time more as if Michelle were a sleeping puppy than a person.

It was a funny business, he thought, this means by which Kindred fed. He laughed at the dichotomy of his thought of the Kindred set apart and above humanity, while it was they who skulked about at night and lived a life akin to much earlier humans, like the ancient forefathers of ones such as Michelle who survived by hunting and gathering.

He carefully shimmied out from under Michelle, leaving her like a rag-doll on the floor. After gathering her clothing and tucking it under his arm, Leopold then stooped and gained hold of each of her armpits and partly dragged and partly carried her toward the stairs and then up into the first-floor kitchen.

The kitchen was a large room, as were all the rooms of the old and worn-out house. Unlike so many bachelor kitchens, though, this one was nearly spotless, though that was from complete disuse and not any sort of perfectionist attitude of Leopold's. For the sake of camouflage for house guests such as Michelle, he did keep a few dry goods such a peanut butter and cereal in the pantry and cupboards as well as a handful of imperishables like cheap beer and frozen pizzas in the refrigerator and freezer, respectively.

As dawn inched closer, Leopold could feel cold trembles in his heart, something as he thought it had felt when his pulse raced when he was yet mortal.

An icy hand clutching at him and urging him to seek shelter.

He hurried Michelle through the kitchen, down a hallway and toward a door he kept shut. He propped Michelle's naked and deadweight body against his thighs and knees and thus freed a hand to work the doorknob. Cool air rushed into the hallway as the door opened. It was the only room of the house that Leopold kept air-conditioned, and he did that only for the comfort of his guests. The expense was little enough and he reasoned that it helped maintain appearances.

The room was a bit of a mess. A bed with blankets and sheets half on and half off the bed. Many articles of men's and a few of women's clothing sprinkled about the floor but mainly gathered in one big pile by closet doors that folded open to the right and left. A long dresser of decent make with empty beer bottles and packed but not yet overflowing ashtrays.

Michelle's clothes fell to the floor and then Leopold hoisted her onto the bed and covered her with a sheet and a blanket. He adjusted the wall unit air-conditioner—the house was too old for central air—and then opened the closet. A small safe was bolted to the floor beneath the draping shadows of shirts and pants on hangers.

Leopold worked the dial and promptly opened the safe. He withdrew a few items, closed the safe and the closet doors and walked to the dresser in order to complete his camouflage.

He spread the items across the wood surface in a somewhat random fashion. Twelve dollars in a five and seven ones. A film of cocaine powder and a nose straw. And the *coup de grâce*: a small bag with several draws of coke still in it. This he placed underneath an old issue of *Time* magazine so it seemed overlooked.

Almost without fail, the desperate women he brought to his house would grab the cash and the coke and flee the premises before the man she didn't remember returned to catch her or perhaps desire intercourse again. Such a small amount of coke was inexpensive enough, but it was an item of great psychological value that allowed a woman to feel it was she who had come out better for the evening. Plus, the coke explained the headache and weakness they would have after losing a fair amount of blood.

Leopold closed the door behind him and locked the front and rear doors of the house before descending again to the basement. The basement door he bolted and barred from the inside. Only one guest had ever been so brave or greedy as to go to the great effort required to break down that door. She had taken a few small sculptures, but Leopold regained them three nights later when he fed a little more deeply than usual. Even then, she had not troubled to tamper with the root cellar wherein Leopold spent his days.

Dawn was less than a half hour away, and Leopold didn't wish to risk the slightest exposure, so he retired to that root cellar. The ancient doors were of heavy and practically unbreakable oak. When he'd moved into the house, Leopold had removed and reversed the doors so the heavy bar to hold them shut was on the inside. A badass Brujah could smash his way through them, and a Kine with a chainsaw could do the same, but he stayed clear of badasses, and women for whom a small bag of coke was worth overlooking a night of forgetfulness did not go to such trouble.

So, Leopold was safe, at least for the moment and the coming day.

Sunday, 20 June 1999, 5:00 AM
Boston Financial Corporation
Boston, Massachusetts

The dark-suited man nervously tapped at one of his cellular phones. It was the newest model, sleek and wafer-thin with sophisticated programming options that allowed Benito Giovanni to perform any number of acts of amazing communications wizardry.

His insistent tapping finally proved too much for the light object and it sprung out of position. Benito's brow furled even more deeply and his intense, angry eyes bore upon the black device. He straightened it and with a few deft moves realigned it with the other two cellular phones atop his massive, antique red cherry desk.

Benito greatly preferred things to be structured and dependable, but something was definitely amiss.

His face relaxed a bit as he gazed about his orderly office. The ivory decorations on the desk were almost fluorescent in the darkness. The perfectly polished and meticulously organized stands of oriental weapons cast strange shadows on the tables to either side of the enormous leather couch. Each end table held a set of matching katana and wakizashi, and the pommels of all four weapons pointed toward the couch. Above the couch, two original Chagalls hung in frames painstakingly aligned at the height of the third that hung behind Benito and between the absolutely spotless windows that overlooked the Back Bay of Boston.

His black suit was pinstriped with blue, and though it was almost dawn, his tie was still wrinkle-free and wound tight about his neck. Diamond-studded cuff links were positioned to be perfect mirror images of one another, and fabulous rings of white gold and diamonds were bound around each ring finger.

Benito was clearly of Italian extraction, and the fullness of such ethnic traits as his Mediterranean skin and black hair and handsome face made it probable that he was not too many American generations removed from his homeland. He wore a slight mustache that helped fill his narrow face, and his hands were clasped with index fingers projecting and pressed together against that line of hair above his lip. He rubbed them slowly back and forth, while his dark eyes glittered in the greenish light of the desk's bankers' lamp. Though in repose now, he looked like a predator, a man who was thoughtful in his stalking patience yet could ambush with an extreme extroversion if the situation required it.

He was also a powerful and wealthy man, and the office could have been that of any such man pondering unwanted and mysterious intrusions. But Benito was no ordinary man. Beyond the fact that the blood of the wealthiest family on Earth once flowed in his veins. Beyond the fact that he had risen toward the top of his family. Beyond the fact that this family was virtually unknown to the world at large. Beyond the fact that he worked only at night. And beyond the fact that he feasted on the blood of any secretary who could not properly maintain the attitude of his office while he slept during the day.

For beyond all these facts, and likely others of note too, Benito Giovanni, like some of his family, his clan if you would, was Kindred. Vampire. And few trifled with Benito's rare mixture of substantial intelligence, devilish good looks, ungodly wealth, raw physical power, and eternal existence. Of course, there were other Kindred from other clans that possessed many of these advantages as well, but they were not Giovanni, and to Benito's thinking at least, that meant a lot. Benito managed a grim grin, for even he—a Giovanni himself—was sometimes scared of his family. Even he, a powerful member of the family, suspected only slightly the extent of the power and influence the Giovanni wielded.

But someone taunted him tonight, and had in fact been doing so all night long. Now that dawn approached, Benito continued to wait patiently but with rising ire to see if more information would be revealed. Yes, someone was clearly stupid or immensely confident because the phone rang yet again.

Benito pulled snug the black leather gloves he wore. They were pinstriped like his suit, and he made certain the lines were acceptably oriented before picking up the phone after its fourth ring.

"Hello." It was not a question like the previous three times he'd answered. Instead, it was familiar, but with a slight bite of anger, for Benito wished the caller to believe he now knew the caller's identity.

There was silence on the other end. Benito did not speak again, waiting silently to press a potential advantage, but also so that he might detect the slightest revealing noise.

The connection clicked dead. Benito knew he'd gained ground. If there was another call—and perhaps there would not be since dawn was so near, though he guessed there would be at least one more so the caller might reassert his earlier dominance—

then Benito believed he could crack the fool. After all, Benito had reached his present position largely because he was a skillful negotiator. He didn't know law particularly well, though that knowledge would come in the centuries ahead, and he didn't have a grasp of the subtleties of international economics, but he did know people. Not what gave them joy. Not what they might want. But what they did not want. What they feared. And once Benito knew that, he cracked them, often seeing them capitulate without the need to raise his voice or make subtle indirect threats.

He knew, of course, that the calls were on purpose. A misdialing caller might have inadvertently tapped the numbers for his left-most phone, with its 212 New York City area code, or his right-most phone with its 310 Los Angeles area code, or even his wireless desk phone with its 617 Boston area code. But the **# area code existed only for use by the Giovanni family, and that was the prefix of his central cellular. It was his most important communications device, for it put him in immediate touch with other members of his family, and they would know the call an important one if it required the use of **#.

Regardless, he turned off the other two cellulars. The ring of the **# phone was singular in its tone, so there was virtually no chance Benito was mistaking the ring of another phone for it, but this was becoming worrisome, so he took no chances.

A fourth time cinched it. This was a provocation. The first time was odd, but perhaps the caller was suddenly detained and delayed his call. The second could have been the call-back that was likewise delayed, though it still aroused Benito's suspicions.

The third hang-up was frustrating, but no one on the other end only worried Benito that a family member was in trouble and could spare but a moment at odd intervals to make a call. The fourth call, though, had revealed it as a game. The delay before disconnection was too great, so Benito began to tabulate possible responsible parties.

No Giovanni would have such lack of respect for this secret area code to play games on an **# line, but Benito did not know who else might possess the secret. Of course, there could be scores of others who did.

Who among these individuals, though, would call Benito thus? A mage, perhaps a member of the Technocracy? An ancient Kindred? Of those who might possess the secret, Benito could only imagine a stinking Nosferatu playing such games. Those vile sewer rats collected more information than they could profitably use.

None of his mortal enemies could have possibly managed to crack the security precautions that protected his phone and its communicating bandwidth from unwanted intrusion. No one accidentally overheard conversation over the **# line, and Benito knew the axiom most appreciated by Madelaine Giovanni, a famed assassin the family called upon when its need was greatest: whatever cannot occur through happenstance will not occur through intent.

Most certainly, no one accidentally misdialed the **# area code. There were no triple-digit area codes, and the only double-digit beginning that was close on a key pad was the 77 of 770 for Georgia.

Nevertheless, the phone rang again.

Benito quickly considered his best strategy. Feigning knowledge had rattled his opponent earlier, so he stuck to that tactic.

"Why now?" he asked of the unknown party. He spoke with some insistence but also with a hint of concern or befuddlement so the caller might perceive an advantage and strike for it.

There was silence, but the connection remained.

*Something more*, Benito thought. *He or she needs some bit more of evidence that I've seen through this charade.* He wanted to press the game to the next stage, beyond the bullying that seemed to give his assailant pleasure, but he might also dramatically weaken his position if his blind guessing revealed a complete lack of credible suspicions.

Therefore, after a moment, Benito added, "I've been waiting. Why now?"

The voice from the other end was surprisingly clear, as if the call was from the next room and not from Chicago, though it was foolish for Benito to imagine his foe was still there and not in hiding. It was this clarity, though, that somehow kept Benito from panicking, or at least from revealing any panic in his voice. If the voice from the past had been muffled and revealed the speaker's identity to Benito over the course of seconds instead of an instant, then he suspected the surprise and fear would have shown.

There was a chuckle first. "How could you know it was me? If only you'd seen through things so well a couple of years ago, Benito."

Benito said, "You used subtlety then. Now without shame you reveal your bullying nature." It was a quick quip of a response, and thank goodness words came easily to him, for he'd have otherwise been lost.

Without further banter, the Kindred on the other end of the line said something more before disconnecting. Benito allowed the phone to clatter from his hand onto the desk. His sense of despair and helplessness was such that several minutes passed before he straightened it and the others which it disturbed as well.

After that first hesitation, though, Benito reacted calmly and thoroughly. First, he buzzed his present secretary, Ms. Windham.

"Sir?"

"Cancel my plans for Atlanta but do not reopen that time for appointments."

"Of course, sir."

Second, he buzzed the head of building security, his strong-willed and militant cousin, Michael Giovanni.

"With particular attention to my own suite, double building security until I can speak with you about more specific and applicable plans."

"Is there immediate danger, Benito?"

Benito exhaled for the effect of impatience. "No, or there would be no reason to save a discussion of specifics for later." Then he hung up.

Benito reclined in his plush leather chair and was momentarily aware of the unconscious gesture to bring his index fingertips to his mustache again. He'd best be vigilant for all such events normally invisible to him.

Then he spun the chair around and looked at and into the Chagall hanging behind him.

**Sunday, 20 June 1999, 10:55 PM**
**East Ponce de Leon Avenue**
**Atlanta, Georgia**

Tireless step by tireless stride, immortal day by immortal night, Leopold incrementally left behind a life like that of the Kine surrounding him. And that was a shame, for he felt more at home among these shadows of his old life than he did inside the halls of Elysium or within the edicts of the Masquerade, which were only two of the trappings of his life among the Kindred of Atlanta.

Yes, he felt more a part of the world, more connected to its vibrancy, its core, when among mortals and not among his vampire brethren. And that was foolish, because better than any other stalking the shadows of this street, Leopold knew these mortals were damn ignorant and completely out of touch with the greatest—or at least the most relevant—truths of the world.

It made him quiver with loathing and hate and resentment, for he knew that he was only incompletely informed himself, yet he comprehended mysteries these people could not begin to suspect, let alone fathom. Yes, the Kine yet wielded great power, for otherwise the Camarilla would not order the vampires belonging to that group to maintain the Masquerade, to make certain the first priority of nightly Kindred life was to continue to hide themselves from prying mortal eyes. The Inquisition had taught the Kindred well. But the essence of mortals was weakness and vulnerability.

Perhaps that's what drew him to them. Especially

these people, the night people of East Ponce. They were on the fringes of human society just as Leopold remained on the fringes of vampiric society. They were the artists, the poor, the mad, the whores. And for his part, Leopold frankly felt he knew too much already, so participation in the events of Kindred society would only increase the uneasiness he felt among his own kind. He did not want to know that Prince Benison controlled the police department so no man or woman or child was safe even from their mortal kin if he desired it to be so, or that Victoria Ash could with a thought so thoroughly pillory an artist's lifetime work that he might be forgotten even on the cusp of being recognized and perhaps immortalized.

These were some of the basic and everyday truths of a world where creatures who lived by night also ruled the day.

Leopold shuddered, but the terribly muggy and humid summer weather did not encourage it. Thank goodness the solstice was but two days away. That would mark the height of summer, but its decline as well.

He stopped walking and leaned against a streetlight post, his back to the roar of too-fast cars cruising in and out of this seductive area of the city, his feet pointed toward the center of the sidewalk.

This heart of East Ponce, north of Little Five Points, stretching eastward from Peachtree Street and Atlanta's downtown, was a congested area. The streets were not wide, though four lanes managed somehow to run through the area. The sidestreets were packed with small houses with patches of green that passed for lawns. And Ponce itself was a jumble of the everyday and the unusual or even unique. Recognizable fast food joints rubbed shoulders with eclectic coffee houses. Just east of Leopold was the neon-lit corner of Ponce and Highland, where the old Plaza Theatre still showed small-run movies and where an ancient 24-hour diner still bustled.

Leopold felt that he should light a cigarette, but he'd quit that when he stopped breathing. It was too much effort to draw and circulate breath, and without that, the fortifying burn in the lungs was missing, and so there seemed little point to smoking.

He watched the people pass by. Many didn't look at him at all. Others glared at him and flared their nostrils in an effort to provoke him. But no one made a special effort to avoid him, as he did not appear threatening.

Except for the clean T-shirt and khaki painter's pants he wore, Leopold might well have passed for a permanent resident of the street. His hair was an unkempt mop of black that looked like it was meant to be short but had grown for six months or more without any care. His hands were filthy with dirt, which was caked under his nails and between the base of his fingers too. He had an unhappy face, like a man who was looking for something but never expected to find it. His mouth was small, and his lips pursed. Though he was quite slender and of average height and build, his face seemed heavy, almost sagging. His eyelids drooped and his too-ample cheeks seemed to contain cotton wads used to calm a toothache.

Mostly, he was just tired. He'd been disappointed to discover that vampires felt fatigue as acutely as mortals.

As he watched the people, he noted that while he felt comfortable among them, he still did not interact with them, except when his various needs of sculpting or dining demanded it. He wondered why. Perhaps it was genetic—or at least the Kindred equivalent of genetics, blood ties, that made him seek human company at all. It was a Kindred's blood—not an egg or sperm—that provided his new genetic imprint, but did that overwrite what he'd been as a man?

Leopold was Toreador, which meant, of course, that his sire—whoever she was, whatever her mortal life had been and no matter how different that was from his own—was Toreador too. And her sire, and the sire before that and before that, back however many generations it required to reach the so-called third, the legendary Antediluvian who founded the Toreador bloodline in some ancient time. This founder was only two generations removed from the hypothetical original vampire, to whom Leopold had read references as "Caine," the man Western mythology reviled as the first murderer.

Leopold could come to no conclusions about whether it was Kindred blood that prompted him to act certain ways, or whether it was a clan's predilection for a certain type of human—like the Toreador's choice of artists, or the Malkavians' tendency to Embrace the insane—that created such a likeness among Kindred of a specific clan. Did his Kindred blood redefine him, or did he fit the Toreador mold even before his Embrace?

Amidst the furor of Leopold's thinking, a thick evening mist of rain rolled in and left the streets and outdoor denizens of Atlanta covered by a film of water. Then cool air rolled in on the heels of the short midsummer storm, and this refreshed Leopold so that he did not mind the dampness.

In fact, the reflections of the street lights in the oil-streaked lanes of East Ponce provided Leopold with a less personal focus for his thoughts. He stared into the wavering ghost images and concluded that he still carried a human program within him—the DNA and nurture his mortal parents had provided—but that was now supported, not supplanted, by his vampiric blood.

Then he forced himself to abandon this line of thought. To some extent, it was a moot issue with him, or at least he couldn't very well look to himself as an example of any side of this internal debate. Perhaps if he felt he knew himself better. Perhaps if he felt the past he remembered was indeed his own. He needed his past. Then, and only then, would he be able to determine more about his future.

Although, Leopold wondered if all Kindred lost touch with their past selves and became a new being at Embrace. If so, then surely he was a mortal reborn in the fire of blood. It was a thought that scared him, for the work of an artist could come only from experience, and without a past he had little to draw upon.

Leopold had fed well on Michelle last night, so there was no need to worry about food tonight. He was glad. It was time he seriously addressed the matter of his sketchy past. It was time for a test or experiment of sorts.

The walk back to his home on Piedmont Avenue was not formidable, but he didn't wish to cover such a distance on foot twice in one evening, especially now that he was resolved upon his investigations. A phone call gained him a cab in little time, so Leopold gazed upon the hot and humid streets of his city from the backseat.

Sunday, 20 June 1999, 11:38 PM
Piedmont Avenue
Atlanta, Georgia

The marble just didn't seem to live beneath his fingers when he tried to sculpt a Kindred. He couldn't say why, exactly. Leopold wondered if this block regarding sculpting Kindred had something to do with the past he could not clearly recall. He remembered "a" past, but he doubted it was truly his own. A neophyte in the complex scheming of the other vampires he called Kindred only because that was the civilized way to refer to a fellow vampire, Leopold now understood that some Kindred could as easily tamper with memories as he could with emotions, so he did not trust the odd past he thought his own.

Foremost, it was too pat, too storybook—an artist willing to sacrifice anything for his work, he apparently ran away from parents who expected him to assume the family warehousing business, and instead scraped together a living in New York City. He barely found the time to pursue his craft amidst the problems of earning money for meager supplies of room and board, fighting the cockroaches away from both of the former, and refusing more chances to sell out than he could even falsely remember.

Then the break for which every such authentic artist dreams: a benefactor, a modern-day Medici. Someone, anyone, with great wealth, who sees the heart of the artist's work and recognizes the greatness therein, and beyond that is humbled by it. Someone who realizes how empty their lives of wealth-attainment have been and fervently feel that in the work of the artist they have discovered is the purpose that will redeem their lives.

In Leopold's case, this benefactor was a gorgeous woman who offered more than just her wealth. Hers was a voluptuous and pristine form that could have inspired even a mediocre sculptor to great heights of prowess, let alone an artist who actually possessed some talent. After six months as the beneficiary of her wealth and posing, Leopold finally awakened to the fact that she had other designs for him as well. Unfortunately, those designs were not sex. They involved his entrance to the ranks of the undead.

One night—for she only posed for him at night, of course—after hours and hours of intense work, she stepped down from her platform and confidently approached her sculptor. Leopold had made some benign remark about how her lovely form deserved to be immortalized in marble, and that was when she approached. As her fangs flared and she drew Leopold toward her, she said, "My flesh shall endure longer than any marble."

The next snippet of Leopold's memory recalled his face being pressed amidst her bare breasts, where he partook deeply of a vertical crimson band that ran along her sternum. Then the waters of memory muddled, and he recollected very unclearly nights of flight and pain that ended in her death and his deposit in Atlanta.

Vampires might have vast powers, but they sure were clichéd storytellers. Or maybe Leopold had in fact lived a storybook mortal life. For some reason, though, he simply doubted that, or at least his subsconscious mind doubted it and gave him a funny feeling whenever he contemplated the story.

So Leopold was attempting to reconstruct his true past, although he had compiled only three details thus far: first, the hollow ring of his supposed past; second, the fact that he could not recall questioning his past until about two years ago, and finally, his inability to sculpt anyone he knew was a Kindred. It was this final matter that most concerned him, and he'd conducted a few experiments to investigate the matter. Namely, he'd asked his friend Sarah, another Toreador neonate who had been new to Atlanta but subsequently succumbed to the Blood Curse, to set up some blind sittings for him. Specifically, he did not wish to be told whether or not the sitter was Kindred. And what had happened? Well, nothing, but that was the point. Half of the sitters had been Kindred. When he did not know their nature, Leopold had little trouble manifesting their likeness in clay. One of the sitters who was unable to be discreet about his nature so shook Leopold that he thanked the Kindred but asked him to leave—an unfortunate incident, as that Kindred was Trevor, one of the Brujah street sergeants who now bore a grudge for the slight Leopold had leveled him.

Certainly, Leopold could imagine that his difficulty sculpting Kindred derived from his work with the beautiful Toreador (who had conveniently insisted on anonymity, he clearly recalled) who ultimately shattered his life by Embracing him and forcing him to save his life by devouring her blood. Leopold was certain even non-Freudian psychotherapists would relent on a dramatic cause-and-effect such as this case, but it didn't seem right to Leopold.

After all, he knew about that event, or thought he knew about it anyway, and the contemplation of it directly did not concern him. Yes, his memories of that time were terrible indeed, and there could presumably be something of the saga he was keeping from his conscious thoughts, something so heinous that the solitary event was stricken from his memory and now unconsciously caused his troubles.

However, he just didn't believe it. Mostly, it was the lame story of the starving artist that did it. Leopold knew that he did fit that archetype. He was unkempt, lost long hours as though a fleeting moment while at work, did indeed starve for lack of blood when he sculpted instead of hunted. But he didn't think he could long overlook a beautiful woman who clearly wanted his hands to enact more carnal pleasures than fashioning her stone likeness.

For instance, though she probably thought him immune to her stunning good looks, Leopold had not overlooked the Toreador primogen of Atlanta, Victoria Ash. If anything, though, she gave some authority to his life story, for she was walking (not living) proof that such gorgeous creatures did exist. Another permutation of his new suspicions regarding his true past suggested that Victoria was his sire, and had concocted this simple cover story to hide that fact from him.

As soon as he imagined that, though, Leopold felt ashamed of such dull-headed paranoia as dominated conspiracy theorists. It's not as if those theorists were not right, for there were conspiracies aplenty, but they should stick to their best guesses, and not indulge any crazy suspicion that happened to catch their imagination. There were vampires behind many of the conspiracies, but not aliens or yetis or whatever silliness was presently in vogue. And just so,

Leopold stuck to his central theory of an entirely other life now unknown to him, and not any number of possibilities he could concoct to fit the evidence. The idea of a missing life just *seemed* right.

Besides, Leopold felt such a brand of skullduggerous activity did not become the ravishing primogen. Victoria seemed stronger than that, and not one to trifle with loose ends. He recognized her obvious beauty, but his gift as an artist was to see more deeply into people than that, and he believed that if Victoria was responsible for his past, then she would not hide him from it. She would simply kill him if he wasn't of use to her.

He suddenly realized that part of this foolishness with Victoria was some vestige of mortal lust. She was just so damned beautiful that he couldn't clear her from his mind. Frankly, it excited him to imagine that he was her childe, and he suspected he would harbor this crazy thought for some time.

In fact, while he had spoken with her on the phone recently, Leopold had never been alone with Victoria Ash, though she was the head of his clan in this city. There was no point. He did the work that seemed important to him and steered clear of politics. Politics got one killed. Better just to follow everyone's rules—the Prince's, the Anarchs', the Camarilla's—and no one would have reason to be hostile, or even offended. The chance that he might accidentally blunder was what convinced him not to attend even events like the Summer Solstice Ball tomorrow night at the High Museum of Art. Such a density of Kindred would surely include one who thought Leopold a perfect foil or dupe for some scheme, and the fewer that knew of him, the better.

That had not stopped him from accepting a commission from Victoria for the party when she called a week ago. She had very specific requests, but suggested that completing the work was doing clan work, so for the pride of the Toreador he was required to accept. He did, and workmen—ghouls, Leopold imagined, for they hefted his sculpture as two mortals could not—had arrived to take possession of the work last night.

He was actually proud of the piece, and wondered if he'd ever see it again. The fifty thousand dollars the ghouls paid him in consecutively numbered new one-hundred dollar bills would have to eliminate or at least alleviate that thought. He already owned this house that served as his workplace and his haven, but eventually he would need more money in order to survive safely as an immortal being. He made pains to cross no one, but one haven was not enough, and until now one was all he could afford.

He almost put his plan aside in order to look through recent papers for clues to good second homes, but for some reason the itch to attend to the matter of his past was severe. Such thoughts had been idle speculation in the past, but now he felt the need to get toward the heart of the matter.

However, this was in all likelihood pure foolishness, for unless there were greater motivations at work—and Leopold doubted he could figure so prominently in any truly grandiose plan—then his fantasy-like life story was probably true. It bored him to think that. Since the past was gone already, he wished for something more vital in it, something he could tap to create truly great art, not just the fine showpieces he could create when concentrating on technical merit, or the outlandish pieces that came when he let himself loose. He was after all a good sculptor, so that part of his possible past was not a charade, for such talent could not concocted, though Leopold knew that some Kindred were capable of patently amazing things. But who in history was the last sculptor to be concerned with plots that might change the world or affect lives beyond those of wealthy patrons or other poor artists dreaming of living as pathetic a life as most skilled but unexceptional artists experienced? Somebody from long ago, Leopold decided. Maybe Leonardo or Michelangelo. Not even the great Rodin shaped international events, or at least so he thought.

So, Leopold decided to engage in an experiment that he hoped would either dissuade him from his theory or recommend it even more strongly. It was his intention to sculpt the bust of his Toreador sire. She was gone, and the memories of her were limited, but there was yet a strong picture of her in his mind, and Leopold decided to see if he could sculpt her. If he could not, then the explanation he would have to accept was that the terrible pains she had inflicted upon him were indeed the reasons for his troubles, and consequently she must be real.

On the other hand, if he could sculpt her when he could sculpt no other Kindred, then he reasoned this would prove a conscious connection to the still unconscious knowledge that his lovely benefactor was not real at all. That is, he believed that if he could sculpt the one Kindred who was presumably the source of the block that prevented such work, then she must not be the real reason and that would be because his unconscious mind might know better than his conscious mind that she did not exist. It would be no different than the likenesses of Bela Lugosi as Dracula that he sculpted, since he knew Dracula did not exist, yet it was a vampire he managed to portray in clay.

He would still not know for certain, but such a result would give him the confidence to proceed with other possible experiments. Perhaps even to go so far as so seek out another—maybe even Victoria—to see what might be done to help him regain his former knowledge. Such a gross move would be dangerous, though, for what if the Kindred he sought for help was part of the charade perpetrated against him? What if it was Victoria, and he revealed even slight suspicions to her?

Leopold laughed to himself. At the worst, he supposed, he might find himself in another city, perhaps on another continent, but maybe the story of his life would be a better one.

And maybe the discovery that his remembered life was a charade would only ruin his life. Should he give up a storybook past in order to learn that the truth might be otherwise? If his sire was a farce, a fable invented by someone hiding something from him, then what trouble, what very possibly dangerous trouble, might he stir up with the return of his memory?

But Leopold was decided in his course of action. Art was about truth, he believed. Though his work of Kindred might never be for public consumption— as such might be considered a dangerous leak in the Masquerade—Leopold felt it might reveal some truth to some few among the Kindred who sought it as well.

But not if he couldn't sculpt those who would see his art, for such an absence would have a clear impact on how his message was broadcast and hence received. Sculptors from Rodin to Brancusi spoke about humans with Kine as the center of much of their work. Maybe there was a way to speak about vampires without Kindred in his work, but for his message to be honest, that method would have to come naturally and not be an impediment around which he constructed a method.

He finally exhaled a great breath and unrolled the cloth covering a large piece of clay he'd cut and covered with a wet towel earlier this night. He was anxious to get to work immediately, for although he was perhaps eternal so long as he fed on blood, his patience to achieve self-discovery was not likewise infinite.

The thought of blood made his stomach tighten, and his throat. He considered delaying his work to seek sustenance, but he resisted the possible procrastination and returned to gazing at the block of clay before him.

He stood and pushed the stool away so he might have freedom to pace about the pedestal upon which the clay rested. He placed his right hand on the clay and then walked clockwise about it. His strong fingers left four slight furrows in the medium, and these he lengthened through several revolutions by spiraling them higher as he continued clockwise.

He played thus for several moments—a cat toying with its prey. And just as suddenly as a cat realizing the game has breached the boundary into tedium, Leopold pivoted and attacked the clay. He was now a bird of prey, his fingertips pressed together like hawk talons as he struck the clay and withdrew a small piece of clay that he tossed to the floor outside the reach of his pacing feet.

Within a matter of ten flurried moments, the ungainly lump of clay was whittled down to a vaguely humanoid bust and Leopold was covered with dollops of the stuff. His fingers were shod in thick shells of grey, completely transforming them from implements seemingly capable of precise work to bludgeons presumably meant only for destructive endeavors. But then there was much that was destructive in sculpting, and Leopold believed in creation through annihilation, perhaps explaining why he was willing to destroy his current life if a new one was created in the process.

He felt himself letting go, though, which was always a good sign for his work. This was a feeling of separation from himself that he could not explain, and he could only describe it as an out-of-body experience wherein he imagined he sometimes looked down upon himself as he worked, though in such cases he had no conscious control over the work he did. Alternately, he sometimes faded completely and only when he grew desperately tired—or, now that he was a vampire, when dawn was near—would he wearily regain his senses and find a sculpture that was a stranger to him.

Invariably, though, this letting go resulted in better works—ones where technical concerns did not intrude and restrict him. It was also this letting go that in his youth had convinced him that he was a great artist and would eventually be recognized as such. The genius of greatness manifested in such odd ways, and he presumed this his eccentricity.

That hubris, however, is what in later years, more recent years, convinced him he would never achieve such greatness. Only when the artist was not aware of his own folly, his own freakishness, could greatness be realized. He realized then that he used this loss of control as an excuse to deserve greatness, instead of a whip with which to flog himself to greatness.

This time, he did at first feel like he floated over his studio. His reasoning was intact enough to be impressed with himself despite his lingering reservations about his talent. He saw a confident artist boldly striking marks into the surface of the clay model. Careful consideration seemed to occur instantly, for the work was steady and constant and there were no errors; at least there was no work that dissatisfied him, for no move was countermanded or covered up.

The form of a woman's face slowly gouged, carved and smoothed its way into existence. It would be a beautiful woman, Leopold understood, so long as the whole of her lived up to the sensuous stretch of the neck and the mischievous tilt of the head.

Then Leopold watched as the sculptor faltered. The rhythm of the work lost its 4/4-time magic and bumbled into a tragedy of inexpert improvisation. The sculptor even dropped his carving blade, and stood slack-jawed and dazed for a moment before retrieving it. Then it was as if an automaton were at work, as if the Leopold floating above the sculptor was the soul of the artist and not the artist's Muse. The sculptor worked methodically, inevitably detracting from the work by virtue of his attention to it, and in fact not adding to the work at all, because Leopold saw now that the sculptor was working in a loop of cutting, smoothing and replacing those same three areas of the bust.

Leopold was then certain that this was his unconscious block asserting itself, and this was without doubt the most demoralizing instance, for never had this fugue state failed to produce something which Leopold held in high personal regard. Even this state, the seat of his fervently desired genius, was incapable of success.

He felt doomed. And lost.

And he felt himself fading farther away, ever higher, though now it was escape, blessed escape.

It was the sensation of gradually losing focus on himself and the clay sculpture. Instead, he began to be aware of the entire studio, and he took it all in without the capacity to concentrate on any one aspect of it. He saw the pattern of the long tables along the walls and the portions of them that T-ed toward the main work space. He saw the boxes of bozzettos and unfinished works atop the tables along one wall, though he was unable to pick out any specific piece. And atop the other tables he could only sense the blacks and greys and whites of clay, stone and marble.

Even these items of the large work studio faded and he gleaned the periphery of his haven: the loosely mortared bricks of the walls of this basement, the warped and water-stained but resolutely sturdy wooden staircase to the ground floor up into which he felt himself drift, and the door to the dry and cool vegetable cellar that went deeper even than the basement and within which Leopold spent every daylight hour comatose on a firm mattress, feather pillows and down comforter.

From the vantage of his height, though, he felt for a moment that there was something deeper even than his root cellar. Something dark and formless and powerful. Then it was gone, but shapeless appendages still tickled his brain as he floated even higher.

He eventually encountered the ceiling that was the ground-level floor. In his present state, the ceiling was also a permeable barrier that separated waking from sleeping, and the blurring details of all he had sensed snowed to pure white in a brilliant flash that suddenly brought Leopold fully conscious again.

Sunday, 20 June 1999, 11:57 PM
An abandoned steel mill
Atlanta, Georgia


The motorcyclist shot over the dark streets of Atlanta. He chose to remain off the main north-south arteries of I-75 and I-85 that cut downtown Atlanta in twain. The better to dodge tails if there were abundant side streets to screech along, and with a virtual Blood Hunt declared on anyone remotely considered an Anarch, it was imperative that the Prince's minions not follow the courier to his destination.

He wove through the criss-crossing streets for which Atlanta is notorious and so only gradually made his way in the proper direction. Satisfied that no one tailed him, the courier made a final dash across a stretch of open ground toward a massive edifice of brick and steel.

He knew this was the time he would be most vulnerable, so he poured on the speed. The BMW motorcycle responded admirably, and the skilled driver edged the wheels around the numerous potholes and breaks in the road.

As he neared the facade—and that's all it was, as the bulk of the old steel mill was collapsed and left only this single proud wall—the courier took a final glance over his shoulder to make certain he was clear.

He was.

But then there was gunfire.

The thunder of large ammunition roared from the wall of brick and steel before him. The courier nearly laid the bike down on the broken pavement, the hard edges and potholes of which would surely have shredded him like a cheese grater.

When he recovered from the shock of being fired upon from his own side's position, the courier noted that the large-caliber weapons were firing into the sky over his head. First setting a course over the road that seemed stable for a moment, the courier craned his neck around and up. He couldn't hear them above the grinding of his own engine, but he could now see the three helicopters. One in the front appeared to be black and unmarked, and that was presumably the one that tailed him. The other two were closing rapidly from a distance, and they appeared to be police copters.

The courier cursed and then pumped the gas handle hard back to unleash all the might of his Bavarian motorcycle. The bike responded with a great burst of acceleration even though it had already been traveling at over 120 m.p.h. Not only was he likely to die for the sake of some fool message—no matter that it was deemed urgent—but he had also failed the most basic aspect of his duty: don't lead the enemy to the hideout.

Bullets suddenly sprayed around the courier like the patter of heavy rain. One of the bullets tore through his arm and lodged in his right thigh. He nearly spun out of control, but the ghoulish strength of his intact left arm was enough keep him in control, at least for the moment. The arm was almost worthless. He could still muster enough hand strength to manipulate the handlebar gas control, but there was no sturdiness in his elbow and the courier knew his ability to drive the motorcycle was severely impaired.

He glanced back again and saw there was a substantial gap between the lead helicopter and the two police ones. If he could maneuver himself into that crease, then he might live.

The courier slammed on his brakes. At the same moment, he laid the bike down on its right side and leapt off the saddle. He landed with both feet firmly planted on the top or left side of the bike and he surfed the road, his sole good arm maintaining its grip on the handlebars.

Sparks and pieces of the motorcycle flew as the courier struggled to maintain his balance as the bike careened over the potholed road. And then the helicopter whirled overhead, unable to check its speed as quickly as the motorcyclist. The courier could barely spare the time to watch the helicopter, but he did see it begin to slow as if the pilot thought to circle back for the kill. Then it sped forward.

Once the helicopter was past and committed to strafing the Anarchs' position in the gutted steel mill, the courier hefted the bike back up with a herculean tug of his left arm. His speed had reduced to perhaps only thirty miles per hour or so, but after he landed back in the saddle, the courier quickly accelerated beyond that meager pace. He fell in behind the lead copter, but ahead of the other two yet swooping in.

The bike was in sorry shape and it wanted to go to the right, but the courier tugged with his left arm to keep the wheel pointed straight ahead.

He watched as the black helicopter dove past the wall of brick and steel. Its forward guns demolished a section of the wall, and the courier saw the figure of one of his Kindred friends fall with the mass of debris.

The helicopter looped around to take another pass, and it was likely to be joined in its next attack by the two police vehicles.

Additionally, the courier was able to see the left-branching I-75 split from the downtown artery to his left, and a long line of streaking cars with flashing blue lights dotted the highway.

He cursed again and coaxed what speed he could from his damaged bike. He let the bike's rightward tendency assert itself and he circled around the wall to seek shelter behind it with his doomed comrades. He wondered briefly if it was any different facing Final Death than the mere mortal's death that stared him down. He might be a ghoul with Kindred blood in his veins, but he would still die in all the normal ways. How would the police handle his friends who wouldn't fall to a hail of gunfire?

It seemed to the courier that the Prince carelessly toyed with breaking the Masquerade by sending his police after the Anarchs.

So much passed through his mind in these final moments. The kinds of thoughts the courier had never had before, and would never have again.

Safe for a moment behind the walls and under a fragment of what might have been the second story's ceiling, the courier killed the motorcycle engine and hopped off the bike. His decimated right arm flopped at his side.

He saw Thelonious and hurried to the mighty Brujah. The man seemed unruffled in his fine business suit. He cradled a cell phone to his ear, but hung up just as the ghoul neared.

Thelonious looked too mild-mannered to be a Brujah, especially one so sought by the Prince that these hordes of police were called into the fray, but the young and congenial black man could be ferocious when required. In fact, he was one of the few individuals—Kindred or Kine—to face Prince Benison in battle and survive. Of course, the Prince survived too, or else the war between the Prince's elders and Thelonious's Anarchs would not be raging.

The ghoul said, "I'm sorry, master. I led them right to you. Once we beat them back or escape, I will submit to your punishment."

Thelonious seemed to not hear the ghoul at first, but then the Brujah said, "Don't be a fool, Thomas. This attack was underway before you arrived. They found us by some other means. A spy perhaps. One of us interested in the profoundly arrogant and demeaning society the Prince has established in our city."

"If that's so, then I'll kill the traitor."

"I've already taken care of that," Thelonious said, holding a bloody palm toward the courier. Then he continued, "As for the police, perhaps we can frighten them off, or at least buy ourselves a little time."

At that, Thelonious raised his hand. Though the ghoul could only catch brief views of the black helicopter through broken windows and holes in the building as it whirled toward the edifice again, he could see that it was making another approach.

The guns began to tear at the bricks again, and Thomas flinched. But then two great whistling noises sounded, and a pair of fiery streaks blazed through the air. One streak whistled out of sight, but the other intercepted the helicopter and a tremendous explosion shook the air and earth.

A cheer went up among the Anarchs, and Thomas saw that Thelonious smiled too.

"Let's see if that makes them think again," said the Brujah.

Indeed, the two police helicopters, which were also ready to make strafing runs, quickly gained altitude instead and shot high over the old steel mill.

The Brujah said, "Now's our chance."

Thelonious let loose a shattering whistle and he waved both his arms. The bulk of the Anarchs on the ramparts immediately abandoned their positions and climbed or jumped to the ground. A couple, however, remained for a moment longer. They readied another missile, and Thomas watched as one of Kindred, a tough Brujah named Trevor, leveled the weapon at the receding helicopters.

The vehicles didn't perform their escape quickly enough and the missile launched from high on the old wall shot directly at them. The missile quickly outpaced one of the helicopters, and the pilot was not a vet skilled in dogfighting, so it too was snuffed in a crackle and thump.

"Here," said Thelonious, drawing the ghoul's attention back to his leader.

When the ghoul turned, he saw that the Anarch leader was stripping off his clothes. The black skin of his magnificently sculpted body glistened in the moonlight. Then Thelonious thrust his forearm toward the courier's face.

"Take some blood. Without it that wound will be the death of you and you'll never survive the flight we're about to take."

The ghoul was astonished, but he did not delay. He grasped the Brujah's arms and thrust his greedy face full upon it. He knew he was fed on the authority of his leader, but he'd never actually tasted the blood of Thelonious, only his underlings. Therefore, the ghoul had never before tasted blood so fine, so aromatic, so full of life and power.

When the blood flooded into his body, the ghoul felt it go to work immediately. In an instant, it knitted his pulped arm and even restored some flexibility and strength. Kindred blood was amazing, he thought. Especially the blood of a Brujah primogen. Well a *former* Brujah primogen. In the wake of the Anarch revolt, the position was no longer official.

Suddenly, the delicious sustenance was gone. A dribble of blood slithered down the Brujah's arm, but the bleeding itself stopped as soon as the ghoul's mouth was removed.

Then Thelonious pushed the ghoul so that he started to jog and then run under cover of night. The entire pack of eight other Anarchs ranged behind the two of them. Five of those were Kindred, and three were ghouls like Thomas. Thelonious had promised the ghouls they would be Embraced as full vampires if this war was won.

As the ragged group ran across the debris-littered grounds of the old steel mill, Thelonious looked at Thomas and inquired, "Do you bring a message, or were you simply returning to HQ?"

Thomas could not so easily speak and run at such a demanding pace, but he managed to say, "I...do...have...a...message."

"Then give it to me," commanded the Brujah leader.

Thomas pulled a sealed envelope from his waist and thrust it clumsily toward Thelonious. The Brujah deftly grasped it and tore it open as they ran. How Thelonious then managed to read it while remaining cognizant of the terrain and maintaining his speed, Thomas didn't know, but it made him wish to become Kindred even more than ever.

"It's from Benjamin," the Brujah revealed.

Thomas was growing weary, but he felt the flush of the last of his leader's blood course through him, and he regained his breath. "Benjamin?" he asked.

"The Ventrue," explained Thelonious. Then the Brujah looked away as if revealing the content of the message only to a part of himself. "He says I should attend the party tomorrow night. Benison will be there…." His words trailed off, but his feet flew furiously and he stormed ahead of the others.

His voice echoed back to the group, "Meet at the next safehouse in two nights." Then the seemingly polished surface of his skin refused to reflect any more moonlight, and as he disappeared into the pitch black of the night, Thelonious wondered if Benjamin's price was too high. Why should the Brujah trade one Prince for another?

Leopold was instantly fully alert and conscious. This particular period of having let go was not marked by the confusion and sluggishness that sometimes greeted him when he reawakened.

He was momentarily confused by the shackles he imagined his hands were encased within, but he soon understood that his digits and palms were simply caked with dried clay. When he flexed his fingers with a slight bit of strength, the dried clay cracked and fell to the dusty floor in shards.

It was this dirty floor of his work area upon which Leopold reclined. His body was covered in the debris of many previous projects, as he was motivated to clean the space only when it accumulated in piles over which he might trip, and that meant once every six months or so.

He looked up at the ceiling, and for a moment imagined that he saw himself floating there. Now it would be the sculptor looking up at the Muse. All he saw, though, were the heavy wooden beams that had supported the ground-level floor for a hundred years and would do so for a hundred more. They appeared indomitable and immune to the passage of time. If only one of his sculptures—just one of them!—would stand up so well to the test of generations of Kindred and Kine.

When he focused his sight nearer the floor, Leopold found that he rested with his head near the pedestal upon which he'd worked the clay bust. A sense of failure still consumed him. And frustration. And foolishness too. How could he have truly imagined that his past held any odd surprises? Was this the dementia of eternal life that some Kindred claimed afflicted the minds of the elders? Leopold had not even scratched the surface of the mortal years allotted to some Kine, and already he was cracking. He imagined himself being served up as an example of the weak-willed Toreador—a poseur sculptor who could not even last four score and seven or whatever it was the Bible promised.

Though clear-headed and strong of limb, Leopold felt no motivation to move. His vantage from the floor provided him as much of a view of his clay bust as his remaining confidence allowed: a slight nose poked out over full and perhaps parted lips.

And there he remained for a good length of time, lost in thoughts that led to little and amounted to nothing. Finally, the grit of the floor and enough of a desire for some sustenance urged him to his feet.

He stood and trod slowly toward the wooden staircase. His hand clutching the railing, he took slow steps up. Then, just as his eyes were going to disappear from the basement over the threshold of the floor above, he looked back at the bust.

An astonishingly lovely woman stared back at him, her head tilted to one side and her neck stretched outward. This was not a piece lost halfway to completion. It was a realized work, something of beauty, and Leopold cracked his head on the ceiling as he started and raced back down the stairs and across his studio to stand before the bust.

The woman's shoulders were bare and slim and smooth, so he imagined her either naked or in a low-cut dress that a woman with such lovely features might favor. Bones easily made themselves known beneath the clay skin of the woman, but something in how the shoulders were arranged or held square indicated strength or at least confidence.

The face was lit by a slight smile, but it was the other woman's other features which gave dimension to this expression. This came mostly from the eyes, which seemed slightly Asian in their bent. There was amusement in them, though it was somewhat hidden within the shadow of their long shape and the fact that they were partially closed. The cheeks were full but tapered to a narrow chin. Above, a single lock of hair fell across her forehead. The remainder of the hair was more controlled, as it was short and slightly curly.

What Leopold failed to note, as he'd not even thought to look for them, or perhaps because he saw them so often now that they did not seem out of the ordinary, were the woman's fangs. They weren't obvious, but the slightly parted mouth revealed the narrow tips of both upper teeth.

That was out of ordinary, and Leopold steadied himself on the pedestal, leaning forward with both palms pressed on the surface that also supported the bust and his legs spread a long pace behind him as if he were about to be frisked by policemen. His head dropped between his arms and hung like a motionless pendulum from his torso.

The teeth not only meant that he had sculpted a Kindred, but it was the particular Kindred he sculpted that disturbed and excited him even though it was not the beauty from the Embrace he remembered.

He couldn't believe what he'd done, nor could he believe he hadn't recognized her immediately.

He raised his head and looked the woman squarely in her dark clay but lifelike eyes. This was Victoria Ash, primogen of Atlanta Toreador. Her lush, pre-Raphaelite sumptuousness was the epitome of beauty in Leopold's sculptor's eyes, though there was enough slenderness in her face to balance it and bring it closer to modern opinions of loveliness. The armless Venus held nothing over her as metaphor for timeless beauty.

He gazed at her for a long time, wondering what this told of his circumstances, his past. Perhaps it had nothing to do with the past, but was an augury of the future. Maybe Leopold would be doomed to know more of his future than his past. However, if Victoria was significant in his future, then Leopold decided he could forgive a lost past.

Then, Leopold slowly stepped away and gave himself the advantage of distance to look again and make certain. It just a moment though. The tapered face, the slightly oriental cast, graceful neck. It was definitely her.

Leopold stepped forward again and bent down a bit. Methodically, as the Toreador savored each moment, he pressed his lips fully against the clay of the bust and held the kiss as he diligently worked his tongue into the clay of Victoria's open and smiling mouth.

Monday, 21 June 1999, 2:02 AM
The Skyline Hotel
Atlanta, Georgia

Benjamin stood on the top floor of his downtown hotel overlooking the beautiful nighttime skyline of Atlanta. One of his dozens of dummy corporations or shell companies—or some combination thereof that even he couldn't precisely quote—owned the building, and this top floor was officially full of equipment and only partially completed because the company's funds ran low before its design could be finalized.

It's true that it was only partially completed, but that was because Benjamin preferred it that way. He could afford great luxury, and he indulged himself with it at many of his other havens, but when Benjamin wanted to think, he required more spartan furnishings. A computer on a desk. A small side table. A large map table with ten flat drawers to store documents. A trap door for a quick escape.

Benjamin gazed north of downtown, past the highrises. He wished he'd been watching when the missiles were launched. His perch would have afforded a fine view of the battle even though it took place two miles north of this haven. The Ventrue adjusted his glasses. It was a nervous habit from his years as a mortal. Otherwise, Benjamin appeared relaxed in his black and white crewneck shirt and black slacks. If not for the crossweaves of white in the shirt, Benjamin, a handsome black-skinned man, might have disappeared in the low light of the room. He would as soon disappear when in the midst of deep-thinking, but something about all black didn't appeal to the Ventrue. Too trendy. Too rebellious. And he was neither Toreador nor Brujah. He'd leave such things to them.

Except he did have to intrude in their matters tonight. At least in the business of the Brujah and whatever other clans might be represented in the group of Anarchs Thelonious led. Perhaps a Gangrel or two, but Benjamin's information pointed to a handful of Brujah and probably a couple of ghouls. And Thelonious, of course. It was a sad army, but the Blood Curse had reduced their ranks terribly, and Thelonious seemed against Embracing others simply to provide shock troops—a tactic preferred by the Sabbat, who cared little for the future of such troops.

No, the war Thelonious fought was a legitimate one, and the Brujah was too scrupulous to stoop to tactics that, if implemented, would risk a long-term victory to achieve a short-term one. Which meant that the Brujah's message must have a longer-term benefit that the Ventrue was presently overlooking.

Anyway, Benjamin was a little more pragmatic. He'd consider the shock troops if they would guarantee victory that would afterwards give the opportunity to more than make up for that wrong.

Of course, Benjamin's grudge against Atlanta's establishment was of a more personal nature, whereas Thelonious fought an ideological battle against Prince Benison. Benjamin fought for an ideology too, but he admitted to himself that the defeat of the Prince and his damned wife Eleanor—his bitch of a sire who would exert control over him if she thought he might never return to her of his own free will—dramatically affected the methods he might employ.

Did Thelonious understand the subtleties of the decision Benjamin was about to make?

The Ventrue walked away from the window and returned the map table. All the intelligence his agents had gathered the prior day was spread across the flat surface. Benjamin had read through it many hours ago and found little of interest.

His hand drifted to a single sheet of paper, which he picked up and read again. Upon it was written, "Now is the time to take steps to block Benison. I know your secret, Benjamin, and Benison could learn of it at tomorrow night's affair."

It was signed, "Thelonious."

The message had arrived via a motorcycle-riding courier about an hour ago. It was enclosed in the letterhead envelope of a non-existent contracting company, and the courier who delivered it had told the front desk it was a work order that should go the top floor. This strange request had naturally gained the attention of Benjamin's ghoul, August Riley, a sharp young woman who managed the hotel and used the blood he granted her to stay on her feet twenty-four hours a day. Benjamin had used to work so tirelessly too, but that was before he was Kindred and could not remain active in sunlight.

Benjamin now accepted that it could be to Thelonious's benefit to reveal the Ventrue's secret at the Summer Solstice party this coming night. Anything the Brujah could do to divert the Prince's attacks and attention might grant Thelonious time to regroup for possible counterattacks. But that still seemed awfully short-term. Still, short-term survival was a necessity for long-term victory.

Benjamin could indeed slow the Prince's pursuit of the Kindred rebels, for while Benison controlled the police force of the city, all of the judicial system was under Benjamin's sway. Any number of steps could be taken by Benjamin's Kine to shut down the attacks Benison was staging with his own puppets. Hell, even a search warrant denied here and there could buy Thelonious several days.

But did Benjamin dare such an action? There was no doubt that he did not care for the threat Thelonious leveled at him. Threat or not, Benjamin would have to do what was best for him.

What it really came down to, Benjamin concluded, was deciding the better pawn—or ally, if he choose to look at things that way—between Thelonious and Eleanor. Whichever way he chose—and he would have to consider the permutations for the remaining hours of darkness this night—Benjamin knew he could take no steps against the Prince before the party.

Benison would know immediately that it was Benjamin's interference that slowed his pursuit of the Anarchs, and the Ventrue reasoned there was no reason to create one's own trouble when others already had the ability to heap it upon you.

Monday, 21 June 1999, 3:18 AM
Piedmont Avenue
Atlanta, Georgia

It was the result Leopold feared the most: an answer. But one plagued with innumerable more questions.

His answer was only that he could indeed sculpt a Kindred, though it required him enter his fugue state, a process he had never been able to control. More than that, this instance of letting go seemed different than ones before it. He recalled the details of what he considered his astral projection with little clarity, but he did remember feeling that his mental block had defeated even this magical state of creation. Then, he had floated even higher until he'd faded back to consciousness.

Normally, his ghostly presence lingered an arm's reach above his working self. Perhaps, though, his Kindred nature was heightening this power of his, or perhaps his was a power with even greater range than he supposed. Perhaps it was potent enough that he could again imagine himself an artistic genius—a creator with enough madness and extreme behavior to qualify.

Whatever had happened and was happening, Leopold knew he needed more answers. His pursuit would be defeating the hydra, for where Kindred were concerned, every answer created two more questions, but perhaps he would stumble across an eventual truth that would let him begin to cauterize the bloody stumps before more mysteries could sprout.

The problem was that his friends were as few as

his enemies. He remained clear of politics in order to avoid creating enemies, but without an area of clout or control he could claim, other Kindred also had no reason to seek him as an ally. There were a handful of mortals he could turn to if desperate need arose—Rose Markowitz in particular, since he had saved her from the street and returned her to a life in art she presumably found infinitely more appealing—but there were no Kindred.

Unless Hannah might help him. He thought on that for a moment.

He remembered thinking of her mansion as he passed it last night. He thought of it as hers, though he guessed it was really the Atlanta chantry house of the Tremere, an extremely hierarchical clan that Leopold believed was bonded together by a common bloodline as well as common blood. That is, he'd heard that all neonates—newly created vampires—were required to drink the blood of all the elders of the clan.

Blood was a powerful force for Kindred, and not just because of its sustenance. After all, any substance that could transform a bloodless human into a Kindred held secrets as yet beyond Kine science. A mortal who drank Kindred blood became a ghoul. A Kindred who drank another Kindred's blood could become the latter's thrall. In fact, Leopold had heard stories of countless ways that the power of Kindred blood could be tapped, and at the heart of a majority of these stories were the Tremere, a clan rumored to be descended not from Caine but from a secret cabal of wizards who had transformed themselves in the Middle Ages.

Leopold shook his head in frustration. There were so many stories. Each likely untrue but carrying within it a kernel of truth. He would need eternal life in order to sort all of this out.

He thought of Hannah and how he was almost glad for his inability—at least at that time about a year ago—to sculpt Kindred. He had never encountered such a morose, unanimated and unengaging Kindred or human. Hannah struck Leopold as combining all the worst characteristics of a prudish Victorian, prissy schoolmistress, and dour Quaker. She was skinny to severity, expressionless to stupefaction, and eerie as a Salem witch who wanted to burn.

She would not have been an impossible subject to sculpt, but Leopold did not imagine she would be an entertaining one. Not that Leopold doubted her ability to sit for hours or even days—interrupted by daylight, of course—if the sculpting required it, but he doubted his ability to find anything within her to animate the soul of her depiction in clay or stone or marble.

But he had tried that evening she suddenly arrived in his workshop. Leopold recalled that he had been having some trouble with an uncooperative model, when suddenly the frustratingly twitchy girl screamed and pointed at a black-clad and hooded figure standing at the base of the stairs. Leopold almost screamed too, but Hannah promptly lowered her hood and Leopold recognized her from one of his very few social engagements among the Kindred.

"I understand that you cannot sculpt the likeness of a vampire," she said in a voice so uninflected that Leopold had to pick the words out of the mechanical hum that was the register of her voice.

The frightened Kine shrieked again, hurling her-self at Leopold and pleading for protection, but her voice gurgled to a halt and she collapsed to the floor with such suddenness that Leopold imagined that her bones must have liquefied.

"Yes, that's true," Leopold believed he'd said, as he crouched to the fallen woman and rolled her over. He brushed some debris from one of her breasts and off her stomach and propped her into a sitting posi-tion against a pedestal.

Leopold must have looked worried about the mortal, because Hannah remarked in passing that she would be fine and would be forever incapable of re-calling the ten seconds immediately prior to collapsing as well as the first ten seconds after awak-ening.

She'd warned that it was actually approximately ten seconds, and then she asked what Leopold might do to her in that time. From anyone else, the ques-tion might have been mischievous or even malefic, but Hannah did not crack the slightest grin or reveal the minutest twinkle of her eye. Leopold gained the impression that everything she did was calculated to draw a response and her presence could not be a vari-able in her experiments, so she remained constantly withdrawn and was present only to record the results.

Leopold didn't recall how he'd answered, but if he had it to do again, and his courage didn't fail him, then he would like to say something outrageous to see how Hannah would react. He shook his head. She would probably take any suggestion, no matter how grotesque or enlightened, with the same stoicism.

This impression of Hannah's methods was confirmed, at least in Leopold's mind, when she then requested that he sculpt her. Leopold protested and a bit testily snapped at her, "Unless you know Tremere magick that can break my block, then you're wasting your time."

She pretended not to hear him, and Leopold was grateful, not resentful, of the fact, for she was an elder vastly more powerful than he. He swallowed his tongue and inwardly berated himself for his foolish outburst.

Hannah had then seated herself in the chair in which the Kine woman had wiggled. Though an impossible subject, Hannah did at least sit still, though the absolute stillness was unnerving. Leopold was used to the Kindred's lack of breathing—though the rise and fall of a Kine chest was a rhythm by which he paced his work—but Hannah's frozen demeanor was eerie.

When the witch grabbed the mortal woman by the foot and dragged her toward the chair, Leopold shivered at the creepy sight. She hefted the naked Kine to her black-robed lap and held her still as well. "Start with the Kine and slowly include me in the sculpture," Hannah had instructed.

Leopold spent most of the night at it, and the Kine slowly revealed herself in his clay, but Hannah's image remained a crude outline without mirroring a single distinguishing characteristic.

Hannah let the torture end when she suddenly stood, toppling the human off her lap into a haphazard pile of pink flesh and jutting limbs. She then walked to the base of the stairs where Leopold had first seen her, and all this without a word before suggesting, "I brought no magic to break your block, but that does not mean that Tremere magic cannot assist you in the future."

Leopold tried to apologize for his failure, but a curt movement of Hannah's hand cut him off. "You have ten seconds," she said, pointing behind Leopold to the human.

Leopold glanced at the woman, then back to Hannah, but the Kindred was gone. The Toreador couldn't recall what he did with the eight seconds that remained to him after that. He chuckled to himself now as he understood that he may have forgotten, but Hannah probably had not.

That mysterious offer—if it was even that—from Hannah was all he had. He had no one else to turn to that he thought would be interested enough to listen to his predicament. He could go to his primogen, but that was Victoria and he would be embarrassed. He did not wish to reveal any of his thoughts regarding her. Besides, if she was involved in some deception, then it would be dangerous.

Not that any deal with Hannah would be anything other than a deal with the devil, but for some strange reason, she seemed to have a personal interest in Leopold, and if his visit could intrigue her for selfish reasons, then she might be motivated to take action that could potentially benefit Leopold too.

Leopold refused to fool himself into thinking Hannah might be cultivated as a friend. She was the type who simply did not have friends, or at least the friends she did have were known only to herself and not to those she marked with such favor. Her attitude was the same toward friend and foe, and in that she was both perfect and imperfect in the world of the Kindred. No one would ever be fooled by Hannah, for she seemed not to attempt deception, and while that removed a wide range of gamesmanship options from her arsenal, she also gained by this attitude. She was not shy about letting others know when their desires or goals aligned, as with Leopold.

The summer solstice was tomorrow, so the nights were short and it had been an exhausting evening, but there was still plenty of time to attempt to visit Hannah before dawn. Besides, the sooner she knew he hoped to see her, the sooner she might deign to do so.

Leopold didn't relish visiting the Tremere chantry, but he wanted to see Hannah before the party that would mark the night of the solstice, especially now that he believed he needed to attend the party. He would be careful and not stray from the piece he had donated, but whether he liked it or not—and at this moment he was definitely troubled by the future—Leopold needed to circulate among the Kindred and better learn the ways of their games.

He was truly damned.

Leopold supposed the mansion was one of the first Reconstruction homes in Atlanta. It was awesomely huge enough to have been the home of an important Kine who saw to his own needs first. Or perhaps it was built at the behest of Kindred who needed safer hiding after untold dangers when Atlanta burned.

The mansion was indeed enormous. Four complete stories high with gables that seemed to crisscross in a confusion of dizzying angles. Great windows capable of illuminating entire ballrooms with sunlight, now cloaked by thick, velvet curtains perpetually drawn. Leopold guessed it must have more than fifty rooms within its walls. Hannah was surely in one of them, but was she too engaged in some bizarre magical activity to receive him this evening?

The Toreador was tempted to assume that was the case and try again another night before it was so late in the morning. But his need for answers drove him from the sidewalk along a short path toward the great iron gate at the foot of a brick walkway that terminated at the massive front doors of the mansion. The gate and narrow-spaced bars of the fence towered more than half again Leopold's height above him.

He noticed two security cameras rotate toward him and stop. They were mounted on the top of the brick columns that held the iron gate. The tall iron fence continued beyond each column.

Leopold looked directly into one of the cameras and hesitantly waved. He glanced back at the street to see if anyone was passing, and when he saw all was clear, he spoke quietly toward one of the cameras. "I am Leopold of the Toreador Clan, and I request an audience with...ah, Hannah." He stuttered because it seemed inappropriate to refer to the chantry leader as simply "Hannah," but he knew no other name or title. It would suffice. Or so he hoped.

And it must have, for in a moment the iron gate creaked open. Leopold looked at the hinges as he stepped through. He could detect no mechanisms that powered the opening, but he didn't wish to ascribe to magic every event he witnessed at the Tremere chantry.

Once through the gate, he walked steadily toward the front doors. The walkway was poorly lit, and a nervous feeling tickled him when the gates behind him closed. As he mounted the first of six brick steps, Leopold detected a shadow out of the corner of his eye.

He nearly tripped on the step in fright when a better inspection of the shadows revealed a pair of black mastiffs. They were both hunkered down and seemed ready to pounce and in an instant rip out his throat. Leopold knew enough about dog attacks to throw his forearm in front of his neck for protection should one or both leap, but the Toreador doubted such tricks would do him much good against these muscled beasts.

He stood for a moment watching them drink in his scent with twitching noses. Then the front doors of the house opened, and Leopold retreated toward the rounded and open frame. Only after his feet were beyond the threshold and his arm brushed one of the mammoth door handles did Leopold turn away from the dogs and regard the interior of the house.

It was dark and incense-scented within the room, though "chamber" was probably more apt for the impressive enclosure. This door too swung shut of its own accord, and Leopold gained the uneasy sense of entering a carnival's haunted house—a place meant both to frighten and invite, so that a guest's discomfort could be turned to the hosts' advantage.

Still, there was no one to greet him, so he paused a moment to examine the decorations. They were all unsettling. A two-dimensional skeleton of the extinct dodo bird in a shallow, well-illuminated and glass-covered crypt in the center of the floor. A framed document on the wall that careful inspection revealed to be the signed confession of a woman who had burned at the stake in Salem, Massachusetts. A small, almost circular table with a half-inch lip around it to keep three perpetually spinning tops from hurtling off the edge. Two black tops seemed to harry a small white one.

Leopold noted a mirror on the wall past the framed document, but despite great curiosity, he resisted peering within it.

The room itself was large and high. The ceiling extended at least three stories up, and various macabre portraits decorated the upper reaches of the walls. A great curling staircase wound along the wall at Leopold's left up to a landing that disappeared into hallways to the right and left on the second story. The stairs did not continue any higher, but Leopold noted a third-floor balcony that overlooked this chamber.

There were also two pairs of great double doors in the room, one set in the walls in front of Leopold and another pair to his right. All four doors were closed.

The Toreador stood for a moment, alternately surveying each of the vantages the room held over him, but spying nobody to attend to him, he took a seat on a large red divan near the table of the spinning tops. The clatter and motion of the tops helped pass a moment or two, especially as Leopold did not desire to gaze upon the recessed bird bones which the divan so neatly overlooked.

Soon, a white-bearded older man entered the chamber through the doors that faced the front door. He was tugging at the sleeves of his tuxedo coat. "Pardon me, sir, but in absence of expectation of visitors this evening I'm afraid the staff has gone a bit lax."

The man was Caucasian and his white hair bristled along the line of his jaw only. He was of average height and rather haggard appearance. As soon as he neared, Leopold ascertained that he was mortal, or at least a ghoul. Probably the latter, but it didn't matter to Leopold. He wasn't gathering information for a future raid on the mansion; he simply hoped Hannah could provide some answers, or even a solitary answer.

"I wish to speak with Hannah, mistress of this chantry."

"Indeed, Lady Hannah has been appraised of your presence, Mr. Leopold, and she has instructed that you be escorted to her at once. You will please follow me, and please sir, do not stray a step from the path we take. If you do, you are liable to come to great harm, great confusion or both."

"Great confusion?" Leopold asked.

"Yes, sir. Though the hallways seem entirely trivial to navigate, a wayward step is likely to deposit you in another wing of this house, or another house entirely. So please do take care."

Leopold dusted off his pants as he stood. Perhaps the dim light of the chamber hid the dust, but a thin layer of it had covered his body while he waited.

The man took a small candle-holder from a low shelf at the foot of the stairs. Also on that shelf were a number of narrow tallow candles. He placed one within the holder and snapped his fingers above its wick. It lit instantly, burning with a steady yellow flame.

The man, or ghoul perhaps, stepped to the base of the stairs and looked over his shoulder toward Leopold before mounting the first step. The Toreador took this as a sign to follow, and he immediately fell in step behind the servant. He reacted too quickly, though, and stepped on the servant's heel, causing the old man to stumble forward.

"Sorry," Leopold said as he moved to help the man to his feet.

The servant accepted the help, but he didn't reply to the Toreador's apology or even look at him. He merely dusted himself off and mounted the first step.

Leopold was still close, so he heard the ghoul whisper a name, "Hannah."

Though he couldn't see the flame directly, Leopold gained an impression of the candlelight from the flickering shadows and an aura of illumination that surrounded the ghoul's body. At the mention of Hannah's name, the light lost its yellow hue and assumed a violet-colored flame.

And because he couldn't see the flame directly, Leopold could not be certain of this, but he suspected that the purplish flame somehow led the servant to Hannah's current location. He surmised this from the way the ghoul's head flinched downward as if he were inspecting the light every time the pair achieved a intersection of possible paths.

The path the flame and/or the ghoul led Leopold along was extremely confusing. They passed through archways, traversed long and empty corridors, entered hallways and rooms through doors that seemed to serve no purpose, and generally took such a circumlocutious route that Leopold retained absolutely no hint of the direction by which he might return.

Additionally, he was so careful not to stray from

the path prescribed by the ghoul that he barely had half a mind to record the route anyway. He would surely rely on this ghoul or another servant to exit the mansion, so there was no reason to risk a misstep that might hurtle Leopold from this Atlanta abode to some other place entirely. That threat was a bit fanciful, and Leopold would have been tempted to ignore it anywhere but in the chantry house of the Tremere.

The ghoul led the way without comment but for occasional polite formality: "Duck here, sir, the ceiling's a bit low," or "Careful of the step, sir." Eventually he came to a halt before an ornate door that Leopold could not clearly see and turned to the Toreador.

The servant said, "Hannah is within this chamber. I will not announce you as it was her request that I not do so. She might be in the midst of careful work, so I implore you to enter quietly and await her to address you. To do otherwise would be to abuse her generosity sorely in seeing you at all this evening, young Toreador."

"I understand," Leopold said. "But should I not simply wait outside the door until she beckons me within?"

The servant shook his head and answered, "Such was not her request. Now please enter." At which the ghoul stepped aside and then quickly strode past Leopold and down a long hallway the pair had traversed a moment ago.

As Leopold watched the ghoul's figure recede down the hallway, he marked the point at which he suspected he might no longer catch the ghoul even if he dashed at his fastest. Once the servant passed that point, Leopold was left with no alternative but to enter as Hannah had apparently requested. Pursuit of the ghoul seemed a reasonable option because Leopold did not wish to interrupt Hannah in the middle of some grisly experiment, and he could imagine no Tremere ritual that might be otherwise.

Again, though, he thought that a foolish excuse to back down from his pursuit of truth, or at least some answers. So he stepped to the door, took a deep breath in a pantomime of relaxation, as he no longer breathed, and slid his fingers through the door handle.

Only now when within a foot of the door could Leopold appreciate the quality of the carving on the oak door. It was very fine indeed, and he would have envied it if he'd ever seriously considered working with wood. He preferred marble and clay—lifeless media from which he could create life. Wood always struck him as too close to living. To carve it was less sculpting than it was experimentation, much as a scientist might do.

The door depicted a scene from the Greek myths, for the three-headed dog Cerberus stood faithfully and realistically rendered in a position before the gates to Hades. His shoulders were pressed low toward the ground, while his hind quarters pressed up. It left the distinct impression that the beast was about to lunge at an interloper, and Leopold was unfortunately reminded of the mastiffs he'd encountered outdoors. Perhaps they belonged to Hannah.

He depressed the latch with his thumb and pushed on the door. It didn't budge. Reflexively, he tried the other direction, and indeed, the door swung outward into the hallway. Leopold's domestic instincts were confused for a moment, as he believed that doors always opened into a room. Almost always, it seemed. The Toreador wondered if there was an explanation for the change. He suspected there was; either that or it was simply another tactic to make a visitor feel ill-at-ease. If the latter, then the dodo plus the tops plus the purple-flamed candle plus this door were certainly doing the trick. However, Leopold felt he was an easy mark for such games.

The room inside was filled with a thin reddish smoke that drifted in diffuse clouds. The room was mostly dark, but candlelight from every corner illuminated the area just enough to cause the smoke to seem to glow. Leopold stepped into the room and quickly closed the door behind him. Now was not the time to be timid, he thought. If this room held danger for him, then he had been led here with purposefully dire intent. Even if he managed to circumvent such intent once, he would not escape the mansion alive if the Tremere did not desire it. Therefore, his brazen move was born not so much of bravery but of resignation.

Before his eyes adjusted to the dim light, Leopold heard the regular ding of some small percussion instrument. The tone of the sound made the Toreador think of finger cymbals like the kind utilized by belly dancers. And wasn't that a thought: Hannah cavorting and writhing like a belly dancer!

As the light became sufficient for him to see more, Leopold did in fact make out a moving figure in the center of the rectangular room. The movement was very slight, though, and the silhouette dramatically thin and pointed. He imagined that it must be Hannah.

The movement was the use of finger cymbals as

he supposed, but Hannah did not emulate the wild gyrations of Middle Eastern dancers. Instead, when her slow and steady beat called for it, Hannah lifted her left arm and mechanically crashed two fingers together. The brass implements flashed briefly in the low light, and Leopold noted this reflection was always in time with the noise they created. He doubted this was coincidental.

The perimeter walls of the room were lined with books, though no kind of book that Leopold recognized. These were of various shapes and misshapes and one close at hand that he could reliably examine bore a title on the exposed spine, but it was gibberish to him. Some oriental language, he guessed. Others he briefly investigated seemed bound in cracked leather, and the Toreador wondered if this wasn't a library of ancient tomes of magic.

Judging by the five candles, Leopold estimated that the room was about thirty feet across, though the presence of five candles suddenly alerted him to its likely pentagonal shape. Five low-rising tables with side edges cut at an angle so they could be pushed flush together sat halfway between the walls and Hannah's position in the center of the room mirrored the orientation of the walls. And through the silky strands of red smoke, Leopold noted that Hannah stood within a pentagram fashioned of metal and inlaid in the floor.

He hoped she realized he had entered, and he somewhat regretted the haste with which he'd entered. He thought it prudent not to disturb Hannah, but perhaps it would have been wiser to draw attention to himself to make certain she would not unknowingly place him in danger. Still, he reminded himself, she apparently knew he would be coming, so if she was unable to maintain her sense while in a meditative state, then surely she would guess that he might be present. Besides, what careful Kindred—and Hannah was surely careful—would let a potential threat remain in the same room when she was vulnerable?

Nevertheless, he continued to worry.

Gradually, the pace of the beat hastened, and Hannah's ringing cymbals seemed louder. Despite the increased energy, though, her motion seemed just as controlled and precise as before.

Then Leopold noted that the candlelight began to flash in time with the beat. First one candle and in a moment a second in unison with the first flared at the musical beat. The flash was not brilliant, but it was noticeable. As Leopold watched and wondered, a third candle joined the first two.

The beat was quick enough now that Hannah was chiming her finger cymbals once a second, and she no longer lowered her arm after each stroke. Instead, it remained lifted and outstretched before her.

When a fourth candle joined the pulsing rhythm, Leopold gained the distinct impression that Hannah's work was nearing completion. Surely, the addition of the fifth candle would complete her ritual.

Just then, a slight wind seemed to blow through the room, and its gusts also joined the timing of the music and candles. The red smoke that had drifted lazily about the room now took a shape demanded by the air flow, spinning as it was blown by each timed gust. Slowly, as if unwilling to kneel to the wind, the smoke coalesced into an air funnel that surrounded Hannah. It swirled in fits and starts, for though its

76                    TOREADOR

motion never ceased, it accelerated each time the strange indoor wind blew.

The beat quickened further, and Leopold grew more nervous than before. Making no great effort to be quiet, while consequently working to avoid a loud interruption, the Toreador shuffled around the perimeter of the room so that he stood facing Hannah. He hoped to at least make eye contact with her, but it was fruitless—the hood she wore hung low over her face, covering it almost to the tip of her nose.

The beat was so rapid now that Hannah's fingers chimed more than three times a second. Then, the fifth candle flared and a blinding flash flooded the room as all the candles spilled intense white light. Leopold's eyes were spared great trauma because they reflexively closed. Some part of him had known that the rapid cadence had built to its crescendo, though he could not explain why or how.

When Leopold urged his eyes to open, he found the chamber mostly dark again, though the steady light from the candles still provided sufficient illumination for a mortal to see, let alone a Kindred with heightened senses. Hannah remained in the center of the chamber, and her hand was yet outstretched, though she did not clash the cymbals again.

The red smoke still swirled, but it had coalesced greatly and now formed an air funnel only a couple of feet high and not that wide that extended from Hannah's uplifted hand. The smoke became denser and denser and the red transformed to ruby and that to the crimson of blood as the funnel compacted further, reducing slowly in size until Leopold could just barely make it out in the light spinning on Hannah's palm.

Throughout, Hannah stood completely still, presumably unable to see what was happening because her hood was still lowered.

When her outstretched hand suddenly snapped closed, Leopold jumped, startled by the movement after the hypnotic spinning of the smoke. As Leopold calmed himself, Hannah threw back her hood and regarded him, her eyes already set in place to stare directly into the depths of Leopold's.

Leopold continued to lock eyes with Hannah, though he did so nervously. Not hiding his uneasiness, he said, "I thought the Tremere did not share their secrets."

Hannah was silent and it was she who broke eye contact to examine the contents of her hand. The brief look Leopold gained revealed only that the smoke must have solidified into a physical object of some sort, and it was something that was still red.

He continued, "Your magic, I mean. I thought the Tremere did not allow others to learn their magic."

Hannah's gaunt, pale and emotionless face turned back to the Toreador. She said, "That is usually true."

"Then—" Leopold began.

"From what substance have the candles been fashioned?"

"I don't—"

"What was the order of the notes my cymbals rang?"

"I'm not—"

"What direction was I facing?"

This time, Leopold remained silent, and Hannah echoed this for a split-second.

Then she said, "You see? I have revealed nothing to you. Not yet at least."

"What do you mean?"

Hannah took a moment to arrange her hood, smoothing it so it would lie flatter against her back.

She said, "Follow me into the next room, Cainite."

The statement was so matter-of-fact that it was something between a request and a command. Leopold followed. Something of the delicacy between coercion and force was in the use of the old term "Cainite." Leopold rarely heard this term used, as "Kindred" was the preferred slang among the younger vampires he encountered more frequently. Leopold wondered if Hannah was really so old that such a term came to her naturally, or whether it was an affectation like that of some Kindred who imagined themselves power-brokers with rising influence despite their youth and general ignorance.

Not that he would call Hannah ignorant. To the contrary, he'd heard her called the All-Knowing before, and while he believed her to be only a few hundred years old, she was rumored to be within a hand's digits in generations from Caine. Probably that was exaggeration, but Leopold, who was no real judge of such matters, suspected she could well be five or six generations removed from the supposed source of Kindred, or Cainite, blood.

Hannah stepped to one of the walls, and when she brushed her hands against its surface, the candles suddenly extinguished themselves. A moment later, the illuminated outline of a door was revealed where Leopold had not previously detected a door. Hannah's thin frame was silhouetted in the light that poured through the doorway, but only for a moment as she stepped on.

Leopold stepped into a room that was in stark contrast to everything else he'd seen in the Tremere chantry. It sported the furnishings and character of an archetypical corporate office. There was a small wet bar; a large, flat-topped oak desk; aerial photos of golf courses hanging framed on the walls; two plush chairs that faced the desk with a small round table supporting a humidor between them.

The ordinariness rattled Leopold more than any of the odd and arcane tableaux he'd encountered already this night. He felt slack-jawed as he staggered toward one of the two over-large chairs and took a seat. Hannah was seated in a leather executive chair behind the huge desk.

She placed the object in her left hand on the desk, and it was immediately recognizable to Leopold as a vial of blood. He unconsciously licked his lips, though he immediately regretted this display. The blood was so obviously thick, and its dark, dark crimson surely meant extraordinary flavor.

Hannah was impassive as she surveyed the Toreador. Leopold expected her to say something, but perhaps a full moment passed and she offered no conversation. So Leopold said, "You said that night you visited me in my workshop that there might be a way you could help me in the future."

Hannah said flatly, "Indeed. There are doubtless many ways I could help you."

Again, Leopold expected her to say more, but he didn't let the conversation idle so long this time. Looking down at his lap, he said, "You're probably right, though I'm sure you could name more ways than

I could." He looked up at that, with a slight grin on his face, but Hannah's face was still an emotional blank.

Leopold continued. "But I'm hoping for one particular kind of help."

Hannah said, "Of course. You seek the identity of your sire."

Leopold was stunned. "Yes, that's true. How could you possibly know?" Perhaps she *was* All-Knowing.

The Tremere sat straight-backed and rigid in her leather chair and seemed to take no enjoyment from the surprise she caused her guest. Again, though, she remained silent.

Leopold's concern was only heightened, and he asked, "Are there others who know of this uncertainty of mine as well?"

"It's unlikely that there are many."

That didn't reassure Leopold.

"I can help you, of course," Hannah said. Indicating the vial of deliciously dark blood on her desk, she said, "That's what this is for, after all."

Leopold imagined himself shrinking into his stuffed chair. Was he so transparent? Did the Tremere witch possess some powers of detection or mind-reading that enabled her to predict him thus? Had he revealed something to her when she visited his studio, something he didn't recall, just as the Kine woman with him would forget some of her time there? These thoughts and others raced through Leopold's mind. Imagining that she might even now be reading his thoughts, he tried to banish them and even replace them with thoughts of confidence.

She raised an eyebrow at him, which on her face seemed to the Toreador an almost stunning display of emotion. "But you must tell me something first."

"If I can," Leopold offered.

"Why should I help you?"

Her voice was so devoid of engagement that Leopold imagined his case closed already. There was nothing he could offer and she knew it, or she must know it if she knew so much else. He felt a hopelessness wash over him. The previous nights suddenly seemed enormously long. His sculpting of Victoria almost vanished on the horizon of his memory. But then he knew what to say.

"As I am clearly the one between us who knows so little, I propose that you tell me why you should help me."

Hannah's eyes narrowed to slits, contracting not like a human's but more like a snake's. She seemed to appraise the Toreador before her.

"Yes, there is perhaps one reason I might help you. You must promise to sculpt me—"

"But you know I cannot sculpt Kin…Cainites," Leopold interrupted. "We established that when you visited my work…shop…that…ni…" Leopold trailed off as Hannah's face registered more and more indications that she did not believe the Toreador's protest. Her left eyebrow raised, then she craned her neck forward a bit, and finally slitted her eyes in that serpent-like manner again, and Leopold cracked. Could she already know about his success earlier this night?

He said, "But I've done it once now, so perhaps I can do it again. I agree to try, but inability cannot be construed as failure."

"Agreed, but there is more to my price."

"Oh?"

Hannah stood and walked around the desk toward the Toreador. "The sculpture must be life-size and life-like. No artistic interpretations. It must also be full-figure, not merely a bust or a portrait."

Leopold said, "I can agree to all that."

"Finally," Hannah added, almost running her words over Leopold's as if unaware that he'd spoken, "it must be from memory. I will not model for the sculpture."

To Leopold, the Tremere's "will not" almost sounded like "cannot," but he couldn't say why he gained that impression.

Leopold pressed himself back in the large chair, for Hannah was practically standing on top of him now. He could tell that the robe she wore was very thick, for part of it draped across his knee.

He said, "That's a bit more difficult, and some life-like details are bound to be lost, but I'm sure I can execute that work with reasonable success."

Hannah stepped even closer, so that her left leg pressed into the seat of the chair between Leopold's spread legs. "Then I will model now, to guarantee more than a 'reasonable' success."

Like a snake shedding its skin, Hannah rolled her shoulders and her thick robe slid off her torso and splashed down to her knees, where it hung only because the chair cushion would not let it sink to the floor.

Beneath the robe, she was naked, and beyond the surprise of this sudden and presumably utterly uncharacteristic gesture of Hannah's, Leopold was startled by the fine features of her body. She was almost painfully thin, but such emaciation was considered beautiful by modern standards. Her skin, like that of many Kindred, was perfect and unmarred, but more than that her narrow waist was wonderfully fashioned and its lines tapered upward toward a stomach that gave way to precious, gem-like breasts, and downward widened slightly at her pelvis before sloping delicately along the length of her legs.

"Touch me," Hannah commanded.

Leopold, suddenly aware that as he drank in her body he had yet to look her in the face again, glanced upward. Some of the magic of her beauty was dispelled by her plain and unemotional face, but Leopold didn't need the suggestion again. He reached the fingertips of both hands toward the Tremere and traced them along the slight curves of her sides.

"No," she corrected, and Leopold quickly flinched in retreat. "More. You must memorize me not only with your eyes, but with your hands as well. Explore me, young Toreador, and think on this promise you've given. Commit my body to memory."

Her words offered that same ground between coercion and force suggested earlier, and Leopold wondered if the puritanical and rigid Hannah didn't offer something more than what met the eye. Perhaps as a mortal she had had secrets of more than a thaumaturgical nature.

Hannah took one of his hands in hers and splayed the fingers wide. Then she pressed his open hand on her naked thigh.

Leopold did as instructed, softly cupping his other hand as well as he did when smoothing over a nearly complete work in clay for the final time. He closed his eyes, rubbing, and exploring.

He was amazed that she was so soft. He'd heard that the skin of many elders became hard in order to protect the Kindred. And though he could feel the bones very close to Hannah's skin, her flesh never-theless possessed a sensual sheen that was a pleasure to investigate.

He closed his eyes and transported his conscious-ness into his hands.

"Enough."

Though softly spoken, the word jolted Leopold back to the corporate office in which he sat. He rubbed his eyes and imagined he'd been sleeping, though he clearly recalled the prior moments when he saw Hannah, still exotic and naked before him. The Tremere dipped to retrieve her robe and secure it over her shoulders again.

She turned her back to the Toreador as she stepped toward her leather chair on the far side of the large desk. She smoothed the robe and sat facing Leopold, her face still as motionless and unanimated as deerskin stretched on a drying rack.

Leopold was in something akin to shock and found himself slow to recover. Hannah's unveiling of herself was so entirely alien to what he expected of her that he didn't know exactly how to react. Nor did he know what to say to her next. Professionally, as a sculptor, he was extremely impressed with her physique. When a mortal, and even until now as a Kindred, he had never had the opportunity to work with such a model. Anyone with a body like that was doing fashion work, not standing for arduous hours while an artist worked over clay or stone.

It struck him as hugely inappropriate to compli-ment her, though, so he simply said, "I sometimes enter a trance when I do my best sculpting. I believe I must have done the same just now in order to memorize the contour of your body as you requested."

"You were quite thorough, indeed," Hannah said, her impassive face not registering any innuendo or pleasure or distaste, or really anything at all.

All Leopold could say was, "The result will be better for it."

Hannah returned her to her silent staring, so Leopold took the initiative again. "So what exactly does that vial contain?"

Hannah glanced at the crimson-filled glass tube and said, "You may imagine it to be synthetic Vitæ. It has not been drawn directly from Kindred or Kine, but it would fuel the former and transfuse into any of the latter without rejection."

"And I—"

Hannah interrupted, acting as if she had never paused, "You will drink it tonight."

Leopold didn't like the sound of that. There was so much power in blood, and the Tremere were the supposed masters of tapping it for unthinkable uses. One such use might benefit Leopold if it addressed his question, but he also knew there was risk in imbibing blood. For instance, he'd been told that if a Kindred ever partook of another Kindred's blood on a half dozen occasions, then the latter Kindred would gain control over the former with a sort of unshakable mind control.

Of course, he'd also heard it said that this happened after two such feedings. Or four. Or, the more times, the stronger the control. Lots of permutations, but it all came down to the basic fact that it was unwise to drink Vitæ—blood—offered by another Kindred, especially a Tremere whose Kindred existence was built on a foundation of shared blood.

"And afterwards?"

"It must remain in your system for a full day, so do not burn it through activity tonight. After that time, a simple ritual I can perform in but a moment at this coming night's party will provide some information that will put me on the track of some helpful information."

Leopold asked, "It will reveal the identity of my sire?"

"Perhaps." Hannah's lack of motion, and hence absence of any sort of body language, did not help Leopold guess whether this "perhaps" was a likely or remote possibility. He had little choice but to accept it either way, though, so he didn't press any further.

"Very well, then, I'd best proceed as it seems that dawn is but an hour or so away, and I must yet return to my haven."

Hannah pinched the vial between a thumb and forefinger and extended it over the plane of her desk. Leopold stood and accepted it.

He weighed it as he returned to his seat. The vial was heavy, so it must have been fashioned from lead glass, and the cap that stoppered it was a very dense cork that instantly reshaped itself after he pressed a fingernail along its edge.

He looked up at Hannah, expecting to find her as she was before, simply waiting patiently. Instead, she stared off into space to Leopold's left. As the Toreador watched, the Tremere's nose wriggled as if she was searching for a scent. Then her eyes briefly narrowed in that serpentine manner and she returned her attention to Leopold.

She snapped, "Proceed." There was no mistaking this for anything but a command. It seemed the patience of his hostess was at an end.

So he drank. Leopold squeezed the cork and carefully pulled it out. With the pop of a champagne bottle, the cork slipped free. A single drop of the thick blood within spattered out as well, landing on Leopold's wrist. It puckered up with impressive surface tension instead of running down his forearm, despite being a sizable drop.

A pleasing rich and earthy odor wafted from the vial, and Leopold found himself desiring the blood regardless of any future benefits that might accrue. Without looking again at Hannah, the Toreador quaffed the viscous liquid. He opened his throat as he had learned to do in order to catch every bit of the spray of blood from a mortal's punctured artery.

The blood slipped satisfyingly down his throat and it was as flavorful as he'd imagined. Leopold felt a brief rush of hypersensitivity, as if his hearing and sight were suddenly more acute, but this faded almost instantly.

He looked at Hannah now as he replaced the empty vial atop the desk.

He asked, "So, there's nothing else that needs be done tonight?"

"That completes our business for now, Toreador. We each have more services to perform for the other, but you understand that your price must be paid regardless of my ritual's success or failure."

"Yes," said Leopold. "I understand, just as you surely likewise accept that I may be unable to execute the sculpture of another Kindred. I hope that I can do so, however, as I look forward to sculpting your likeness. Your *exact* likeness."

Hannah said, "My servant awaits outside the

door. He will escort you out—a journey I believe you'll find somewhat simpler than your entrance."

Leopold nodded, but as he turned to leave, the Toreador paused and looked squarely back at Hannah. He asked, "When you first visited me that night a year ago...?"

"Yes?" she asked to answer his pause.

"What did I do to the girl after you left?"

Hannah smiled, and that made Leopold visibly shiver, for she had never done that before, and he wished she wouldn't again because it was far, far more frightening than a thousand hours of her stoicism.

Leopold said, "I don't recall, but for some reason I'm certain you know."

"I do indeed possess that knowledge, young Cainite." She leveled her gaze directly into his eyes. "You got down on your hands and knees and begged for her forgiveness."

Leopold stood still for a moment, surprised that Hannah told him so bluntly, or even told him at all. And he was partly shocked that Hannah would be privy to what he understood should have been a private display, and partly ashamed for begging thus at all.

Leopold glanced at the floor and then back up at Hannah. "Did she grant it?" he asked.

Hannah's smiled slowly eased from her lips. She darted a look over her shoulder and then returned her gaze to the Toreador. "I'll tell you that tomorrow night as well. Now begone."

Again her tone left no room for dissension, and Leopold turned quickly on his heel and left, closing the carved oak door gently behind him.

# part two:
# victoria

**Monday, 21 June 1999, 9:36 PM**
**The High Museum of Art**
**Atlanta, Georgia**

Victoria was delighted with herself. She savored the final few moments of her chauffeured ride by settling even more deeply into the downy-soft leather of the seats. It was high time she made an appropriate impression on the Kindred of the South, and she knew that tonight would be that time.

She had filled the vacancy of Toreador primogen earlier this year after the Blood Curse killed the vapid and witless Marlene—along with the majority of the Kindred in Atlanta—in 1998, but she needed a coming-out party, and this summer solstice celebration would serve wonderfully. It had been a delightful suggestion, one she gladly embraced, and she was demonstrating her thanks by actually inviting the handful of Atlanta Nosferatu to this party. The hideous Kindred were not normally welcome at Toreador affairs because of their often gruesome appearance.

There was difficulty planning the celebration on such short notice, but she appreciated that in such spontaneous implementation the event seemed stamped even more strongly as a Toreador affair. Her delight in this fact was not one of clan pride—though she would argue the merits of her clan against any other, and she expected she would be forced to do so this evening—but instead she was happy to take advantage of the Toreador stereotype. Victoria preferred "archetype," but the result was the same: by making cunning use of others' expectations of Toreador behavior, she was able to lull them regarding the ways in which she subtly strayed from such convention. If the spotlight of Toreador allowed the candlelight plots of Victoria Ash to flicker unnoticed, then Toreador conventions could be very valuable to her.

After all, who would imagine that a Toreador taking pleasure in the sumptuousness of the evening would really have an ulterior motive regarding the Prince and the envoy of Jarislav Pascek, the Brujah Justicar, who would also attend? Victoria was not so dim as to fail to realize that there would be some who would suspect such underhanded play, but there was great difference in suspicions and proof. Victoria enjoyed providing room for plenty of the former, but opportunity for others to find little of the latter.

She stretched a slender arm toward the central control panel, her slender limb covered from her upper arm to the tips of her fingers in a silken glove that accentuated the poise and flair of this beautiful woman. Pressing a speaker button on the enormous central armrest, she lazily commanded, "Go by the front first. Slowly."

Victoria kept the interior of the car dark as she observed the High Museum of Art on this final pass. The white structure rose four stories on a small rise in downtown Atlanta. The entire building appeared to be dark and empty for the night, but her party was well underway on the fourth floor.

Special spy lenses that looked like ordinary opera glasses allowed Victoria to penetrate the seemingly opaque glass set inside the High's standard windows on that top floor. That special glass hid the party from mortal eyes, but not from her own, though only when she used the special lens to pierce it. There was something technical regarding wavelengths of light and interference that she didn't quite understand, but what she did completely understand was that the glass was opaque to her naked eyes even when she utilized her very heightened sensory capabilities.

No doubt others possessed even greater abilities, but she was confident her spying method was foolproof. Her decision whether or not to utilize the glass had been decided by a simple coin toss, a far cruder means than she usually employed. Not everything could be put to an elaborate or elegant test. Not like the moves she might make tonight.

The glasses revealed approximately a dozen Kindred already present, which pleased Victoria. The number wasn't great, but considering how the Blood Curse had ravaged the ranks of local Kindred—Camarilla and Sabbat alike, thankfully—she was pleased nonetheless. In fact, if not for a number of out-of-town guests, despite the cancellation of some of the more interesting ones like Benito Giovanni, then this dozen or so might be all she could expect. Pathetic, yet that's what made Atlanta perfect for her.

She was the hostess of this party, but she damn well wasn't going to be early to meet every low-life Kindred who might drag himself in for a cultural experience. No, she would arrive so the Kindred would see her according to her own plan. Then, she could seek out those who deserved or at least required her special and personal attention, though she had not yet decided who had earned her "special" attention for this evening. Perhaps it would be one of the out-of-town visitors. Or perhaps there would be no such games tonight, if her plans were executed and especially if they blossomed to fruition.

As she tucked the lens away in an inconspicuous compartment, Victoria wondered if this little trick was technically against Kindred law. The High Museum was regarded as Elysium, and that meant no violence was allowed within the building, but the Toreador was unsure if this status meant her shenanigan was frowned upon as well. She suspected it was probably pushing matters too far, for while she perhaps did not break the letter of the law, the intent was certainly being subverted.

She doubted anyone would ever know, however, so that was the same as its being acceptable. Besides, how else did Kindred get ahead in this world but by guile? The brute power many Kindred possessed was too dangerous and more often than not caused lasting harm and possibly death to its user as well as the adversary. Guile, cunning, and deception were expected, and so long as a Kindred could operate without undue attention, then she might proceed with her plans.

That was the difficult part, of course. She would have to be careful, for instance, when she used her apparent opera glasses, but it was with them she could look through the dividers of glass that for others would provide an illusion of privacy.

She pressed the button again. "To the elevator now."

The car turned right at the next cross street and then shortly turned again on an even smaller street that ran behind the museum.

As the car slowed to navigate speed bumps at the entrance of an underground parking garage, Victoria checked herself in the mirror a final time. Her curled hair was perfect. For that matter, her face was too, but that part of her never changed. It was pleasingly rounded, with a narrow and interesting chin. Hers was not a noble face, but the face of the lovely servant girl whose beauty outshone her haughty, royal-blooded mistress.

She batted her green eyes and overlooked the slightly Asian appearance that had once troubled her. In this more cosmopolitan world on the verge of the twenty-first century, a subtle cast like hers only enhanced her beauty. Then she directed a little blood to flow into the flesh of her cheeks. She preferred the color of mortal women. The red that all Kindred knew was blood made mortals appear vivacious, and that was especially inviting to Kindred males.

Finally, she curled her fingertip through a ringlet of lustrous brown hair. Her own servant (this one not nearly as lovely as her haughty mistress) had succeeded in exactly reproducing the style of one of the statues displayed at her party. A statue of Helen, if the Toreador recalled correctly. Victoria grinned devilishly. Her hair seemed weightless in its curled suspension, for it hung above her shoulders but jostled down to kiss the silk of her faux-Grecian yet stylish dress when she moved. If Helen with this hair launched a thousand ships, then the vain Toreador suspected it would take a modern nation's armada to do her proper justice.

She let her eyes drop from the mirror, though she watched herself do this long enough to enjoy how demurely she executed it. For the remainder of the night, the eyes of others would speak to her of her beauty, for she was as gorgeous as ever even after over three hundred years on this Earth. Of course, the bulk of those years—349 to be exact—had been spent in this peculiar form of unlife that characterized the Kindred, in which she no longer aged as a Kine might, but hers was timeless beauty that won her as many stares and as much wanton lust as it had those handful of centuries ago.

As a mortal, Victoria's splendid beauty had won her all that she needed. It was much more difficult to use sex to control a Kindred, as limp vampire males could prepare themselves only by means of special magical disciplines. She knew these means, of course, and could apply them, but something in the nature of the Kindred's instinct for survival overwrote the almost unendurable compulsion of mortals to copulate and procreate. Kindred were rewired to care only for themselves, for even a childe created through the Embrace seemed to hold no special place in a vampire's heart unless the vampire retained a great degree of human nature, or unless the childe reminded the more bestial vampire of something lost from an earlier, lesser lifetime.

But lust was still an easy sell. Most Kindred were very young—less than a hundred years old—and these were often still mortal in their minds. Their physiology would not react as Victoria wished, or cooperate as the vampires themselves often desired, or thought they desired, but their feeble brains were still wired for the copulation important to the Kine. Thus they were often easy marks.

It was a game no different from the one she had played in her mortal youth. All her husbands had been older men. Their stings could not prick her, but oh, how they must have imagined it might have been as she cuddled her slender yet appropriately rounded body against their bony and broken shells at night!

They would have paid anything. In the end, they had all paid everything.

It became much more difficult to ply her schemes the higher she moved into the hierarchy of the Camarilla. The men who controlled the organization were ambitious and time had dulled their memory of the pleasures Victoria might provide them. And it was mostly men, for the changes that occurred in the mortal world by virtue of the succession of generations did not affect the Kindred world as quickly as that of the Kine. On the other hand, they were still male, and their brains were still wired in a way that could prompt them to strut like peacocks.

Hence events like this one tonight. Certainly, she needed to continue the usual exercises of discovering allies and ferreting out enemies. Regardless of her greater plan, Victoria needed to become a locus of Kindred society in Atlanta. Soon the Kindred would come to rely on her parties—and not the insipid or insane, or both, Bible-studies gatherings required by Prince Benison—as the excuse to gather and discuss strategies and debate activities. Once she controlled the forum, it would only be a matter of time before she controlled the content as well.

And now was the time to do it. It looked as if the Kindred population of this Southern city would recover enough to make it a worthwhile starting point. A Reconstruction of sorts was underway in the wake of the Blood Curse, and now was Victoria's opportunity to shape the protocols and traditions that would continue when the Kindred population doubled and tripled and grew beyond that again.

Victoria wiped the smirk from her face.

"Why didn't you tell me we had arrived?" she demanded.

There was no reply, of course. The chauffeur would be silly to do anything but accept the blame.

Victoria noted that her car was parked before the elevator doors in the High Museum's underground garage. How long it had idled there, she did not know. And while she was irritated at first, she decided to withhold punishment because the time likely did her good. It couldn't hurt to hold clear in her mind some of the many plot threads that wound through this evening. Doubtless, she did not know them all, but the ones in her control would hopefully be woven a bit tighter before the night was done. Perhaps even knotted.

A second later, the door nearest Victoria soundlessly swung open. The Toreador kicked one sandalled foot through the opening and slowly extended her hand as well. Her hand was immediately accepted by a strong grip as one of the doormen helped her out of the car. Like her driver, these were ghouls in her employ. Because they were still half mortal, they thankfully did not suffer any of the sexual retardation of the Kindred, which meant Victoria did not always have to work so hard. However, she paid them with blood and cash as well.

Without her blood, they would age and suffer all the weaknesses of the mortal form. Because they were not strong enough to take her blood from her, she had absolute control over them. It made the sex boring, but she refused them more than an iota of free will because their proximity and intimacy to her meant anything more was too dangerous. In this she took the lessons of the elder Kindred around her.

Rarely were egalitarian vampires among those who long survived.

As her car pulled away, Victoria scanned the parking facilities. The amazingly wide variety of vehicles parked in the underground garage demonstrated in a snapshot the range of social strata of her guests. Her chauffeured Rolls silently backed into a space between two similarly ostentatious vehicles—one a great limo with driver waiting patiently within, and the other a sexy Dodge Viper for a Kindred of more solitary or adventurous nature. Only two of the off-road, or sports utility, vehicles so favored by the Brujah and Gangrel were evident. The Gangrel, who actually utilized the off-road nature of the vehicles, were unlikely to have more than one or perhaps two representatives here. Victoria didn't mind if none made it. Likewise, Victoria doubted either of these SUVs belonged to a Brujah, unless one or more of that clan had decided to make use of the Elysium here to protect themselves against the retribution of Prince Benison, whom the Brujah had brutally attacked in the waning days of the Blood Curse last year. The few Brujah rumored to have survived the Curse were yet in exile among the Anarchs of the city who were all being subjected to the Prince's crackdowns.

Finally, nestled here and there about the garage were the pathetic vehicles of the neonates. These Kindred were so recently Embraced that they still possessed the automobiles of their mortal years. Either that, or museum employees had abandoned those sad clunkers.

"Send me up to the party," she said, pirouetting gracefully on her heel to face her ghouls and the elevator they managed.

"Of course, milady," said the one who had helped her from the car. That was Gerald, a handsome and muscular manchild from Canada, who held one elevator door open.

She asked, "Has Benison arrived yet?"

"No, milady."

"Julius?"

"No, milady."

Victoria nodded happily. She hadn't expected either of these major players to arrive so soon. It would have been difficult if one had arrived before her, and perhaps ruinous if both had. It was a chance she had taken.

She asked, "What about Benjamin?"

"He's here, milady."

"And Thelonious?"

"Yes, he too, milady."

She *was* surprised they were both here already. They were also major players, though not in the league of the other two. The fifth great power that would be in the gallery tonight was Eleanor, the Prince's wife. She was a linchpin for Victoria's plans, but she and the Prince would arrive simultaneously, so no further inquiry was required.

Victoria stepped in and the other ghoul, Samuel, a lithe and dark-complected Bostonian, stepped in behind her. As Victoria leaned against the mirror-glass at the back of the small enclosure, Samuel quickly stabbed the "4" button. The elevator doors closed and Kindred and ghoul began to rise.

Victoria sighed as she gave further consideration to the laughable automobiles of the neonates. They were so human still. So young and still playing such foolish games. Young Kindred were truly like mortal children. So undisciplined. So confident. So foolish. They felt the universe was at their fingertips because they were now a part of something previously unknown. A world unknown even to presidents and famous actors and men who had walked on the moon. But there was little they could do that would seriously impact the greater machinations of their elders. Despite their feeble attempts to gain power or wield influence, neonates inevitably found themselves outguessed and outplayed by those of Victoria's ilk—Kindred who spent less time relishing their position than taking advantage of it.

Yet she knew she was a fool as well. Many elders probably laughed at the petty games she and her contemporaries played. Vying to control a city as if that meant something. Cities, nations, entire cultures were but fascinating baubles for the oldest Kindred, the so-called Methuselahs and even their elders, the Antediluvians. These latter were the unknowable and probably mythical vampires of the third generation— Caine's grandchildren.

From their perspective, Victoria's generation and even those older than she were but playthings discarded when their usefulness was over. At least, such were the stories the elders had told when Victoria was herself a neonate. She had little reason to distrust such rumors, for as in mortal life you are always second best to someone no matter your area of excellence, in Kindred life there was also always another who knew more or possessed greater powers. Whether this theory was true or not, it was a mirror Victoria always used to look at herself. To second-guess herself. She played delicious games with those weaker than her, so why could she not herself be part of a greater power's game?

Unhappily, she always admitted that she could be, and that was what drove her. Perhaps this very party was an event someone mightier than her had put in motion through her. It seemed natural to her because it suited her ends, but were her ends the means to another's goal as well? Might a Methuselah or even an improbable Antediluvian have good reason to see Victoria claim greater power in Atlanta or the Camarilla? Victoria could only hope so, but at the same time she shuddered to think her careful plots, her deceptive double-crosses, her ruthless games were not her own.

And this was why it was good to be a Toreador. She could be fickle and mischievous without anyone looking more deeply than the blood that ran in her veins. Being Toreador was her excuse to be unpredictable, and she tried to keep herself guessing as well. Well, not unpredictable, for that was the role of the Malkavians, the madmen among the Kindred. As a Toreador, Victoria was allotted a certain leeway to rationalize changes of heart. So long as any change of direction she chose bore the signs of a whimsical carelessness, then Victoria could execute her plans with less scrutiny.

In fact, she was about to make a huge decision regarding her future this evening. She pushed herself off the wall of the elevator. The door was beginning to slide open, but Victoria already knew what she would see. There would be two portals, and each led to a different future.

As the doors began to open, Victoria hesitated at the brink of the elevator. Her big moment was approaching and she was suddenly apprehensive.

Samuel asked softly, "Did you forget something, milady?"

"No, no," Victoria answered in a voice without its customary commanding tone. Despite the sanctuary of the elevator, this quiet exchange was overwhelmed by the music that drifted from beyond the lift. Victoria gained confidence from what she heard. It was Ravel's *Bolero*, a piece first performed in 1929 or so, she couldn't recall the exact year. Those were years when the Masquerade had been easiest to uphold because the times were fast and carefree in Paris, much like the '60s in the United States. She felt emboldened as she recalled her successes of those distant evenings.

Chin high again, Victoria stepped out of the elevator and swiftly turned to face Samuel. Her voice more certain again, she said, "Quickly now, go back down and fetch the next guests. But remember, now is the time to create a pretext to wait until two people are ready to be lifted to this floor. More than two is acceptable, as we discussed before, but a single guest would be disastrous."

Samuel was suitably perplexed by this command, just as he and Gerald had been when Victoria first explained the procedure last night. However, she was certain he would perform this duty even without satisfactory explanations. This was all part of Victoria's safeguards, and explanations would only cause others to believe her as mad a Malkavian hatter. Therefore, she kept the specifics of her odd behavior to herself and hurried Samuel along.

"Disastrous," she remonstrated him again with a wagging finger as the elevator doors began to close at

Samuel's depression of the first-floor button. The vacuum of the elevator tube whooshed as Victoria turned to examine her handiwork.

Indeed, two pairs of enormous doors faced her. They were propped up as part of a temporary wall that divided a shallow entry area from the remainder of the gallery beyond. All of the huge doors were closed, and though the ceiling of the gallery beyond could be seen over their tops, they nevertheless fulfilled their function as entryways.

And that was the crux of it. Which door did each of her guests choose? More importantly, which door would the next guests select? For that would determine Victoria's entryway, and *that* would have great consequences for the remainder of her evening and her life.

The doors on the left were by far the largest, and at over thirty feet high they taxed the altitude of the High's upper ceiling. These monstrous doors were of beautifully sculpted bronze, and they displayed ten individual scenes in eight separate panels arranged in two columns of four, over which a stretched a lintel divided by a central bearded figure flanked by two more scenes.

The fact that this central figure was biblically bearded, swathed in draping robes, and held aloft an engraved stone tablet, fixed his identity for even the densest of Western viewers as Moses.

Victoria knew, of course, that this was Henri de Triqueti's *The Ten Commandments*, but she had little idea which of the ten scenes represented which of God's commands. One notable exception was the second panel up on the left side, for this was the panel that allowed these mirror-opposite doors to fit another underlying theme of the displays in the gallery beyond the doors.

"Thou shalt not kill," God said, but it took only a handful of humans to already be too many before Cain took matters into his own hands. For Kindred, though, Cain was "Caine," and legend extolled him as the first of the Kindred, the reason Kindred were called such at all, for if Caine's blood was passed to his progeny, and they passed their blood containing some of Caine's to their progeny, and so on, then even Victoria Ash, six generations removed from her biblical ancestor, carried with her some of the First One's blood. Even so diluted as it surely was within her, it was the source of her amazing powers, as well as the attendant curses over which some Kindred pouted but which Victoria had years ago decided to accept as part of this surpassingly grand existence.

All of this warbled through Victoria's mind for two reasons. First, the scene on the gargantuan doors that illustrated the Sixth Commandment was in fact that of Abel's death. In it, angels descended to transport Abel to Heaven while Caine was outcast. Second, because Victoria strongly held the fear that her actions were often not her own. If the blood she carried within her was so potent, then how else might that blood hold her in thrall? If not in Caine's service, then what of one of his awesome progeny of the fifth or sixth generations whose blood she also carried?

And this fear was what made her game tonight so important. It was why the opposite of *The Ten Commandments* was so important.

Victoria turned slightly to the right and took in once again one of the most incredible works ever created by the hand of man. Since it too was sculpture, the man who fashioned the work could be none other than Auguste Rodin. Though shorter than the thirty-three feet of *The Ten Commandments*, Rodin's *The Gates of Hell* did not seemed dwarfed despite its mere twenty-four-foot height.

This lack of diminishment was entirely due to the genius of the work, for it was a true masterpiece. The kind of creation Victoria sought but doubted she would ever achieve in the artwork she created.

This great door also possessed a lintel divided by a central figure. In an early, but already almost complete, form of Rodin's great *The Thinker* of later years, the figure was seated and leaning forward, his chin braced on the inwardly curled knuckles of his right hand, and his elbow supported by his left thigh. It was Dante, and he imagined the scenes of his *Inferno* on the door about him.

Standing upon the top of the door frame were three figures, essentially three views of the same man from different angles. Their heads were bowed together and their hands clasped in a moody and lethargic reenactment of the Three Musketeers.

Beyond these distinct trappings, the remainder of the door was indeed as if from Hell. Wells and troughs of barely discernible figures and scenes covered each of the doors, as well as the door frame. Within the turbulence was both the passion of creation as well as the pain.

Against the white walls and ceiling of the High Museum's gallery, the darkened bronze of the two sets of doors made them seem even more ominous. Their massiveness served only to heighten the impression that a decision of a serious nature was before the one who approached. And as a pair they created quite a contrast: *The Ten Commandments*' symmetrical design of panels and its generally clean sculpted lines against the blurred and difficult-to-comprehend *Gates*.

And Dante, in the pose of *The Thinker*, above the *Gates* made contemplation seem natural.

Victoria's plan was foolishly superstitious, but in order to believe that she was free of the invisible shackles of a power greater than herself—a Kindred greater than herself who might imagine the lovely Toreador a chess piece on his field of play—she rigorously applied randomness to much of what she did.

The pitter-patter of *Bolero* was gaining healthy momentum when she heard the rumble of the elevator and stepped away from the doors. Which door would her next guest use to enter the gallery beyond? Would he or she step through Heaven or Hell? The forthcoming answer would determine much about what Victoria did this evening; specifically, whether or not she should make her bid to become Prince of Atlanta in the place of an ousted Benison. The Prince was not here yet, but his arrival was a certainty. Victoria's scheme to supplant him, or at least to move closer to the top, was risky, and she would only feel secure about implementing it if she could be certain that the idea was her own, and not one planted in her subconscious mind by another.

Perhaps there was no way to be certain, but Victoria always felt better if her plans survived random testing, such as the trials this very party faced. Like the idea of this party, plenty of plans did pass Victoria's test, but others did not. Numerous seemingly good ideas and opportunities had been lost or gone unrealized, but the Toreador felt no regret. Implementation of those schemes might have led to disaster. They might have been set into motion by others who used her merely as a pawn. Besides, there was nothing irreproducible about a good idea. When randomness bade that she not take some course of action, then another, sometimes better, option always presented itself. And she had an eternal lifetime to explore them all.

The whole matter was uproariously superstitious, and she understood that, but there was also a grace to Victoria's games which pleased her and suited her artistic sensibilities. Perhaps she was on the verge of becoming a great artist after all, for there was something in the chaos of her actions that was itself beautiful. After finding a comfortable pattern of her own in decades of randomness, Victoria was delighted to discover that the Kine themselves were finding that chaos could be structured too. Most sciences eventually became arts, so perhaps this theory of chaos waited to be rendered into beautiful form by an undying mind that could attend to cycles no Kine could hope to witness.

Or perhaps it was simply ridiculous. Victoria knew of Kindred who were mightier than she, but their number was not beyond counting, nor was their power beyond reckoning. Perhaps there were no Kindred greater than these. Perhaps the theories promoted by the Sabbat—that the Antediluvians were real and must be destroyed for any free will to exist among Kindred or Kine—were groundless and Victoria's advance to power was slowed only by her simpleton games.

And there were evenings when she thought how

improbable her eventual command over any number of Kindred was. How could she hope to rule when her plots were hatched under the auspices of chance events no more believable than the signs a Greek oracle once gained from the intestines of birds or sheep?

Finally, the elevator doors hushed open, and Victoria turned to see who would decide the fate of her latest plans. Her methods were crude in one light, but the Toreador always preferred to judge them in the light of what might be. Chances were that if she hid secrets from neonates, then someone held secrets from her, so she would circumvent their plans by proceeding only when her guile aligned with fate.

And Victoria laughed to herself when she saw whom chance delivered her.

First out of the elevator was Cyndy, the Toreador who had inherited the adjectives "vapid" and "witless" once Marlene passed on shortly before Victoria's arrival in Atlanta. Victoria reasoned that these titles primarily fell to the short and athletic little bitch because Marlene was Cyndy's sire, and misfits begot misfits, but they were also accurate enough no matter the exotic dancer's lineage.

Cyndy, who had apparently been speaking in a friendly manner to her fellow occupant, fell sullenly silent when she saw Victoria. Then she looked quickly away, but she did not resume her conversation.

The Toreador was indeed short of stature and supple in body. Her figure was lithe and she possessed some grace despite what any knowledgeable observer would note as a complete lack of formal dance training. Her face was attractive, if a bit too rounded and cute in that way of slightly overweight college girls—

she was a bit too big really to catch the male eye, but she looked fresh and young and that would catch a man's imagination. And because she was Kindred, she would always look so young.

Whatever potential she possessed, however, she threw away in her huffy willingness to be crude, as when she clutched her crotch when she walked past Victoria without a word.

Victoria allowed her deprecating chuckle to be faintly audible. To think that this upstart Embraced by Marlene on some careless night in the strip clubs and lingerie shops that formed her territory on Cheshire Bridge Road actually imagined *she* should have been named primogen of the Atlanta Toreador.

Victoria chuckled again, though this time sourly and silently. She had become Kindred and left London only a handful of years before the Black Death decimated that city, and she had been in the United States in the deep, dark sleep of rest and recovery known as Torpor during the years of terrible influenza earlier this century, but she realized with what randomness such plagues struck. How could this hussy of a Kindred—she barely deserved the title—have survived the Blood Curse when other, eminently more capable and deserving, Kindred had fallen to it? Not that Victoria regretted the loss of these others. In fact, she chuckled again—and this snort of laughter earned a baleful glare and forceful spit from Cyndy—because such randomness clearly worked in Victoria's favor this time.

The second occupant of the elevator, who emerged as Cyndy stomped past Victoria, was just as interesting. He was also a relative low-life in Atlanta, but he was at least an individual of some merit or talent. Victoria watched with further amusement as Leopold stepped slowly from the lift. This Toreador was an apolitical sort, but even he surely understood there was bad blood between Cyndy and his primogen. He kept to cover until the potential confrontation passed.

Victoria turned away from Leopold for a moment to watch Cyndy choose between the mammoth doors. Victoria noted with chagrin that the simpleton barely paused to absorb the wonder of the portals before her. Then Cyndy glanced back, apparently confused, but when she saw Victoria studying her, she huffed and stamped a foot as if these odd doors had been placed here solely to torment her. Victoria let a wan smile flicker across her lips, and Cyndy practically dove through Rodin's presumably more manageable-looking *Gates of Hell* after tugging open one of the great doors.

*So she enters Hell,* Victoria noted as she turned to face Leopold, who had taken one step more only because the elevator doors threatened to close upon him. When they did slide shut, the young Toreador paled and seemed to shrink away for want of a hiding place. Wise enough in her judgments of men— Leopold was so young a Kindred as to be practically Kine in her mind—Victoria recognized some of Leopold's discomfort as an attraction to his primogen. She had noticed this on a past occasion as well, but before his evident desire had been more straightforward—an uncomplicated urging from the parts of his mind that retained some portion of physical need, perhaps.

As she thought on the matter, Victoria turned her head slightly to the side and raised her eyebrows a fraction—body language to invite the timid Toreador from his hole. She decided that there was definitely something different in Leopold's attraction now, but she couldn't quite put her finger on it. She would eventually, though, as she was very good at reading people, a talent she had possessed as a mortal but even more so now when her heightened senses detected so much for her to analyze.

Leopold attempted a friendly but not too personal smile as he approached Victoria. The latter's acute hearing read fear in the surprising flutterings of Leopold's heart, and it wasn't the stage fright that might normally disarm such an introvert. Victoria decided there was something more poignant to this fear. She also decided it wasn't a fear of Victoria herself.

She asked, "Are you all right, Leopold?"

Leopold's smile hung on his face a little too long. Realizing that, he wiped it away and said, "Yes, Ms. Ash. Just, ah… nervous about the, ah… premiere of my work tonight." The smile returned as Leopold unconsciously attempted to reinforce his lie.

"Of course, of course," Victoria graciously accepted. And then she reached forward to embrace him, which, as she anticipated, startled Leopold. His body went rigid, but he managed to relax as Victoria kissed him lightly on each cheek.

Still holding him, her face close to his own, with *Bolero* advancing toward its climatic notes, she said, "And it's a remarkable achievement, considering the short notice I provided. I apologize for that."

Leopold did not answer, but instead returned the hug. Victoria was greatly amused by his schoolboy ineptitude as he tried to use clumsiness as an excuse for holding her very close and placing his hands very low on her back.

Then she suddenly disengaged, which further startled Leopold. Victoria would have delighted in playing more games with the whelp, and his sculpture was indeed a respectable one, but she needed to attend to the matter of the doors before she embarked on any course of action this evening. Even if that course were as simple as the befuddling or seducing or embarrassing of a young Toreador.

She said, "But, please. Don't allow me to delay you. There may be Kindred even now admiring your sculpture. I hope I will have the opportunity to speak to you again later."

"You're not coming in as well?" Leopold asked.

"No, no, Leopold. I'm the hostess, so I'm greeting my guests. Now run along. I hear the elevator returning with more guests."

Leopold listened but could hear nothing except *Bolero*, which was achieving the peak of its enthusiasm. He stood so long that he blinked twice before nodding and walking toward the doors.

He immediately pulled up short. His mouth was agape when he turned to regard Victoria with disbelief. He jabbed each index finger in the direction of one set of doors and silently tried to elicit explanation from his elder.

Victoria just smiled and nodded before opening her own mouth slightly and pointing at it to help Leopold correct his unappealing expression. Then she waved the back of the fingers of her left hand to scoot him along. Leopold did a doubletake once more, but then he approached the doors without further encouragement.

Victoria watched him intently, for her plans now essentially hung on his shoulders. Cyndy had limited Leopold's ability to determine how Victoria would proceed this evening, but the final determination was the young Toreador's, for he was the second to choose an entrance.

Victoria ran the permutations of her eccentric rules through her mind. The fact that the two individuals who arrived on the elevator were of opposite sex and the same clan necessarily dashed an entire assortment of possibilities, so Victoria ignored those and focused on those involving a male and a female who were both Toreador, and beyond that a male who entered after a female.

The rules were extremely complicated, but they were so thoroughly codified in Victoria's thinking that the complexity did not occur to her, just as the obscure rules of cricket did not befuddle a fan of that peculiar sport. And so Victoria did not imagine herself obsessive about the measures she took to protect herself from unwary cooperation with the plans of another.

She grew somewhat impatient with Leopold as he dawdled in his examination of the scenes depicted on the doors of Heaven. He seemed particularly engaged by one of the panels—the lowest one on the right standing door—but his body obscured it and Victoria frankly did not know the piece well enough to recall the Commandment depicted in that spot. She wanted to rush Leopold along, but she dared not do that. Hurrying him was only an option when he was not before either door, and if she did so now she might as well not have staged this elaborate game, as Leopold was likely to duck through the nearest door.

In this case, Heaven would mean she would should cancel her plans, for it was the taller door and would be entered by the taller of the two, who was male, which meant Victoria should enter through Hell and cancel her plans.

However, if Leopold entered through Hell, then Victoria could not follow, and her entry through Heaven would mean her game was afoot. It seemed likely to her that that would be the case as Leopold examined Heaven first and would presumably enter through Hell after inspecting it too.

Satisfied with his appraisal of Heaven, at least for the moment, Leopold did indeed move to *The Gates of Hell*. Victoria grew a bit nervous and excited over the approaching moment. She sometimes wondered if she prepared these elaborate games not because of fear of being given direction by others but because she feared to give herself direction. She always rejected the notion, though, because she was not timid person. Just cautious.

Victoria had not really heard the elevator before, especially over the final throes of Ravel's eighteen-minute-give-or-take masterpiece, but now Victoria did register the *cling* of its doors on the ground floor in the near absence of further music. It sounded as though some piece that made the Toreador vaguely call Beethoven to mind was beginning, but the early portion of the piece was very faint.

Leopold seemed just as curious about the near-formless masses that swirled across the face of the doors of Rodin's masterpiece as he had been of the starker images of Triqueti's. He even glanced back at Victoria another time to shake his head in awe and wonder.

He started to ask, "How did you acqui…" but trailed off when Victoria turned away and toward the elevator as if she had not heard him.

When she glanced back, Victoria murmured a quick, "What? Did you say something, Leopold?"

The younger Toreador waved the question away as if he realized he was pestering her. "Nothing. I'm sorry to keep you from your other guests." He then placed his hands on the doors and slowly moved them over the surface as if imagining it was suddenly forming under his fingertips. *Or perhaps he imagines what he would have done differently,* Victoria mused, as that reaction was often a great or even good artist's reaction to the work of a master. They saw not so much the work, but how the work differed from and therefore defined their own.

Having successfully deflected Leopold's question, Victoria now turned in earnest toward the approaching elevator. She was frustrated to be caught here actually greeting her guests. It was a formality better suited to receiving lines, not a small gathering of Kindred. Besides, if new guests arrived, then they would become complicating factors in her game, though the permutations that presented were also predetermined, of course. However, she would much rather the decision be a less complicated affair. It was just like reading the auguries of a lamb's bowels where too much blood—too much sign—might obscure the important facts evident in the intestines. The fewer guests the better.

Victoria smiled when she heard the elevator doors open on the third floor. Samuel was playing the delaying game as she had instructed, for not enough time had passed. Victoria had known that certain guests were beyond the ability of the ghouls to delay in the garage, so a few tactics like this were necessary.

Victoria turned again to watch Leopold more directly. She had not, of course, taken her eyes from him, but her gaze had been inconspicuous for a few moments. She wanted to strangle the young Toreador when he returned to the larger doors of Victoria's self-styled Heaven. He looked closely at the lowest right panel again, and rubbed it as he had Rodin's work, but then quickly stepped back to take in both gargantuan sets of doors.

Victoria did not know whether or not to be appalled by such apparent contemplation. He actually seemed to be choosing which door to use as an entrance, as if it mattered to him.

Victoria was curious about why he finally chose Hell, but he did indeed return to Rodin's work and slip out of the hallway after a brief struggle with the heavy door. She would have to inquire of him later, for now that his choice was made, she could freely discuss the doors with him, if not her true reasons for utilizing the doors.

When Victoria neared *The Ten Commandments*, she looked with interest at the panel that had most interested Leopold. She didn't like what she saw. The panel showed Naboth. He was dead—stoned to death because Ahab and Jezebel coveted his vineyard.

The Commandment came to her mind because she knew it well. It was one that had troubled Victoria during her mortal years.

*Neither shalt thou desire thy neighbor's wife, neither shalt thou covet thy neighbor's house, his field, or his man-*

*servant, or maidservant, his ox, or his ass, or any thing that is thy neighbor's.*

Victoria swallowed hard. All she did was covet the things of her neighbors.

Victoria tried vainly to make herself feel better rather than read this as a sign that she was being misled after all. For indeed, it was Naboth, not the covetous Ahab or Jezebel who was dead in the panel's depiction. And this was one of the more powerfully executed scenes on the door, so perhaps Leopold examined it merely for technical merits, not because he was attuned to anything greater than the feeble powers a young Kindred such as he might possess.

In the end, Victoria shrugged. She was committed to her choice and to her methods. If she superstitiously feared every sign she saw, then she would indeed be a timid person who must surely rely on the games to make decisions—not just safe decisions—for her.

Victoria Ash entered a Heaven where she found only demons.

The handsome Italian man reclined behind his mammoth desk of cherrywood. Benito's phones were organized as always, and while two nights ago he had sat here in irritation that he was receiving phone calls, he was now equally upset at the lack of one.

Lorenzo Giovanni was normally very reliable. In fact, Benito had already put a good word in for the ghoul. Lorenzo desired the Embrace, of course, as did virtually all Giovanni who learned there was more to their very extended family than undreamed-of wealth. Benito might have to rescind that recommendation, though, if Lorenzo did not call soon, or at least have a very valid excuse for his tardiness.

There was only so much time Benito could carve from his family responsibilities in the last forty-eight hours to devote to a matter that was, after all, a personal issue; but after a long discussion about security issues with his cousin, Michael, Benito had contacted Lorenzo in Atlanta.

The ghoul was engaged in some secretive mission there for the family that Benito did not grasp—nor did he wish to if the family deemed he was not one who needed to know—but as one of the few permanent Giovanni in that sole bastion of civilization in the South, the ghoul still had time to fulfill the special requests of other family members. He was only a ghoul, but he was a formidable one, so Benito felt no qualms about sending him to spy on the festivities at the High Museum.

Spying was necessary, as there was no way Lorenzo might be invited, or even accept Benito's invitation in his place. The affair was for Kindred only, and while Benito could have made a stink if the Toreador bitch in charge, Victoria Ash, denied permission to Lorenzo, Benito also realized this would bring disfavor upon his family by his having pressed the matter at all.

And now Lorenzo was late—very late—reporting back to Benito. He wanted fresh information, not something as stale as the night after, for that might be too late to take actions if the damned neonate who held Benito's life in his hands was in fact spotted at the scene.

He tapped his finger impatiently on the phone that had rung so often two nights before. Still nothing. Benito clenched his fingers and smashed his fist onto the desk. He almost cried out in rage as well, but he reined in his emotions. He was under tremendous stress, and this was not a time to give the Beast an opening.

He slowly returned his attention to the financial documents on his desk. At first, the numbers swirled and didn't make any logical sense, but with concentration, Benito devoured the information they held.

He quickly lifted his head and looked to the right, toward the door to his office. Something, just a flash of shadow perhaps, had passed. Without hesitation, Benito hovered his finger a millimeter above an alarm button under his desk. Meanwhile, he watched carefully for any other sign of movement.

Even though there was none, he remained poised.

Benito spoke toward the empty spaces of the

room. "Randall?"

And again, "Randall?"

The inhuman whisper that replied was barely audible, but a fractured, almost demonic echo, repeated the word. "Yes," came the secondary voice.

Benito demanded, "Was that you moving just now?"

The same dark echo replied, "Yes."

"For what purpose? I am not in a state to tolerate such activity."

"The shadows were speaking to me. So I conversed."

Benito remained irritated, but the wraith was bound here to provide protection, so it was best to heed it in times like this.

Benito said, not without a hint of sarcasm however, "And what do the shadows tell you?"

"Not much," the formless wraith said. Then added, "Yet."

Benito sighed, then said, "Well, heed whatever signs you must, but do so without disturbing me. I am wary, but I still have work to complete."

There was no reply, and Benito expected none. He resumed his work immediately upon completing his command.

More time passed, and Benito suddenly interrupted his work to knock the central cellular phone, the one connected to the Giovanni network, onto the floor. "Call, dammit!" he shouted at the facedown phone where it had landed on the plush rug covering a portion of the hardwood floor.

Benito stared at the phone for a moment, and then stood to retrieve it. He reached it in two strides, and as he bent to grasp it, Randall's inaudible whisper precursed a deep amplification sounding a warning. "The shadows are speaking!"

Startled as much by Randall's voice as the note of alarm it sounded, Benito squatted on the floor, balancing and preparing himself for whatever might come next.

"What does the shadow say?" he demanded.

Randall said, "It says it is too late. They are here."

Benito's eyes flared in fright, but he quickly gauged his distance to both the desk with the alarm button and to the nearest stand of samurai swords. The nearest stand held the blades supposedly wielded by the so-called Tiger Warrior, a samurai who had hunted and exterminated ninja more than a half century ago. *How appropriate*, he thought to himself, as he saw ninja-like figures, four of them, step from the shadows of the room.

The nearest seemed to peel off the wall behind Benito's desk and stood crouched between the Giovanni and the alarm button. Two others welled up like black blood oozing from weeping welts. One was by the couch, and the other by the door out of the office. The last one seemed to sprout from a rug near the center of the office like a vine viewed through time-lapse photography.

"Unbelievable," was all Benito could manage in the first instant. Then, he took the offensive, for these might indeed be mortal assassins, and if so, then his lack of response would be the only way they could defeat him.

"Randall!" he shouted. "Duel!"

Benito saw the figure near the door, the one with the best vantage, look quickly about the room. When the Tiger Warrior's katana leapt from the stand at the near edge of the couch, the figure at the door shouted a warning to his comrades, or at least that's what Benito imagined he did. No actual words could be heard; instead, darkness issued from the figure's mouth and formed a sinister mockery of a comic book's dialogue balloon, though one filled with the almost invisible pulsing of darkness.

However that darkness disseminated information, it was not in time. Appearing to float in mid-air, but actually brandished by an invisible spirit of the dead brought back to Earth by Benito from a hellish existence, the Tiger Warrior's katana whistled through the air. The weapon's blade was honed to a perfect edge, and the scores of folds of its metal executed by its creator made it strong. Strong and sharp enough at least to divide an assassin's arm from his torso even though the wraith called Randall could barely summon enough strength to manipulate the blade, let alone drive it through a foe.

The target of the attack was the assassin at the near edge of the leather couch. However, the assassins were evidently well-trained, for the apparent leader at the door was the only one to react to the attack. He reached into the tangle of darkness that stretched like old spider webs from the shadows around the door to wrap and obscure much of his body. Benito's glance lingered long enough to glimpse a long-nailed hand as it emerged and flipped deftly in the direction of the Tiger Warrior's katana. A flash of metal sped in that direction—presumably a knife or shuriken—as the commander must imagine an invisible yet nonetheless corporeal opponent wielding the blade.

That split-second was all Benito could afford, though, because the other two assassins ignored their comrade's plight and pressed the attack directly at Benito. This meant it might well be a suicide mission, or else the foe in the center of the room would have turned to assist his nearer and now one-armed ally.

The Giovanni focused his attention on the assassin nearest him, the one behind the desk who posed a more immediate threat and who also blocked the route to the alarm. Michael and other members of the security force might well be dead and destroyed already, but no alarm was ringing, so Benito imagined his best hope was to activate it now.

When Benito turned, he locked gazes with his foe for the barest portion of a second. The assassin aborted his attack in order to turn his head and stave off the powerful mind-control Benito could exercise.

"So, you know I'm Kindred," Benito shouted angrily. Their knowledge didn't matter. That millisecond their eyes had met was enough.

Benito succinctly commanded, "Retreat!"

The defensive posture of the assassin was abandoned as he somersaulted to a dead stop before rolling backward without a pause. He did hesitate a moment near Benito's chair, but the assassin seemed unable to resist the Giovanni's command, and his flight carried him past the alarm button, which Benito promptly scrambled to reach.

Meanwhile, the assassin set upon by Randall was too slow reacting to the threat, as he too assumed he merely faced an opponent he could not see, not one he was also unable to touch. With his remaining arm he threw punches to every side and height around the floating weapon, looking to land a blow against his assailant. The efforts, of course, proved fruitless, and the assassin's astonishment left him open to another sweep of the hardened and honed blade. This time, the arc of the katana carried it through the neck of its victim. The ligament, muscle and bone there gave way with the same ease as had the victim's arm.

Benito caught sight of the bloodless decapitation as he hustled toward his desk. The lack of blood was bad news, for it meant the assassins were likely Kindred, and Benito was not old enough or powerful enough to handle four Kindred even with the assistance of an intangible ghost. Although, it was now two on two if the effectiveness of Benito's order to "retreat" persisted.

As if driving that point home, the other assassin who had targeted Benito grasped him from behind as the Giovanni scurried toward his desk. Instead of resisting, as Benito assumed his opponent expected, he quickly turned to his assailant. He whirled and dropped, hoping his quick move would allow him an opportunity to gaze into this one's eyes as well.

However, the maneuver was only marginally successful. The assassin reacted well, so he did not stumble over Benito's prone body, but he did not avert his gaze in time, and Benito widened his own orbs as if that would make his hypnotic compulsion do its work even more easily.

But Benito was disoriented as he stared into the face of his foe. There was nothing familiar to grasp, no normal landmark of facial contour to guide his reflexive attempt to lock eyes. The assassin's face was shrouded in an unnatural darkness, and though he desperately tried to stare through this haze from a mere handful of feet away, Benito was unable to penetrate it. This bewilderment cost him as it had cost the assassin who counterattacked Randall—it opened the Giovanni to an attack he could not defend in time.

The assassin's clenched fist caught Benito on the very tip of his chin, and the Giovanni reeled backward so awkwardly that he could not even respond to break his fall. His large chair did that job for him, the thick arm of it savaging a bloody welt in Benito's back. Benito then flopped facedown onto the floor, and just as he tried to roll to right himself, the great weight of the assassin dropped onto his back, pushing him back into the thick shag of the rug.

The attacker then clutched at Benito's arms, trying to secure them by the wrist or forearm so they could be immobilized behind his back. The first was gained quickly, and Benito writhed like a snake to keep his right arm free.

From his vantage of the floor, Benito saw the decapitated head of the other assassin lying in front of the desk. Then there was a flash of metal and the Tiger Warrior's sword fell to the ground beside the head. Either Randall had abandoned the weapon or it had been taken from him. Benito lifted his head to scream a new command to the wraith, but he was then clutched by the hair on the back of his head, and a strong arm jammed his face into the floor. The rug softened the blow somewhat, but since the assassin maintained the pressure, Benito was effectively blinded.

Benito's right arm was still free because its capture had been abandoned in favor of his head, so the Giovanni reached toward his desk, groping blindly in hopes of reaching the alarm. His first random flailing connected with the edge of the desk, and he immediately realized he was too far away to reach the button.

His only hope was the strength of the blood he held within him. With the briefest concentration, Benito sparked the conversion of some of his blood stores into the capacity for tremendous physical strength. His vision clouded with red and he felt a tingling in all his extremities. Then Benito bucked like a wild stallion.

Despite the commanding grip he'd held, the assassin was thrown like an incapable cowboy. Benito did not pause for even an instant to survey the wreckage of his office. Instead, he immediately pressed the silent alarm button. Only then, with his augmented strength still coursing through his body, did he examine the scene of the battle as he stepped backwards to put distance between himself and the assassin he'd flung off.

The leader was no longer near the door. Instead, he stood in the center of the office, straddling the headless corpse. His hands were thick with blood because he was using his own obviously prodigious strength to bend the wakizashi that was the companion to the Tiger Warrior's katana. Not with all the blood his body might hold could Benito generate the kind of strength required to bend so formidable an object—a sword crafted by a master metalsmith. Only the other wakizashi still rested in its display stand, which meant its katana companion was probably already warped beyond use. Nevertheless, that blade soon animated as Randall seized the sole remaining weapon.

The Kindred Benito had commanded to flee was nowhere in sight. He must have been a weak-minded fool to be affected so thoroughly. Perhaps these assassins were physically powerful but vulnerable to mental attacks.

The assassin Benito had escaped moments ago stood his ground, facing Benito from about fifteen feet away. The Giovanni realized he was simply waiting for his commander to dispense with the invisible threat before they both advanced to take him. But Benito hoped Randall could hold out until Michael Giovanni arrived.

The wraith's weapon arced toward the commander, who still seemed to literally drip with darkness as with a physical thing. Indeed, when he side-stepped to avoid the strike, the sword left the puddle of darkness trailing an inky track like an octopus might leave in its wake. And before weak-armed Randall could regroup for another strike, the commander pounced and clapped his hands on opposite sides of the flat of the blade. With a quick and powerful turn of his hips, the assassin wrenched the blade from its invisible wielder, promptly grasped each end, and bent it.

Benito wryly reminded himself to display much lighter weapons in the future—perhaps epées—so Randall might press an attack more effectively.

The commander surveyed the room briefly and then spoke in another puff of black. The second assassin nodded his head slightly while keeping an unflinching watch over Benito.

Benito said, "What do you want? My death will only guarantee the endless baying of hounds at your heels. The Giovanni family will not idly set aside my death."

The Giovanni hoped to gain some time, but the effort was in vain. The two assassins, presumably Kindred assassins, advanced. Benito cursed. Where was Michael? And did this attack have anything to do with Lorenzo, or Atlanta, or Chicago? Had other assassins gotten to Lorenzo and killed him too?

Then the commander cocked his ear toward the door, and Benito exhaled in relief. He imagined the assassin must hear assistance drawing near.

When the door caved in from the impact of a thunderous kick, Benito reacted immediately. He thought to use the distraction to rush past the commander and gain the safety of Michael and guards. But it was he who was surprised, for though he reacted first and seemed to gain an advantage for it, in mid-flight he realized the commander had simply decided to pay no heed to the disintegrating door and legions of guards behind him. Instead, he slyly waited and pounced on Benito as the Giovanni attempted to pass.

The assassin commander grabbed Benito around the waist and neck, and both holds quickly tightened so that the Giovanni worried he would be crushed to death before Michael might extricate him from this restraint. The grip grew no tighter, though, than what was required to choke off Benito's windpipe and gain absolute purchase around his midriff. Considering the strength of the commander, there was no hope that Benito might slip away.

The remaining masked assassin was suddenly at the side of his commander, and once they turned to face the figures issuing through the doorway into the office, they stood perfectly still. The security guards efficiently lined the back wall of the office and trained their weapons on every available inch of the area. In addition to the rifles and pistols they brandished, they were outfitted with bullet-proof vests, visored helmets, and gas masks. Benito knew another member of the security force waited in the hall, ready to lob in gas grenades if such was required.

Benito could not imagine what the assassins planned. They were severely outnumbered and outgunned. Even a Kindred as powerful as the one who held Benito could be felled by enough bullets. If not permanently, then for long enough for other means of permanent disposal to be arranged. Killing Benito now—which the Giovanni supposed his captor could do in an instant—would only make their death certain. So perhaps they would use him as a hostage.

As Benito's thoughts spun and spun, he realized that time was passing and nothing more was happening. No dialogue. No fighting. No recognition. In shocked disbelief, Benito regarded the line of security officers that stood with weapons.

They looked in every direction throughout the office. Some of them even seemed to make eye contact with Benito, but they looked right through him. With growing apprehension and then terror, Benito realized that none of the guards saw any of the three figures before them. Somehow, the assassins must have hidden themselves, and that was powerful magic indeed. It must have been by this same means that they circumvented the security measures in the first place.

Benito kicked his legs and batted his arms and tried to scream despite the cinch on his throat. He managed only a sputtering whisper, and neither that nor his wild gyrations drew a single glance.

Benito watched as the guards suddenly eyed the desk and trained their weapons upon it.

"Mr. Giovanni?" one of them asked.

The Giovanni ceased his struggling then, for he knew it was in vain. Through some means unknown to him, the assassins were cloaking themselves and him. But surely the security guards could see that the place was a wreck. That a struggle must have taken place. But if so, why did they delay to alert others?

It was then that Michael stepped into the office. Benito's cousin was a bit less distinctively Giovanni than himself, but the resemblance was undeniable. Michael was a bit too broad-shouldered, too rugged, too muscular. In short, he was a bit too quintessentially American, and that was because Michael's grandmother had married outside the family, a mistake for which Michael's father had spent his lifetime atoning so that his son might be welcomed back into the family and granted the greatest gifts the family could bestow. Michael's father was punished by knowing what it was he could never attain, but he'd been a strong-willed man—more Giovanni than his treacherous mother—and he used that knowledge not to rail at his own misfortune but to goad himself toward redemption.

Michael was Kindred, his family's debt repaid, but he was yet low in the hierarchy, so he merely commanded the security force. Nevertheless, like his father, he did what was required of him and he generally did it well. He obviously had the loyalty and respect of the men in his employ, for when he stepped into the room they remained relaxed and in position. Not one of them adopted a more effective stance or a more professional demeanor. They all obviously gave everything they had without concern for appearances.

"What's the situation here?" Michael asked.

One of the men replied, "Mr. Giovanni's office is secured, sir, with the possible exception of beneath the desk. We called out for him, but there was no reply."

Michael turned to look at the desk as well. He squinted his eyes for a moment and seem to concentrate his senses on it, staring with such force that he seemed to expect to peer through the solid wood construction. Benito knew his cousin possessed extraordinary senses, even a sixth sense of sorts, so if anyone could pierce the shroud obscuring these assassins, then it might be him. If he failed, then he was undone. And likely dead as well.

The assassin commander seemed to reach the same conclusion, for he shuffled from the center of the room toward the far wall where the couch stood. The other assassin followed carefully, seemingly placing his feet where the commander's trod as well.

The life-preserving instincts in Benito's mind demanded that he make a final effort to draw attention to himself, no matter how helpless the chances, but the Giovanni ignored them; he was too fascinated by the powerful forces at work now: the environment-piercing senses of Michael Giovanni versus the cloaking veil draped over the area by the assassins.

The assassins won handily, for though Benito's cousin seemed ill-at-ease, his powers were too feeble.

Michael Giovanni's intense gaze lingered on the desk for a moment more, and he said, "No one is there." Benito watched as the guards relaxed their weapons. But before the tension drained from their bodies, they were re-alerted, for Michael—eyes still fiery slits to illuminate the deepest shadow—continued a slow appraisal of the room. "Something..." he muttered.

When Michael's wary gaze passed over Benito, the captive Giovanni did give into his life-preserving instincts and he struggled mightily by kicking and twisting with as much energy as before. But the assassin choked and restrained him even more viciously, and in that second, Benito understood he was doomed. In the face of such power, nearly any Kindred would be, and Benito decided he could not mourn a death that drew the attention of one so mighty as this commander. It would be like a newborn gazelle expecting to live despite the determined predation of a healthy cheetah.

Finally, Michael stopped and said, "Damn alarm is driving me to distraction." The Giovanni made a slashing motion before his throat as he glanced into the hallway outside the office door. A few seconds later, Michael relaxed. Benito realized that, though the alarm was silent to most, it was only so to those who possessed senses as ordinary as his own, while Michael must hear it even in this room. Benito wondered if the assassins heard it, and he concluded they must.

Then Michael suddenly craned his head toward the ceiling again. "I said turn it off," he shouted testily through the open office door. "Don't play games with me now, Daniel."

A voice carried from the hallway, "I didn't reactivate it, sir. The schematic indicates that the alarm was activated from Mr. Benito's office again."

At that, the security guards immediately readied themselves once more. Benito even believed the assassins seemed troubled by the news. Benito was certainly confused.

Only Michael appeared unflapped, and he spoke in the direction of the desk. "Spirit, quit your hauntings. Benito has never confirmed your existence to me, but I've always known you must be here. Quit these games now, or your master, who will be informed of your impudence as it is, will have no reason to show you mercy."

A pause, then Michael's eyes glanced toward the ceiling and back to the desk. "Good," he said. Then, to his men, he said, "Find Mr. Benito. Even a false alarm such as this must be investigated thoroughly."

Benito shook with helpless, hopeless rage. Randall clearly saw an opportunity to extricate himself from Benito's service. He wasn't doing anything contrary to Benito's commands, and because Benito's voice was choked off, no new orders could be given. Randall was therefore protected from the safeguards Benito had in place to punish the wraith. If the Giovanni ever escaped this predicament, then Randall would pay for this; but treachery in a crucial moment was the price of forcing spirits of the dead to aid you.

When the guards dispersed to investigate every corner of the office and the other rooms on the floor, the assassins slipped from the office and into the hall. They moved down the hall and passed a trio of men who crouched over computers and other instruments.

Then they moved to the stairs, to the first floor, and finally out of the building.

Floating unseen amidst so much activity, Benito felt as a shade passing from life to death. Perhaps only as a wraith would Benito gain revenge on Randall.

Monday, 21 June 1999, 10:22 PM
The High Museum of Art
Atlanta, Georgia

Victoria smiled as she closed the door of Heaven behind her. The black portent of the Tenth Commandment was forgotten at the sight of her party. It was glorious.

From her slightly elevated vantage atop the few steps on the gallery side of the doors of Heaven and Hell, Victoria took in the sight and scenes of her party. Statues and sculptures so grotesque that their assembled whole made the gallery seem the lair of a decadent and mad king. Vampires dressed in rags. Vampires dressed tactfully and expensively. Servants bearing trays of crystal flutes filled a hairsbreadth shy of the lip with rich ruby blood.

All of this was amidst of a veritable maze constructed from sheets of the same opaque, shatterproof glass that lined the outer windows of the High. The eight-foot-high and ten-feet-long sections of glass divided the gallery like crooked snakes. Here were long stretches interrupted only by a narrow portal. There were numerous broken sections that created a maze capable of hiding an individual no matter the direction from which one attempted to view him. Anyone not armed with lenses like those in Victoria's glasses, that is.

All this was spread before Victoria, and for a moment the scene seemed a choreographed dance. With Victoria's arrival, though, the rehearsal was over, and these dark and dangerous figures amidst the gothic and terrible set would begin to play games in earnest.

Or at least they had better, for Victoria played no other way, especially tonight, when the auspices were right and she planned a bold move to catapult her toward the Princeship of Atlanta. The secondary ambition of becoming a powerbroker in this city—becoming an integral part of the new structure—was very secondary now that her entrance had been made through Heaven. She was an angel accepting a fall so she might rule this rabble.

The population of Kindred in Atlanta was still greatly diminished from its level prior to the Blood Curse, but the dozen or so Victoria expected within seemed a suitable lot. Even the sole Caitiff Victoria noted was dressed pleasingly, although like many other Kindred, Victoria harbored vague fears about these clanless vampires. This new breed of Caitiff was often not clanless for the traditional reason of a dead or missing sire who might otherwise claim the childe, but because they were too many generations removed from the source of Kindred power and their blood was too thin to support the kind of differentiation and power that a clan identity provided.

*The Time of Thin Blood* was one name Victoria had heard applied to the recent proliferation of Caitiff. But this one—Victoria believed her name was Stella—showed some class. She was a dainty little thing and sported little in the way of defining feminine attributes, which to Victoria meant Stella lacked voluptuousness, but the Caitiff was dressed in a tuxedo which granted her petite frame and short-cut hair a certain charming and sexual quality. Victoria determined to keep her eyes on that one.

It was such Kindred that populated the fourth floor of the High Museum of Art. The room seemed suddenly larger now that people were within it, for they suggested scale to the vaulting ceilings and the sometimes enormous sculptures spread across the room.

The room was long enough to justify the use of the opera glasses Victoria carried in a pocket sewn into her pseudo-Grecian garb. She did not utilize the special lenses of those glasses now, but she knew there were a handful more Kindred present than those she could see at the moment, so some must be tucked into the alcoves of glass.

These alcoves would allow the Kindred here some sense of privacy, for they would imagine themselves safely out of view for a few words with a friend or foe. And they would be thus protected from everyone but Victoria, who was a marvelous lip-reader.

Also set within some of these alcoves were the sculptures that were the artistic attraction of the evening. No Toreador party was possible without such pretension, and Victoria was worldly enough to understand a portion of it was pretense. But whether it was her variety of Kindred blood or an appreciation built over centuries of watching change that caused her to feel thusly, Victoria did hold a true respect for this art form. The profound conflict of time in sculpture was what attracted her. Each piece cast in bronze or carved from marble or granite was as eternal and enduring as the Kindred, yet the brief gestures and fleeting moments captured within the pieces were archetypically mortal.

For guests who could not appreciate the work, the sculptures would at least provide a semblance of an excuse to strike up a conversation on other matters entirely.

Where Victoria looked across the room, a hooded figure held his champagne flute aloft in a silent toast to Victoria. The Toreador knew this must be Rolph, an unfortunate yet noble-hearted member of the horribly disfigured Nosferatu clan, who had obviously accepted Victoria's invitation. Victoria regretted the invitation for a moment, for like most Toreador, she preferred beauty, and the hideous Nosferatu hardly passed that test. But she wanted the Nosferatu in her power bloc, and when it came to political allies, the information-grubbing Nosferatu were among the best to count as friends.

The robe Rolph wore was far from sumptuous, but Victoria expected that at minimum it did not smell of the sewers and underground the Nosferatu preferred to frequent. That was consolation enough for Victoria; she could expect no more.

She nodded back to him in acceptance of his appreciation. She could not see a face within the dark folds of Rolph's hood, but she imagined him smiling before he took a small sip of the fresh blood that thickly coated the crystal flute.

"Milady?"

Victoria absently took a flute of her own from a tray a servant offered. She looked to return Rolph's toast, but he was gone. Nosferatu had a way of doing that. They were masters of moving unseen. Their wretched ugliness demanded it, for otherwise their mere presence would shatter the Masquerade.

Victoria did another quick sweep of the room. She saw Cyndy trying to insinuate herself into the proximity of Javic, a Gangrel new to Atlanta who had requested and received permission to dwell here from Prince Benison. Javic was a Slav, and Victoria knew his story included something of the recent events in Bosnia, but she did not know whether this Kindred had been on the giving or receiving side or even whether he had been mortal or immortal at the time.

He carried himself confidently enough, so perhaps he was an elder. That plus his dark and rugged good looks was what must have set Cyndy after him, Victoria supposed. That and the mystery of him, for he was still practically a stranger. Like many Gangrel, or so Victoria believed, Javic appeared to prefer his own company to the virtual exclusion of all others, as he made no effort to entertain Cyndy. Victoria wasn't even certain where he dwelt, though Atlanta was green enough to support a clutch of Gangrel within as well as outside the city.

Cyndy noticed Victoria watching her and beyond that, looking at Javic. She made a dismissive gesture toward Victoria and tried to place herself between the Slav and her hostess. All she managed, though, was to draw Javic's attention to Victoria.

The Toreador allowed a coy but lingering smile to move her lips. Javic's expression did not change, but the fact that he held her gaze for longer than a glance was as good as a smile back. Besides, it infuriated Cyndy, who tried to take Javic by the arm and step him elsewhere. But that was too much for the Gangrel, and he shook her off so quickly and deftly that Cyndy almost fell. In fact, she would have, but Javic recovered before she did and saved her from a disgraceful collapse. His help was mechanical, though, and had nothing of the intimacy Cyndy might spend a long night trying to engender.

Victoria noted Leopold stepping into the hidden confines of a nearby alcove that contained a bronze enlargement of Jean-Jacques Feuchére's *Satan*, which Victoria had arranged to borrow from a Los Angeles museum. She thought she might not return it, but she wasn't sure what the ramifications of that would be. There was presumably a means to make the proper people out West forget it had been loaned, or at least to whom it had been loaned.

Victoria watched with amusement when Stella stepped in that direction as well. They would be hidden from plain view, but Victoria suspected nothing would pass between them that required the use of her opera glasses.

Leopold sought the first cover he could find, a decision for which he ruefully chided himself when he realized he should have pushed farther into the room and away from the crowd of Kindred near the entrance.

But he was flustered. Stomaching Cyndy's whining and posturing on the elevator ride from the parking garage had made him so. He'd been first into the elevator, and though Cyndy was some distance off, the rude ghoul who operated the lift refused to take Leopold up and then return for Cyndy.

If ever there was a Toreador who gave the clan a bad name, then it was Cyndy. A poseur, and beyond that a poser. Her and her damnable strip joints. No wonder Victoria barely took notice of the girl.

To add to his discomfort, he was then thrust into the presence of Victoria Ash as soon as he stepped off the elevator, again at the rude behest of the ghoul. When Leopold noted Cyndy's reactions, then he knew Victoria must have been there waiting to greet her guests. Why he had thought it would be otherwise, he wasn't certain. It seemed Victoria ranked higher than most of her guests, so why not await them beyond the entrance?

The ghoul had insisted, however, so Leopold was forced to meet her with scant preparation. He was amazed that he had calmed himself so well, but even so he'd wanted to blurt out that he'd sculpted her. That she was the key to the unknowns that plagued him. But it would have been ridiculous, because in all likelihood, he was ridiculously wrong.

Leopold prayed that Hannah would have something to tell him. He shuddered to think of the Tremere's odd behavior the night before, but he could still feel her alabaster flesh beneath his fingertips. He suspected he'd never be able to look at her again without imagining that exchange, but perhaps that was as she wished it. The machinations of Kindred were largely beyond him, and those of the Tremere surely were, or at least this one Tremere.

Thankfully, it wasn't Cyndy who cornered him in an alcove of the strange glass that created borders and walls around the chamber. Instead, it was Stella, a clanless one, a Caitiff, whom Leopold would have welcomed had he not preferred privacy right now.

The Toreador had met Stella on three previous occasions—a high incidence rate for his normal pattern of fraternization with other Kindred. Leopold preferred to dwell on the last of those three times only, for the first two had been gruesome occasions. Regardless, when he saw the pretty young woman approach him, his thoughts flashed back briefly to all prior occasions.

The first was shortly after her Embrace, when some Anarch whose system was flooded with drugs and alcohol must have forgotten he was Kindred, for he'd tried to rape Stella before he Embraced her out of frustration.

The second meeting had been much the same, though this time it was a mortal who had tried to be rough with her. In her fear she'd reverted to mortal patterns as well, and she forgot that she was now the hunter and the hoodlum the prey. It was only when

Leopold stumbled upon the attack during one of this tours of the narrow streets that ran perpendicular to Ponce that she'd unleashed some of her might on the thug. Leopold's cry snapped her out of that trance, and Stella had sucked the man dry. Leopold then helped her destroy the body, which fortunately turned out to be no one anyone else wanted to find.

The third time had been only a few months ago when the two Kindred discovered that they were both attending a showing of the black-and-white classic movie "Metropolis" at the Fabulous Fox Theater, which was only a few blocks down Peachtree from the High. Leopold went as much to see the interior of the Fox as to see the old science-fiction movie. The stars that seemed to twinkle on the ceiling of the theater would have been more interesting if Leopold's entire life wasn't spent under the night-time sky, but the ornate decorations of the place—especially the Egyptian Ballroom with its hieroglyphic-inscribed ceiling—fired Leopold's imagination.

Leopold had seen Stella first, and he sat apart from her during the show—almost left altogether—because he didn't want to be a reminder of the previous encounters. However, after the movie, the Caitiff had approached Leopold as if he was a valued friend, not just a timely rescuer. So after seeing who could better feign drinking an espresso at a nearby coffee house, they returned to Leopold's home and talked for much of the night.

Leopold had tried to sculpt Stella's likeness, but she was one of his many failures. She'd been sympathetic; but more than that, she would have been an excellent model, for Leopold knew enough of the tragedy in her life to lend depth to any work she modeled.

Stella was a small woman, perhaps only four and half feet tall. Her hair short and attractively styled, she was just old enough to look mature and to possess little crinkles around her eyes, but youthful enough to pass for someone perhaps not even of drinking age. She'd been timeless as a mortal, and now as a Kindred she truly was.

Unless the Caitiff were not like other Kindred. It was claimed that the blood was getting even thinner now, but a Kindred like Stella used to be the lowest grade of vampire. The blood her sire had fed her was too weak to transfer much other than the trappings of vampirism—the need for blood, vulnerability to the sun, and a little more. No indication of clan was passed, though, and so she was clanless unless a primogen would claim her.

Leopold had thought about presenting her case to Victoria, but he shied away from that because he didn't want his discussions with Victoria to center on a different woman. It was damn foolish. He knew that, but it didn't change how he acted.

He thought Stella deserved to be a Toreador because she saw the world through artistic eyes. She'd made a poor living as a decent photographer as a mortal, and it was work she continued, though she now specialized in night photography for unavoidable reasons.

"Let's hope this sets things even," Stella said as she approached Leopold.

"What do you mean?"

Stella grimaced, the memories hurting her too, but she said, "Two bad encounters and then one good one. This will make a second good meeting, and things will be even."

The Toreador laughed. "Don't expect karma to be part of a Kindred's life, Stella."

She was close now, and Leopold hugged her. When she warmly returned his friendly gesture, Leopold reprimanded himself for thinking so horribly about her clanlessness. He admitted to himself that she was the kind of girl that would suit him if they could both still be Kine and never have been exposed to so much more of the world than he wished he knew even now.

Stella's grimace was intact. "I don't expect anything out of Kindred life, Leo." She was the only person who called him that. The only one who had ever called him that who had not been immediately corrected. It was the name she'd cried that night after she'd drained every drop of red from the man who had assaulted her, and Leopold hadn't wished to make an issue of it then. For some reason, he continued to let it slide.

"Let's hope we get better than this guy got, at least," Leopold said, thumbing his hand at the two-and-a-half-foot-high bronze sculpture in the center of the alcove.

"It's the devil, I suppose," said Stella. "Seems like all the sculptures here tonight are rather demonic."

"As are the guests," Leopold suggested. "But, you're right. The piece is called *Satan* and was sculpted by a man named Feuchere. Look at him." Leopold pointed to the center of the work. "Satan, that is," he added.

The leathery-looking wings of the statue were partly unfolded so that they hid Satan's face. Inside this region of shadow, the horned and taloned plotter sat with his chin in a hand and his head cocked akimbo. And though the representation was that of a beast, the human qualities of the figure showed through and Stella felt a swelling of compassion as she gazed upon that face at Leopold's request.

Leopold said glumly, "It's the kind of work my condition should allow me to realize."

Stella gave him a sad look. "Your block is still stopping you from sculpting Kindred? I'm sorry, Leo."

Leopold was tempted to tell Stella about his recent success as the urge to share the news with someone friendly to him was great. Instead, he remained glumly silent, and he let that silence tell his lie for him.

They stood in silence for quite some time, and Stella used the opportunity to examine *Satan* more closely.

"You can do work at least this good," she said at last.

Leopold nodded, graciously accepting her praise.

Then he said, "Have you seen my new piece on display here tonight?"

Stella brightened, delighted to move the conversation onward and away from oppressive thoughts. "No. No, I haven't. I would be honored if you would show it to me."

Leopold took Stella's arm and moved to exit the alcove. Then he stopped and suddenly inquired, "You've not seen Hannah here tonight, have you?"

Stella said, "The Tremere? No I haven't. In fact, come to think of it, I don't believe any Tremere are here yet."

"Is that odd?"

"Oh, very," she said. "The Tremere are very political, and I can't imagine a gathering like this at which they did not have someone here early in order to spy on everyone else. I call them gadflies, which is what Rolph must be for the Nosferatu."

Leopold didn't know such things himself, but he trusted Stella to know. She was working hard to learn the ropes of Kindred society. Nothing else was working to her benefit, and her willingness to tackle such situations suggested to Leopold that she would find a way to overcome her clanless status, even if supposed friends like himself continued to be assholes.

Stella asked, "Did you need to see her for some reason? If so, I'd be careful. She drives hard and dangerous bargains. At least that's what I hear."

And then they both heard something more. A commotion just outside the alcove was drawing the attention of all the nearby Kindred, and Leopold and Stella stepped out just in time to catch a royal entrance.

Stella's mouth dropped and she stared at the emerging figures. Leopold, though, had other things on his mind, and he still needed a moment alone.

He whispered in Stella's ear, "I'll meet you at my sculpture later." She nodded slightly, so she at least heard him, though he wasn't certain if she listened too.

The attention of many of the guests was suddenly drawn toward the center of the room. Victoria was grateful for something that gave her direction so she did not have to linger at the entrance any longer, or choose her own first conversation. There would be charges of favoritism if she chose poorly. Now fate had intervened, so any expectations of social niceties would be forgotten.

She approached the ruckus. Sipping from her red-filled flute, Victoria smiled at Clarice, a young Ventrue who stood nearby. The blood coated Victoria's lips and she carefully licked it off before saying, "Something interesting, I hope."

Clarice was polite, "There's much of interest here tonight, Ms. Ash."

"'Victoria' is fine," the Toreador corrected. "As a Ventrue you should learn that most Kindred prefer titles in keeping with their apparent age, not their actual age."

"That's odd," Clarice admitted. She was a tall and heavily built woman. By no means fat, she was full-figured, though she retained a degree of physical grace which Victoria appreciated because this rather plain woman needed something to compensate for her deficiencies. Clarice's drab, conservative clothing certainly did not alleviate her need.

Victoria disagreed, "It's not so strange really, if you consider the instinct for the Masquerade that many Kindred have accumulated for several centuries now. It seems a small thing perhaps, to avoid a scene where an older man calls a younger man "Sir" or "Mister" when they appear to be of the same station, but I suggest to you that it would seem less foreign to you if you lived in a climate where the existence of our kind was not forgotten or overlooked as it is today."

Clarice didn't have any means of responding to such a statement that carried so much authority. Nor was she seemingly prepared for the length of the retort. She could only salvage her Ventrue pride with a quip: "Your case appears sound to me, Victoria."

And then they reached Jean-Baptiste Carpeaux's *Count Ugolino and Sons*. A small crowd of a half dozen Kindred besides Victoria and Clarice had gathered. A tall, slender man, whom Victoria imagined was the Setite she'd been convinced to invite, was among them. Javic, not yet free of Cyndy, stood aloof from the rest of the group, but he had been drawn by curiosity as well. The other three Kindred were the African-American Ventrue Benjamin, who was a close friend of the Prince's wife Eleanor; the sole Brujah, Thelonious; and the center of attention, the Kindred known only as the General.

This was only the second time Victoria had seen this last Kindred. All she knew was the common knowledge: he was Malkavian; he was recently awakened from Torpor, which he had evidently spent inside Stone Mountain, a huge chunk of granite east of Atlanta; and he had been witnessed by the Gangrel called Dusty stepping from the mountain.

In years past, or so Victoria had been told, Benison had been relatively loathe to accept new Kindred into Atlanta. The destruction brought by the Blood Curse changed all that, and indeed a majority of the Kindred in attendance thus far this evening were either new to town, including Victoria herself, or even newly Embraced. The General was part of that group as well, but Benison doubtlessly would have granted him permission to remain regardless, since the Prince too was Malkavian.

Such Kindred were invariably demented in some manner, though like many madmen they could often appear sane. Some, like the prophet of Gehenna named Anatole, hid their madness behind no such facade, and he and other Malkavians claimed their madness came from too often seeing the truth overlooked by other Kindred who still dwelt too much in the world of Kine. In essence, Malkavians like Anatole insisted there was a Masquerade greater than the one perpetrated by Kindred on the Kine. With her healthy fear of unseen powers, Victoria accepted this madness of the Malkavians as wisdom. Most others did not.

Because Malkavians intrigued her so, Victoria had made certain the General received an invitation to this party. She was delighted he had attended. Authentically delighted. Unlike some Kindred awakened from Torpor—the deep sleep a Kindred slips into for as long as a century at a time—and especially ones waking now, when the last hundred or fifty or even twenty years had brought so much change to the world, the General seemed at ease with the new world and took little time to adapt. Either that, or he was powerful enough to overcome a deficit of knowledge.

Victoria and the others assembled watched the Malkavian with interest. His clothes already stripped from his body and strewn across the floor, the General clambered onto the podium that held Carpeaux's great work. His muscular and naked body was not unattractive, and though he sported a grand physique, Victoria saw nothing that particularly dazzled her. Her charms worked better when men were more impressive than this.

The General crouched at the feet of Count Ugolino, where he summoned a grotesquely inappropriate *têtes d'expression* in conjunction with the four naked sons of the Count who crouched, reclined, or fainted at his feet. His expression of comical happiness made Victoria shudder, for the son nearest his position held a plaster incarnation of fear and even terror upon his face. Completing the *têtes d'expression*, the other sons displayed other emotions, none of them joyous, for the Count above them was soon to devour them. The Count himself sat above his sons, but his powerful body was hunched and his face twisted with madness, and he ripped at his face with fingers bent like claws.

The General was as wild-haired as when he had first presented himself to the Prince and the council of primogen, though he no longer wore the uniform of the Confederate soldier he claimed to have stolen from the racks at a souvenir store in Stone Mountain Park, but which the Prince greeted as a sign that the General had fought on his side and perhaps at his side in the War of Northern Aggression. At the time, the newcomer introduced himself only as the General, which of course led everyone to wonder if he had been one, though Benison did not recognize him. He refused to answer most questions put to him, and when the Brujah Primogen Thelonious demanded better answers, the General nonchalantly ripped the tongue from his own mouth and placed it on the table before the nonplussed council member.

Benison had laughed and granted the General permission to remain. If Benison needed another reason, an insult to his constant enemy the Brujah was reason enough.

With his tongue presumably regrown, the General now climbed to sit alongside the Count, his butt cheeks wedged over the face of the fearful son he'd mocked a moment before. The Malkavian was in much better health than months before. In fact, his previously wasted frame now rippled with muscles so that he seemed a twin of the plaster Count. And as the Kindred spectators watched, the General literally became one with Count Ugolino. As some Kindred had the ability to sink into the earth—and clearly the General possessed that ability, if he had slept within Stone Mountain for the one hundred and thirty-plus years since the Civil War—he either became somewhat discorporeal or otherwise attuned to the structure of the plaster, and slipped within the Count. As this transition took place, the Count's expression of madness slowly shifted to the beaming jocularity preferred by the General.

Victoria tried to make sense of this potentially profound, potentially whimsical, potentially ridiculous gesture of the General's. She looked around and the others seemed at a loss too. All except Javic, for he stepped away from the scene shaking his head. He could have been dismissing the event as ridiculous, but something in his earnest refusal struck Victoria as knowing. Javic's irritation with Cyndy finally overcame him again, and he shook the Toreador from his arm with a swift jerk that sent Cyndy to the floor. This time, he did not catch her. Victoria would have laughed aloud and pressed her advantage over the young Toreador, but she did not wish to transform Cyndy from a passive to determined enemy. A Prince needed friends, which was exactly what Benison largely lacked.

The only Brujah present, and likely one of only two that would be present throughout the night, was Thelonious. He seemed somewhat irritated by the General's performance, though perhaps it was only the General himself whom Thelonious opposed. Victoria found that funny, for the Brujah were usually in favor of any variety of disruption, especially if it might offend others. But then, Thelonious was an atypical Brujah, which perhaps explained why he had once been the only Brujah Prince Benison would recognize as an official member of Atlanta's Kindred. That, or it would have looked unseemly not to have at least a Brujah Primogen. Brujah typified the Anarch movement among Kindred of the Camarilla. They were the rebels who wanted to see an end to the conservative, usually Ventrue, control of the organization, and they dressed as rebels will—in clothing that allows them to stand out prominently from those they oppose.

One of the reasons Thelonious was so atypical was his conservative dress. He favored modern suits and small, round-rimmed glasses. He was a young black man, one who was surprisingly soft-looking for a Brujah warrior, but Victoria had heard tales of how this man had fought Benison, and knew better than to be fooled by the large, doe-like eyes that seemed to make evident a meek and compassionate heart.

Tonight, however, Thelonious was arrayed in traditional African clothing. The loose-fitting robe was bright orange with colorful bands of pink, yellow and green swirling across and around it. He wore a small round hat on his head, and tonight he disdained the use of his usual eyeglasses. Coming back to this fact now, Victoria realized it was actually the first thing she had noticed, for without the glasses amplifying the gentle expression of his eyes, Thelonious seemed suddenly capable of ferocious glares. It was such a look of intense disfavor that he now bestowed upon the General.

Benjamin seemed very puzzled and extremely disturbed by the General's display. Victoria felt Benjamin was a very attractive man. In fact, he could have been a poster-boy for the successful modern African-American, which was why Victoria was surprised Benison had accepted him into Atlanta even if he was supposedly an old acquaintance of the Prince's wife, Eleanor, for what might the Prince hate more than a successful black man, or black vampire? The truth was that Benjamin was Eleanor's childe, and Benison didn't know it. At least, not yet. Victoria's entrance through Heaven demanded that the Prince no longer remain bereft of the truth. Thank Heaven, so to speak, for Hannah's amazing ability to deduce or somehow determine a given Kindred's sire.

Like Javic, the two black men departed as well, but they did so together. Victoria smiled. It was particularly important that these two speak to one another. Her plan called for an African-American alliance, and it would be best if these two started before Julius arrived to provide the final glue or impetus.

The scene flashed in her mind's eye. Benison killing Eleanor, Eleanor killing Benjamin, Julius killing Benison. If Benison could take Thelonious with him, then so much the better. She smiled at these thoughts.

Beside her, Clarice shuddered and said, "It's ghastly. Those children seem so unhappy and now… that smile."

Victoria glanced back to the sculpture. It seemed as though the General was going to remain within the Count. If so, she would have to remember he was there, because it wouldn't do to reveal any of her plots accidentally when no Kindred were apparent. The ghoulish smile beaming at the plaster children was indeed disconcerting, but much was this evening, which was perfect for Victoria. A little nervous tension would help her pot boil later. Besides, Victoria felt this party was an opportunity to reveal to everyone what fearless stuff she was made of. Did they expect impressionist paintings or classical nudes? Every piece on display tonight alluded to a terrible story, whether it was Satan's fall, the wicked Count's feast of children, or Caine's murder of Abel.

Victoria answered Clarice, "Perhaps the General is only displaying his own artwork for our amusement—his own interpretation of the Count's terrible predicament."

"The Count?"

"Come now, Clarice. Surely you know your Dante?"

The Ventrue smiled. "That book about Hell, you mean?"

"Yes," sighed Victoria. "Count Ugolino and his sons were imprisoned in a tower to starve to death, so, to save himself, the Count devoured his children."

Clarice shuddered, and Victoria found she liked

this large woman very little. The works on display separated the wheat from the chaff, and Clarice had been winnowed.

The Setite was clearly wheat, for when Victoria looked his way she saw a thin smile divide his face. He also noted Clarice's shivering reaction, and that apparently was what amused him. His eyes then darted to Victoria's, and the two regarded one another momentarily. Victoria was suddenly glad that Rolph had told her the Setite would be visiting the city. She smiled coquettishly at the tall, straight and narrow man. To that, the man's smile grew impossibly longer, as if his face might indeed split like a serpent's.

Then Clarice was on top of Victoria again, and the exchange ended.

"He really ate his children?" she asked nervously.

Victoria was perturbed by this incessant prattle. "Yes," she insisted firmly. "Just as we Kindred eat mortal children. Aren't the parallels between art and reality refreshing and engaging?" With that Victoria stepped away decisively.

She swept her gaze around the room to find the Setite again, but he was under cover somewhere. Victoria adjusted the brooch on her right shoulder that was all that held her Grecian gown on her body, then reached into that garment's pocket for her opera glasses. It was time not only to find the Setite, but also to see what else she was missing. Particularly the conversation between Thelonious and Benjamin Brown.

Victoria was the last to slip away from *Count Ugolino and His Sons*. The General was presumably still within the statue, because the new expression of delight remained. She glanced again at that face and once more sought significance in it. Was this another message concerning her mission tonight? In the end, she accepted it merely as the means by which two of her hopeful threesome came together, not that either of those men would be able to withhold their accusations for long.

She was much humored to discover the two black men—one Brujah, considered the clan of rebels, and one Ventrue, thought of as the clan of aristocrats, usually a volatile mixture but one brought together by a mutual disregard for Prince Benison—pondering the implications of the General's mad display.

She watched the two men through her opera glasses from a position safe from discovery. The migration away from the General and the disruption the Malkavian's display had caused in the first place granted Victoria time and cover enough to slip into a special cubicle she had prepared during set-up and construction. It was a small area about five feet by five feet, and perhaps eight feet high, that was surrounded by the opaque glass utilized throughout the larger chamber. Entry was quick and easy via one of the glass planes that doubled as a sliding door.

The potentially most important touch was the trapdoor on the floor. She expected to use the interior of the cubicle to safely view those outside it, but in case she feared discovery, Victoria could always slip down through the floor and then lock the trapdoor from beneath.

Now inside the small but ample area, Victoria could freely use her special glasses to pierce the shadow of the glass and view anyone attending the party who had not taken other precautions to remain unseen. On that count, Victoria was especially wary of Rolph, as even among Nosferatu Rolph was considered a master of his art. Victoria tried to keep an eye on Rolph, not with the expectation of actually seeing anything interesting, but more to deduce his actions by his physical omission. That is, when he disappeared, it was possible that he was still at the party, but attending to his or his clan's goals more stealthily.

For the moment, though, Victoria was only concerned with Thelonious and Benjamin. These two men, along with the Brujah Archon Julius, figured intimately into her plans. The bright orange robe Thelonious wore was the first object to come into view in the Toreador's opera glasses, and she adjusted the zoom and focus so she could clearly see the sides of both men's faces. Lip reading was difficult, but hardly impossible.

Benjamin was saying, "Perhaps it's that robe you're wearing, Thelonious. It brings out the shaman in you."

"If I were wearing my business suit, then I wouldn't try to find messages in the General's odd display?"

The two men eyed each warily and with a hint of threat as well. It was no wonder, as each thought the other had recently posed a threat. But Victoria knew they would speak despite her faked messages, especially when those threats came the night before Elysium presented the opportunity to inquire about or face down those threats.

Benjamin shrugged his shoulders and said, "Maybe. Maybe not. The madman's behavior seems like nothing more than a Malkavian's warped sensibilities being put in the open for our amusement."

Thelonious shook his head. "That's just it. Why would he wish to entertain us?"

"It *is* a party."

"That doesn't matter to a Malkavian. It may be a party in this world, but not in the dark interiors of his addled mind. No, whether his performance actually means anything to us or not, I guarantee that it means something to the General."

Victoria grew frustrated with this small talk. Either the two men knew one another better than Victoria realized—and that would probably only further her plans, so it didn't concern her at all—or they were staging this small talk. Staging it to pass real messages by code, perhaps. None of that seemed right, and by widening the view her glasses allowed so she could read their body language as well as their lips, Victoria decided that they were both anxious to be about the business of an earnest discussion, but neither seemed certain how the other would receive a frank statement.

Victoria mouthed the words she hoped Benjamin would say. And either her powers had grown more than she imagined possible or Benjamin took the plunge on his own, because the Ventrue glanced about them and motioned Thelonious deeper into the alcove formed by the glass panes.

The Brujah squinted his eyes fiercely at the Ventrue, but he accepted the invitation and also said something Victoria missed. She quickly zoomed in on the pair so only their heads were displayed in the magnified field of the glasses. She caught more of the conversation.

Benjamin said, "I'm surprised you're here tonight, Thelonious."

The Brujah's mild face grew a touch more hostile and he prepared to bark something, but the Ventrue cut him off.

"Obviously, you're not frightened of the Prince. If I wished to insult you, then I would not do it so crudely. I am not a centuries-old Confederate soldier." It wasn't necessary, but Benjamin emphasized his obvious reference by a tilt of the head and a raised eyebrow. Thelonious and Victoria both understood he referred to Benison, not the General.

Thelonious's features smoothed again, and the Brujah actually grinned, though only briefly. In her cubicle some distance away, Victoria smiled as she continued to eavesdrop. The real conversation was beginning.

Benjamin continued, "I don't respond to blackmail."

Thelonious cocked his head at this. He was caught a bit off-guard, but then he snapped, "Nor do I."

It was Benjamin's turn to be taken aback.

This was great fun and very revealing for Victoria, for she knew the basis upon which both of these men spoke. If everything worked according to plan, then these would be her remaining rivals in Atlanta, so any clue to their methods was a boon to her future.

The Ventrue said, "But you expect others to be swayed by such strong-arm tactics? I must say I'm disappointed, Thelonious. I thought you were less typically Brujah."

Thelonious chuckled, "'Typically Brujah'? How typically Ventrue."

"Nevertheless, I remain disturbed by your tactics."

The Brujah said, "Our difference, then, is that I'm not surprised by your tactics."

Benjamin gritted his teeth and said, "Is there something unusual about using the protection of Elysium to confront you? Elysium may be a concept invented by and for elders more than Anarchs, but your presence here tonight, in spite of the Prince's efforts against you, reveals your faith in this convention as well."

"No, there's no shame in Elysium. The integrity of your offer, on the hand, is disputable."

"My offer? Is that how you wish to view the matter? Your letter didn't give me any indication—"

"My letter?" Thelonious interrupted.

"Yes, your let—"

Thelonious interrupted again, "You mean your—"

"Stop interrupting me!" Benjamin hissed. But then he recovered as Thelonious's words registered. "Mine?"

And at the same time, the Ventrue and the Brujah took their eyes off one another and looked around, and looked out the open end of the alcove. Victoria imagined they could be brothers, they were acting so similarly. She wasn't sure yet whether that was to her advantage or not.

She continued to watch them, safe from their dread gazes. Or so she hoped. And so it seemed.

They reappraised one another when their eyes locked again.

Thelonious said, "I take it you didn't send—"

"No, and nor did you?"

The Brujah asked, "So who then?"

"I don't know," admitted the Ventrue. "Nor do I know whether this trick was meant to unite or divide us."

Thelonious seemed puzzled. "To divide us, I presume."

Benjamin pointed out, "On the eve of an affair at Elysium? Might we not possibly have a discussion and revelation exactly like the one we're having now?"

Victoria grinned in appreciation. Perhaps Benjamin was the deeper thinker.

Thelonious nodded his agreement.

Gasps suddenly rang out from Kindred near the entrance of the party chamber, and Victoria reflexively turned to look that way. The great doors of Heaven and Hell were swinging open simultaneously. Such was the clamor caused by the four great doors opening at once, that everyone near the entrance turned to behold the source of the commotion.

# part three:
# the eye

Backlit by the light from the outer chamber, which outshone the diffuse light spread by the spotlights focused on the sculptures, the figure in the open doors crafted by Rodin was revealed in silhouette to be a woman, or at least it was a thin-boned person with pleats of piled hair and outfitted in a great hoop dress. The outline of the man backlit as he stood in the open doorway of *The Ten Commandments* should have been dwarfed by the awesome creation, and though the man was truly not a giant and stood only some few inches over six feet tall, J. Benison Hodge, *Prince* J. Benison Hodge, projected so powerful an aura that no mere portal could overwhelm him.

Victoria cursed. A few moments more and she might have learned much of how her unknowing allies would proceed. As it was, she took advantage of the commotion to slip back out of her hidden room and move toward the doors.

The drama of the arrival rippled through the ranks of the assembled Kindred. As both the Prince and his wife stepped forward, Victoria found that she needed to steady herself against the dizziness that tickled her head. Both these Kindred were such potent presences—the Prince powerful and commanding, his wife lovely and radiant with something other than physical beauty—that her struggle to attend to them both was impossible. They each demanded—no, deserved—her full attention. And even though Victoria knew the instinct to deify them both thus was an effect they purposefully created with their Kindred powers, it was hard to resist.

Finally recovering for a moment, she looked around and to her amusement saw that she was resisting far better than most. Clarice and Cyndy were particularly obsequious as they practically threw themselves on the floor in an attempt to show proper respect and worship for these two godlings. Others, like Javic, Rolph and even Thelonious, showed the strain of resisting. Most interesting to Victoria was the Setite's response. He seemed not to flinch or quiver, and perhaps straightened himself to appear even taller.

When Eleanor revealed herself completely by gliding into the direct light, Victoria shuddered. The Toreador did not like to admit she possessed an enemy so much her equal, and even superior. Perhaps Eleanor was not quite as beautiful as Victoria, but the Toreador knew any actual physical shortcomings—and they were few indeed, for the woman was delicately crafted and boasted exquisite qualities that left men speechless, such as her milky pale skin, her glittering green eyes, her high, regal cheekbones— were more than compensated by phenomenal control over many of the disciplines of Kindred power that Victoria too possessed.

Where Victoria might use her beauty to snare even wary men, Eleanor could enhance her beauty to enrapture men, and even women, who considered her their enemy. In fact, Victoria wondered how it was that she herself remained safe from this insidious effect she'd personally witnessed infecting Kindred whose hatred for the Prince's wife was well known to Victoria.

For in truth, no one could hate the Prince and not also despise Eleanor. She was obviously an equal partner in the relationship, and that meant she ruled equally, though the Prince was known to make rash decisions over which Eleanor presumably had no sway or council. They were so patently opposite yet so perfectly suited for one another: He a cunning American land-owner with ambitions of royalty, and she a noblewoman with ambitions of power. Both had achieved their dreams, and both were fantastically powerful.

When the Prince strode full into the light, by contrast, there were no revelations beyond what the silhouette impression had conveyed. He was powerfully built with a bull chest and long, thick arms and legs. His hair was long and auburn, and he wore a full beard that with his generous mustache and bushy eyebrows swamped his face. He was very forthcoming when the conversation concerned himself, so Victoria had learned some time ago that he was Embraced when in his mid-thirties, yet the touches of gray in his hair, his receding hairline and a barrel-chested body just slightly relenting to a thick waist revealed to Victoria that he must have lived a hard life as a Confederate soldier those many years ago.

Nevertheless, as now, there could be great kindness in his face. When he smiled thusly and had good color in his face, he seemed like a Kris Kringle before age had brought snow-white hair. Victoria doubted there were any present who had not also seen their Prince fully in the grip of his great and sudden rage. Victoria momentarily pictured an enraged Benison in her mind, but the image was too terrible, so she instead dwelt upon the beneficence of the present incarnation of the man.

As those two impressive individuals continued their slow entrance into the room, a pair of Caitiffs that Victoria barely recognized as Grant and Fingers had the misfortune of stepping into view through the still-open doorway of *The Gates of Hell*. While the two men seemed strong and capable individuals, they looked so ordinary and feeble in the radiance of their Elders that their intrigued gawking was comical.

Thelonious was the first to laugh, but then he was probably looking for any legitimate excuse to embarrass the Prince. Prince Benison's eyes flew wide in shock and hatred, and Victoria wilted before the heat of the very transformation she had denied in her imagination only an instant before. The collision of reality and her thoughts made the Prince's terrible rage even more frightening.

The color rushed from Benison's face, revealing a whole host of scars across his forehead and eyes. His cheeks fell in, his eyes seemed to shrivel into their sockets, and his massively bearded jaw clamped with great force. The effect was that of seeing a humble, kindly man suddenly transformed into something more akin to the Prince's true existence—something that sought revenge from beyond the grave.

"You dare!" he exclaimed loudly. One of his large hands curled into a sledgehammer fist that pounded once, then twice into the open palm of the other hand. "You dare show yourself before me!" he continued. It was not a question, but a statement, pronouncement of doom.

Victoria was delighted to hear it, for it meant the Prince was indeed on the edge this evening, probably anxious because Julius would be present, and that would make her work simpler.

Despite himself, Thelonious shrank at the challenge. He was frozen in his tracks like doomed prey, and the Prince's swift verbal assault seemed certain prelude to annihilation.

Until Victoria intervened. She stepped close to Benison and said, "Great Prince, please do not forget that the law of Elysium holds sway here because you yourself have declared it to be so."

Benison glowered at her, and it took every ounce of Victoria's will and the fortification of the desire to see her plans to fruition to withstand the incendiary presence of the Prince.

"I revoke my declaration," he snarled.

Victoria took a half-step back. She needed to keep the peace until all the elements were present, and Julius, the Justicar's envoy, had not yet arrived. On the other hand, she did not wish to put herself in the path of the Prince's anger, and she did not desire him to feel that she played any part greater than that required of a concerned primogen and the hostess of this party to stay his hand.

Victoria looked to Eleanor for help, but the Prince's so-called wife had her deadly gaze full upon Thelonious as well. There was no alliance between *this* Ventrue—the Ventrue primogen—and the Brujah primogen. Some Kindred suggested that it was her hatred of the clan that prompted Benison's savage attacks.

As the Toreador considered what to do next, she saw the two Caitiff slip around the angry scene and join the crowd of spectators. It might be that the Prince had not seen them earlier and would not know where he might seek revenge for Thelonious's laughter.

Then Victoria stepped close to the Prince again and whispered so only he and others of extraordinary auditory abilities might hear her. She said, "Please, great Prince, I worry for your safety on this night that Julius, the Brujah archon, visits. But, of course, you know best how to handle such tricky and political situations."

More quickly than she had imagined the Prince might register her words, his face transformed again. The rage and hate did not melt away, but instantly evaporated, and the Prince wore an expression of magnanimity. The look was too exaggerated to be real, and everyone knew it. Such serenity did not sit well on the Prince's face, and not for the first time Victoria imagined that he must truly be mad, must truly bear the scars of the Malkavian clan, to change his emotional clothes so quickly and easily.

Then the Prince looked at Thelonious as he somehow grinned a bit more broadly. The Brujah involuntarily recoiled a step and Victoria saw him shiver. *Benison must have put a little mojo into that look,* she thought.

Then the Prince stepped toward Eleanor and put his left arm around her. His right arm lifted skyward and with a flourish he declared their presence again.

Benison said, "Let us enjoy the shortest night of the year, and let us find that every moment tonight carries the weight of two on any other."

Champagne glasses tinked and chimed and there were mutters of "hear, hear" and "cheers", and though the moment of the solstice had passed some hours before, as the time neared half past eleven and the crowd pushed toward the rear of the gallery, the party was officially on.

Victoria helped usher everyone away from the entrance and then stayed to make sure the servants would be quick to supply the far end of the gallery. When she turned to join the guests, Victoria saw that Eleanor was waiting for her.

The Toreador primogen approached her Ventrue counterpart. When she neared, Eleanor gave Victoria a hug in greeting. Or rather, the Ventrue made it plain she was favoring Victoria with a hug.

When the Kindred separated, Eleanor said, "This looks like a wonderful party, my dear. You must be very satisfied." Her face was animated with all the false sincerity she could muster, which was enough to fool and flatter anyone but one as perceptive as Victoria.

Victoria wanted to gut the bitch right here, but she knew she had to be careful. On the other hand, too much care might alert Eleanor as much as a blatant warning, so she had to play along with the Ventrue's double-entendre politics.

"Well, thank you, Eleanor. Such compliments certainly mean something when they come from you. But I'm not really satisfied yet. Why, I'd say the entertainment and fun has really yet even to begin. My only regret is that I dressed in this Grecian style, when Roman would have been so much more suitable."

Eleanor narrowed her eyes. She too knew Julius's background as a gladiator in ancient Rome.

Then the Ventrue said, "It is certainly quite a cast of characters you'll have on hand tonight."

"Oh, indeed," Victoria agreed. "But all of them, those from out of town too, have been strictly informed of the High's Elysium status. I'm sure no one would even consider breaking the Prince's peace."

Eleanor bit her bottom lip. "Of course not. The Prince is a vengeful Kindred, and it's not wise to cross him."

"It's true that no one is safe when opposed by the weight of Camarilla law," Victoria admitted, obviously less concerned now about Elysium than other recent events in Atlanta, such as the dubious crackdown on the anarchs and the Brujah in particular.

When Eleanor was silent for a moment, Victoria continued, "Atlanta used to be such a backwater that the Camarilla probably cared little what happened here. But our Prince has done an excellent job of drawing attention to us all."

"Oh, he has done a fine job, hasn't he? The Olympics, of course, were a splendid coup."

Victoria brightened with feigned realization. "That's right, maybe my Grecian clothing is appropriate after all."

The edge of Eleanor's lip trembled, and the Ventrue had clearly had enough. "I'd best rejoin my husband," she said as she turned her back on any farewell Victoria might offer. But after a few steps she turned right back.

"You know," the Ventrue said, "it will be good to have a Camarilla representative here tonight. I find the long memory of the organization to be simply amazing, and I'm led to believe we'll all have some interesting surprises tonight."

Victoria didn't have a response. Her eyes just blinked a few times in rapid succession. Eleanor smiled and walked away, alternating her thumb up and down in the style of a Roman Emperor. After several repetitions, all barely but completely within Victoria's view, the Ventrue decided on thumbs down and she half turned her head to flutter her eyelids at Victoria one more time.

The Toreador was stunned. Eleanor had allowed Victoria to steamroll her in that conversation in order to make that last blow even more unexpected and telling. More than that, she was worried about what Julius might know, because there were a couple of well-concealed secrets of her past that were best left buried.

Victoria had expected to be on the offensive all night, and this sudden twist made her fear her own defenses were inadequate.

Monday, 21 June 1999, 11:24 PM
The High Museum of Art
Atlanta, Georgia

The gesture was virtually frictionless: nearly poreless, alabaster skin stroking smooth, cool marble. His hand gliding to a stop, Vegel gently and methodically clasped the wrist of the sculpture, his attention so fixed on this simple act that it became meditative.

Vegel stood thus for many moments. As his fingertips resumed their fluttering along a forearm of one of the sculpture's figures, Vegel lost his thoughts in the display of emotion captured in the marble expressions of the grieving parents. The son's head cradled in the lap of the seated father. The childless mother—for now one was dead and the other exiled—collapsed on the ground beside her limp son, clutching his arm, burying her head in his shoulder. Her anguish was acute, almost cruel in its portrayal, while the father's questioning eyes gazed up, looking for the God he knew with certainty did exist.

Transfixed though he was, Vegel noted two things: first, the lighting for this sculpture was too diffuse, failing to reveal the detail of Canova's chisel marks completely; and second, someone was approaching him from behind. Whoever drew near stopped, though whether loitering to speak with Vegel or lingering in courtesy of Vegel's presumed reverie, the Kindred did not know.

Not willing to disengage wholly from his appreciation of the sculpture, Vegel hoped to dismiss the need to converse with a mutter of small talk that might encourage the uninterested to leave him uninterrupted. "There is no marble smoother than Canova's." As was his habit, to annoy those fond of stereotypes and to encourage those drawn to legend, Vegel drew his "s" out a bit, so his "sssmoother" had something of a hiss.

He was answered mirthfully, "Nor any skin so ripe for plucking by the serpent fangs." A woman's voice—he recognized it immediately from the charming laughter he'd heard earlier: Vegel's hostess, Victoria Ash.

Vegel gathered himself, allowing the emotional residue of his interaction with the beautiful sculpture to drain away. Turning, he said, "Good evening, Ms. Ash. Were you observing, expecting me to nip Eve's marble flesh and double the caterwauling of the Kine as their descent from God hastens?"

"My, my, Vegel. I do believe this piece has you in a philosophical frame of mind." Victoria Ash stood before Vegel. As a peacock could outshine an emu, then surely the most beloved of mortal models would be lonely for lack of admirers when Victoria Ash was nearby. Her features were as perfect as only those of a beautiful Kindred could be—the perfection Antonio Canova had reserved for the mythical subjects of his sculpture: Eve, Psyche, Venus, or even the magnificent Head of Helen elsewhere in this room, which Vegel instantly realized was Victoria's guise of the evening.

With exaggeration so lavish as to border on embarrassing, Vegel's eyes traveled up and down Victoria's slender yet sumptuous frame, which was clothed in a silken and sleeveless variation of a classic Greek robe. Then Vegel mock-bowed and recited:

"In this beloved marble view
"Above the works and thoughts of Man
"What nature could, but would not, do,
"And beauty and Canova can!
"Beyond imagination's power
"Beyond the Bard's defeated art
"With immortality her dower
"Behold the Helen of the heart."

An enchanted smile warmed Victoria's face, though Vegel knew it was deceit no greater or less than he could expect from any Kindred with whom he spoke this evening.

Victoria stepped closer, whispering, "I would not have recognized that bit of Byron's before planning this little display for tonight." To emphasize how "little" her display was, Victoria gracefully fanned her hands to her sides to indicate the extent of the huge chamber. Meanwhile, she elegantly stretched her neck—revealing a marvelous profile—to absorb the scene along with her guest.

Naturally, Vegel looked about as well, though he took a half step backward, since his instincts found his hostess's proximity a little too cozy.

The entire top floor of Atlanta's High Museum of Art had indeed been transformed into a neoclassicist's dream. Vegel knew that the quality, let alone history, or rather historical impossibility, of most of the pieces on display was lost on the hollow-eyed and cheerless crowd that formed the majority of Victoria's guests.

There were many more Kindred here now than earlier. The crowd was beginning to differentiate with the arrival of a less couth element of the Camarilla society. No longer were the only guests those interested in political maneuvering. Some of the Kindred were actually examining the sculpture rather than the minute facial ticks of a debate opponent, though Vegel noted the specifics of one such examination of the artwork—a black-leather-clad idiot was sniffing the hindquarters of Adriano Cecioni's *Dog Defecating*.

The works of art were amazing, but no less so than the fine ringlets of dark hair arranged on Victoria's head in perfect duplication of Canova's Helen. Vegel didn't know Victoria's true age, but her stunning hair framed a face that could be that of a woman in her mid-twenties. She was slightly rounder than the athletic good looks held in vogue by modern American women, but she surely came from a time well before this century, and hers was a classical beauty sure to please no matter the trend of the decade or day. There was a bit of a Mediterranean hue to her, but Vegel couldn't be sure if that guess was overly influenced by her similarity to Helen of Troy. Perhaps it was the hint of Asia in her eyes.

Victoria caught him looking. "Am I a dancing cobra to transfix so easily another serpent?"

Vegel's response was witty and quick. "I have no doubt that you could deceive as proficiently as the serpent who claimed Eve, but if we are to remain on this theme of my Setite clan, then I will admit the snake-like coils of your hair do indeed mesmerize me. However, my fascination with the Eve of this *Mourning the Dead Abel* has nothing to do with cold-blooded kinship. The available knowledge claims the piece was never executed in marble from the terracotta *bozzetto* Canova prepared."

Victoria's response was enthusiastic. "Delightful!" she exclaimed. "Perhaps my innuendo of snakes was misguided. Perhaps I should treat you as an honorary Toreador, so extensive is your knowledge of these masterpieces. But of course, the knowledge to which you refer is merely *mortal* knowledge, and we are both clearly in a position to possess much more than that."

"That is true, Ms. Ash."

"Please, just Victoria is fine, or for tonight 'Helen,' if you prefer, and it seems that you might as I noted earlier that you were quite taken by the bust and now quite by my own…resemblance to it."

Vegel smiled sourly at Victoria's stutter. "That is true as well, 'Helen.'"

Victoria did not acknowledge her guest's expression, but only said, "How is it that you come by such knowledge of art masterpieces?"

Vegel stepped away from the sculpture as he answered the Toreador. It made him uncomfortable to have such a trifling conversation so near the heart-rending anguish that was Adam and Eve's for their son Abel. Especially since Vegel had been warned before that such were the reverberations of the black essence of the first murder, that Caine himself—if he indeed still wandered the Earth—was connected to every portrayal of it and even the mere mention of the event was a clarion call to him. According to the stories Vegel heard, many were the neonate fools who tempted this legend, and enough were the unfortunates who were dead soon after to give superstitious credence to the legend's veracity.

If Victoria noticed his discomfort, then she made no sign of it.

Vegel answered, "In the service of my master, of course."

"Hesha?" Victoria asked, though she clearly knew the answer.

"Yes."

"I was so looking forward to meeting him," Victoria pouted, a behavior splendidly suited to her attire and grooming.

Vegel nodded, and then smiled as he said, "Is that why you treated your guests to Clesinger's scandalous *Woman Bitten by a Snake*? Is it poison or is it ecstasy which makes her writhe so?"

"You're dreadful, Vegel," said Victoria. "But why is it that Hesha would require his progeny to be so mindful of art like dear Auguste's *Woman*? While it is a piece of no small notoriety, and perhaps some innovation for its time, it surely has no special value to a treasure-hunter such as Hesha. If nothing else, then surely its age must be a deterrent. I mean, it's only 150 years old!"

Vegel casually explained, "It is a new piece, 'Helen,' but Hesha desires we be aware of the old and the new. Besides, though 150 years is youthfully refreshing to us, it is quite an ancient age for the new money of the United States. I'm certain there must be a information-age millionaire loaded with silicon dollars who is eager to reveal none-too-subtly to his guests via his new sculpture that he is a hearty man of sexual appetite and not merely a cerebral gentleman of meek physique and diminutive manhood."

"You're very funny, Vegel," Victoria said, smiling. The smile seemed more genuine this time, but that only served to help Vegel maintain his wariness. She continued, "It's no wonder Hesha's wealth is rumored to be so vast. With huntsmen as able as you flushing out the game, he need only scheme the means to obtain it."

Vegel said, "If I seem a show-off, though, it is because you have struck upon a particular fancy of mine—the heads of Helen."

Victoria raised an eyebrow as invitation for him to continue, but Vegel demurred at first.

Still shaking his head, Vegel continued to resist, "No, no, the explanations really reveal much too much about me. I must decline in general, only to say that her divine smile, so finely wrought by Canova, communicates the very essence of self-knowledge. This Helen clearly knows something about herself, her world, and the others who inhabit it, that the others have yet to discover for themselves."

"Perhaps, then, dear Vegel, you should keep the head I have on display tonight. A memento of the evening, shall we say?"

Vegel's back shuddered from a chill wrought by Victoria's face. Her surprising offer was imparted while reproducing exactly the impossible smile of the Head of Helen. It was so perfectly performed that it seemed entirely natural for the moment. Precisely set were the lips wherein the smile was virtually nonexistent but for the slightest cast of the eyes that lent the curious illusion of a smile.

Flustered though he was, and realizing for the first time that he was far, far out of his league when dealing with Victoria Ash, Vegel managed to stumble haltingly forward with the conversation. "A totally unforeseen and unreservedly generous offer, Victoria, but I must decline. Not least of all because I already possess a copy, but properly so as well. You clearly deserve the piece more than I have ever imagined I might."

"Thank you," Victoria said sincerely. "I believe I would have regretted my gift had you accepted. Funny how a piece that has simply served its place as part of my collection could suddenly come to mean something more to me. Thanks go to you, Vegel, for that gift."

Something or someone caught Vegel's attention and he glanced left before returning his gaze to Victoria, though it was not a distraction that escaped her attention.

Vegel said, "As I stated, you clearly deserve it, and now your bust deserves you. However, I fear that as delightful as I find your company, I should remind you that you have other guests here tonight as well. More than a handful of them have cast me baleful gazes for distracting you for so long, so for my sake, perhaps I could encourage you to bless them with your radiant smile."

"Yes, yes," agreed Victoria. "I'm certain we both have other business to attend to tonight. However, I don't regret this time spent with one who was previously a stranger to me. I hope I'll hear from you again, Vegel."

Intrigued, Vegel asked, "Pray tell me, on what pretext, 'Helen'?"

Victoria answered, "Why to examine Helen's bust, of course. Or to bring word of any treasures not fit for Hesha that might on the contrary make a fine contribution to my own collection."

Motioning toward the previously unknown Canova, Vegel said, "Perhaps we should trade positions. I will put my knowledge of art and art history to use as a vain Toreador poseur, and you can put your treasure-hunting wiles to work as a slippery and conniving Setite who pretends many friends but truly has only one if allowed to count himself."

Victoria didn't appear to find such a rude comment surprising, or if she did she hid it with silence.

So Vegel continued, "Therefore, I bid my snake-charmers adieu." Turning to the anguished marble woman, Vegel continued, "Lovely Eve, save us all an inordinate amount of trouble and forgive Caine his transgression."

Then Vegel stepped close to his hostess and whispered to her, "Do not give up your innuendo of serpents, lovely 'Helen.' Though I suspect it will serve you better with mortals than an immortal snake such as myself."

With that, Vegel quickly turned on his heel and strode away. As he did so, the Setite noted with chagrin that the poor lighting from earlier seemed to have been corrected, which was impossible unless the reason for the problem was unassociated with electricity and light bulbs. That made Vegel very uncomfortable.

But Victoria summoned his thoughts back to the moment. A petulant lip pouting at Vegel's back, the Toreador was quick with a parting quip: "Mortals do not interest me, Vegel, and neither do ordinary snakes." Looking back to catch these words, Vegel imagined Victoria as a day-dreaming schoolgirl as she delicately curled a bobbing ringlet around a sleek finger, and then with a deft toss of her neck flicked a kiss at Vegel's receding back.

Vegel wondered what magic she had wrought when he felt the kiss's sensual warmth melt on his neck. How could she have guessed that her sophomoric humor and innuendo would be effective on one as seemingly cultured and intellectual as himself? More than anything else—with the definite exception of the mimicked smile that still haunted Vegel with its aftershocks—that was what Vegel found most frightening.

Such fear be damned, though, for Vegel was hastening to meet his Nosferatu contact—the only reason he had accepted the invitation to this party on Hesha's behalf in the first place.

The proliferation of corpses of Abel on this top floor of the High Museum of Art disturbed Vegel. He was too superstitious to chuckle along with the majority of the Kindred in attendance at the vulgar indecency of the displays.

After Vegel left Victoria Ash at Antonio Canova's *Mourning the Dead Abel*, he was passing an apparently freshly carved sculpture when he realized it was another death scene of Abel. And this was yet prior to his planned rendezvous with the Nosferatu Rolph at the side of Dupré's *The Dead Abel*, so Vegel knew at least one other sculpted corpse awaited him.

Just as much as the mass grave of Abels was disturbing, Vegel was realizing more fully the great danger of Victoria Ash. She was clearly, and more importantly, easily, seducing him. Not since his long-gone days as a mortal had his lust been so out of his control. The curse of her effect on him was that, even while he understood intellectually that she was clawing her way to his heart, the sensation was too delicious to resist. Few were the dangers to the Kindred greater than nostalgia, and reliving so vividly the forgotten tangibles of desire was invigorating and irresistible.

Slackening his pace before he passed the newly carved Abel, Vegel warily rubbed his neck where the Toreador's kiss had massaged him. Was it magic, or merely the flush of lust that warmed his neck?

The new Abel was monstrous for reasons entirely

opposite to the *verismo* of Dupré's work which Vegel would soon behold again (for he first viewed it years ago when it was first moved to the Louvre). Where Dupré's Abel was horrifically rendered in absolutely realistic detail, the carving before him now was a shocking caricature.

Vegel normally preferred to view new works with an unfettered access, but he found himself slowly absorbing the details of this strange piece despite the presence of another viewer. Fortunately, the slender Kindred was quiet. In any event, Vegel paid but passing attention to him, instead focusing his concentration on the sculpture before him.

His analysis was annoyingly interrupted when the stranger said, "A piece of garbage, don't you think?"

Curtly, Vegel said, "I'm yet undecided. I'll draw my own conclusions after ample viewing."

Vegel caught a glimpse of the other Kindred sneering, glaring down the length of his too-long nose as Vegel turned his back to him and continued his observation. The Setite sensed the other shuffling back a handful of paces, but the gesture was clearly one of irritation meant to draw attention to himself, instead of one of courtesy to allow the clearer access Vegel preferred.

The most startling aspect of this death scene was the anatomy of the two figures. The limbs of both Caine and Abel were soft and fleshy, and the torsos possessed little definition. Also, the heads were overly large—much too ponderous for the frames of the figures' bodies. As the sculpture was carved from a textureless black stone, this purposeful disproportion was enhanced.

The implement of death was a knotted rope of sorts, and the means strangulation, so this felling of Abel was a bloodless one—presumably not the sort that in reality had occurred.

The expressions were intriguing, and were well executed; so much so that Vegel was surprised he did not recognize the piece or even the artist. Abel's face was lit with a cheery bliss without even a hint of resignation. Clearly, he anticipated the journey to heaven. Vegel wondered if there wasn't something to that. Yes, this was the first murder, but was it not also the first death? Abel was the first of God's likenesses to stand beside Him in heaven. Or was this prior to mankind's admittance to heaven? Vegel was unsure of this specific of Christianity.

This intriguing premise made Caine's face even more decipherable, for the murderer's expression was one of resolution and determination but with an upper lip that was slightly wrinkled to denote some amount of distaste. The sculpture told Vegel a story of Caine slaying Abel at the latter's request.

Pacing back to the front of the piece, so the other Kindred was behind him again, Vegel noted the bronze plaque with the imprinted title of *Abel Condemns Caine*, which potentially confirmed the Setite's interpretation of the piece. From this vantage, Vegel could also see that the "rope" was in fact an umbilical cord still attached to Caine's belly. That revelation made it ridiculously clear that the brothers were not misshapen at all, but were actually infants.

Vegel wrestled with how this discovery affected his interpretation of the piece.

From behind, he heard, "I shouldn't have made them children, should I?"

Vegel groaned inwardly and lied, "I admit that aspect of the work was initially confusing, but in light of the title I find it entirely appropriate, and more than that, a very novel approach."

Rarely did he enjoy discussing a piece with its creator, especially one so clearly stalking those who approached his work and fishing for comments. Even in the rare cases when Vegel's appreciation for a piece was not immediately soured because of the personality of the creator, though the piece itself might be extraordinary, he preferred to be on equal ground when discussing a work with another. When that conversation was with the creator, Vegel's interpretation could only be accurate or even reasonable if it had much in common with the creator's own interpretation of his work. It was difficult to argue with a self-proclaimed expert. Artists could not be experts on their work for everyone, for much of art was in the eye of the beholder.

The Setite turned toward the artist as he continued, hoping his lie would extinguish the other's need to discuss the sculpture, "You must be the artist. I am Vegel, a collector of antiquities."

"Not interested in new work, then," said the thin man, his tentative smile dripping away to a frown. "My name is Leopold, and yes, the work is mine."

Face to face with him now, Vegel took a moment to examine the artist. Though a Kindred, and presumably a Toreador, or else Victoria Ash would not allow his piece admittance here (for though flawed, the work was too good to make a mockery of him in the event Ash allowed the showing with the intent to embarrass him), Leopold had the look of a starving artist. He was thin, drooping, haggard and unkempt as only a person who generally cares little for his appearance but who tries to tidy himself prior to an evening like this, could be. Vegel noted a gleam in the artist's eyes, though, that told him this Toreador was an authentic creator. The gleam could be madness, but often that light was the same as the one that guided inspired artistic work.

Vegel was tempted to reveal his lie to the artist, but there was much more pressing business tonight than even a remarkable potential talent. So, eliminating any tone of engagement or interest from his voice, Vegel said, "It is a fine piece. Now, if you'll excuse me…"

Leopold seemed barely attentive to what Vegel was saying, and staring at the piece, he muttered, "These harder substances still don't respond well for me. Perhaps I should try something more malleable, like wood. Can you imagine this in wood? The umbilical could be so much more dynamic! I just couldn't impart any energy…through…the…stone…."

But Vegel was gone. He didn't turn even as the artist's words trailed indelicately into silence. The Setite did not wish to meet the Toreador's sad eyes.

Monday, 21 June 1999, 11:47 PM
The High Museum of Art
Atlanta, Georgia

The scene seemed one from an early Hollywood monster movie: a dark-clad and hooded figure crouched beside the nearly naked form of a man. Monstrous facial features were not readily discernible because of the hood, but backlighting silhouetted a knotted and crooked nose and a much too sharp and long chin from within the hood as the head pivoted slowly about.

Vegel imagined the copse of elegant white birch trees that would complete the eerie scene. Their slender white trunks could be giant, bleached bones jutting skyward, visible at night with even the barest hint of moonlight.

But there were no trees. Nor was there a corpse. However, there was a monster: Rolph of clan Nosferatu, the Kindred whom Vegel had expressly journeyed to Atlanta to meet.

Rolph indeed crouched as if poised over a corpse—another one of Abel. This was Giovanni Dupré's Abel, *The Dead Abel*. It was not a romantic interpretation of the dead man. His arms were akimbo, his eyes rolled back in his head, and his mouth gaping open. Some missing fingers and fingertips were not to the design of the sculptor—those losses had occurred in the century and a half since the piece was completed.

As for Rolph, there was little to see because of the robe, though Vegel knew him immediately from past acquaintanceship. There was no mistaking the bulbous nose crooked hard to the left, or the chin so long and pointed it seemed a horn grew beneath the Nosferatu's thin lower lip. These were features no hood could hide.

Rolph was average height, perhaps a couple of inches shorter than Vegel's six feet, though he remained crouched even after he noted Vegel approaching. The voluminous brown robe draped the floor around the Nosferatu, so Vegel could not determine how he was dressed beneath.

Rolph spoke first. "Greetings, Vegel. I've watched you make the rounds and wondered when you would settle down to the real business of your trip."

Vegel replied, "Hello, Rolph." Then, after a few more paces that brought him to a comfortable distance as the Nosferatu finally stood up, Vegel defended himself, "My instructions were to meet at *The Dead Abel* as midnight approached but before it neared. If armed with more precise instructions, I would have happily satisfied you more fully."

"No matter," Rolph said. "You are here in plenty of time. I wondered if perhaps you were addled by the confusing quantity of Abels strewn about this chamber, though I saw, in fact, that you were distracted earlier by living, or at least nearly living, concerns in the form of our redoubtable hostess."

Vegel was embarrassed by this accusation, but there was little he could do to refute it, so he lied while at the same time stabbing back at Rolph. "Yes, we conversed for some time. I feel she may of immense help locating important artifacts which Hesha seeks."

"I see," Rolph said. "Perhaps it's time then that we got down to business."

"Of course," replied Vegel, pleased to be past pleasantries, for he disliked small talk, and smalk talk with Nosferatu least of all. He didn't trust members of this clan, though they in general and Rolph in particular had provided assistance in his endeavors. The defining ugliness of the clan tricked one into believing that everything about a Nosferatu was just as visible. They often exaggerated this with a rudeness of the sort Rolph had displayed when he mentioned Victoria Ash.

They also pretended to be transparent in their schemes. Vegel knew from experience that they could be the wiliest of Camarilla vampires. The Ventrue might claim to be masters of deceit, as their arena was anything political, but this claim was one the Nosferatu granted the Camarilla's leaders in a move that even further obfuscated the achievements of the Nosferatu clan.

Rolph said contritely, "I'm sorry to drag you into this den of thieves, but it was honestly my only means of providing some material that Hesha has long sought."

Vegel did not inquire about the privacy of their conversation even though it unfolded in plain view in the gallery. This was a detail Rolph had surely covered, and if the Nosferatu had not—that is, if Rolph wanted this conversation to be overheard—then there was nothing Vegel could do about it. He could speak to some other Setites in a hissing whisper that no one outside the clan could translate even if they could hear it, but he doubted the secret of that tongue was known even by the prowling Nosferatu.

Rolph continued, "However, I know your risk will be worth it, for tonight, Clan Nosferatu would like to repay an old debt to Hesha. What I give you should even matters regarding the Bombay affair some centuries ago. This incident was before either of our times, but I guarantee that your master will know of what I speak."

Vegel said, "Very well. I will relay notice of the debt repayment and whatever information or material you hereafter provide to my master. If he deems the matter unfair or unsettled, then I am certain he will contact your masters. But if no direct payment is demanded of me, then I will gladly entertain whatever you reveal next."

"Understood," Rolph said. The Nosferatu then took a few steps to the side so that Dupré's sculpture was no longer behind him. The move afforded Vegel an unimpeded view of the piece.

"What I offer tonight, friend Vegel, is an artifact greatly desired and long sought by your master. I offer none other than the Eye of Hazimel."

Vegel couldn't help but be caught by surprise. Whatever had happened in Bombay long ago must have placed some important elders among the Nosferatu in Hesha's deep debt, for the Eye of Hazimel might be *the* Evil Eye, the artifact that served as the basis for all the silly posturing of gypsies and superstitious simpletons. That there was usually truth at the heart of such legends was something Vegel had learned early in his service of Hesha.

"It is much too late to hide my surprise, Rolph, so I will admit my shock. If what you offer is truly the Eye of Hazimel, then I of course will take your information to Hesha so he may pursue the item wherever it rests."

"Pursuit is not necessary," Rolph laughed. "The Eye is here in this statue of Abel." Rolph waved his hand at the plaster corpse at their feet.

Vegel said in surprise, "So it belongs to Victoria Ash?"

Rolph explained, "Certainly not. At least not in any real sense, for it's virtually certain that the lovely Ms. Ash does not even realize the Eye resides within her sculpture, if in fact she's aware of the Eye's existence at all."

Suddenly feeling odd about examining the sculpture too closely, for fear his gaze would be a tell-tale heart, Vegel nevertheless thoroughly examined the piece, though he did so without moving from his present location. He remained dubious. His best detection techniques—powers that had once located slightly enchanted jade earrings sealed somewhere in a five-mile expanse of the Great Wall of China, and then when they were embedded some forty feet above the ground—did not note the presence of the puniest magical bauble anywhere within the plaster Abel. And the Eye of Hazimel, especially if it was *the* Evil Eye, would probably have registered to Vegel so long as Vegel approached within several dozen paces even if the Setite weren't actively searching for it.

So Vegel asked, "Can you explain then why everyone seems oblivious to its presence?"

"Certainly," smiled Rolph. "In its present state, the Eye is undetectable."

Vegel inaudibly groaned. As if that explained anything. Though it did explain something. *In its present state...*

Rolph continued, "That's why it's unlikely that Ms. Ash realizes she possesses this item. It's also why it's necessary to give you this gift at so public a locale where we have access to this sculpture, or for that matter, why we arranged for you to be invited to this celebration in the first place."

Nodding so Rolph knew he was listening, Vegel scanned the large open chamber. If he was to take possession of so potent an artifact, then it was crucial he know who was about. For the Eye might be undetectable in its present state, but what about when it was removed from the sculpture? At least Vegel hoped it *could* be removed. There was little chance of him slipping away from the party with a plaster corpse tucked under his arm, and that was assuming he had Hesha's strength and could lift Dupré's masterpiece at all.

Vegel noted several details of importance as he examined his surroundings. First, he was pleased to confirm that this display of *The Dead Abel* was on the periphery of the chamber. No clusters of Kindred stood between him and a nearby emergency exit.

Second, he was relieved to see that Hannah, the Tremere chantry leader, was still absent. If any of the Kindred of the city were capable of detecting the Eye, then it would be her. And the Setite knew that she would discard her own two eyes without a second thought in order to possess this single, ancient one.

Third, he was disconcerted to catch Victoria Ash glancing at him so that their eyes locked briefly before he glanced past her—with difficulty.

Finally, Vegel was alarmed to note that the huge bronze clock set over the windows looking down to Peachtree Street in front of the Museum was but a handful of ticktocks from midnight. While no midnight timetable had been absolutely set, Vegel's impression was that midnight was something of a deadline for this exchange.

"If I may, I have a number of questions," Vegel said.

Rolph glanced at the same clock Vegel had checked seconds before. "Certainly, but our time is short, so let's be brief and relevant."

Without allowing much pause, Vegel said, "Why midnight?"

"Because we have arranged an escape route for you. If the route is to serve its purpose, you must be passing through that emergency-exit door at precisely one minute before midnight."

Vegel briefly nodded, then asked, "Will the Eye be detectable once removed from the sculpture?"

"Not for some time. Certainly enough time for you to make your escape. So long as it resides in an inanimate object it may not be detected, even by its progenitor. Actually, especially by its progenitor, but presumably others who use the same methods as well."

Slowly dredging up memories of the legends of the Eye, Vegel asked, "And if placed within an animate being?"

"It will come to life in the empty socket of an animate being."

Hoping to glean some information he did not possess but the Nosferatu might, Vegel ventured, "For this purpose, is a vampire considered an 'animate' being?"

"Most certainly. The Eye comes from one of our kind, after all. Quickly now, last question."

Vegel thought for a moment. He didn't like the idea of others providing an escape route for him. Frankly, he was even nervous when that task was left to Hesha. There had been no trouble, of course—who would dare cross swords with his master?—but leaving such serious business as his existence and a precious artifact in the hands of Rolph, even if he was a sometimes ally apparently repaying an ancient debt, made him nervous.

Brandishing a cell phone he withdrew from his dress coat's breast pocket, Vegel asked, "Why your escape route? Why should I not accept the Eye and then summon my chauffeur to depart as I arrived? After all, if the Eye will remain undetectable—"

Rolph's face discolored with impatience, then it flushed with what Vegel could only interpret as confusion. Rolph recomposed himself, glanced at the clock, looked at Vegel earnestly and said, "Listen and listen closely, for after I answer I will hand you the Eye and direct you to leave immediately via the emergency door nearest us on the wall—an instruction I strongly advise you to heed. Please do call your chauffeur, but let him arrive and depart again as a decoy. I promise that you will not see him again."

Rolph looked intently into Vegel's eyes for a moment after these pronouncements. Vegel understood the gesture held no intent to subjugate his will, as some Kindred were capable of doing, but was instead merely a check to see if the sincerity of this message was impressed upon the Setite. With a slow nod, Vegel indicated his understanding.

"Good," said Rolph.

Moving quickly, Rolph threw his hands skyward, and with his fingers spread so it seemed his hand might split as if quartered by horses, he drew back the large hood to reveal a face as disgusting as Vegel recalled. The Nosferatu cared little about Vegel's reaction, and in fact did not notice it at all. He seemed as unconcerned with everyone else in the galleries as well.

Indeed, as Vegel looked around, briefly taking his attention off Rolph, he saw that Rolph's sudden and exaggerated movements had drawn absolutely no attention. In fact, everyone seemed to be pointedly looking *away* from the two of them.

Vegel took great pleasure in being at the epicenter of the Nosferatu's power. The abilities of various Kindred never ceased to amaze him. He might be able to find a jade earring in China's Great Wall, but Rolph could effectively make himself, and apparently others too, vanish.

The Setite's enjoyment was cut short as he watched in awe as Rolph retrieved the Eye of Hazimel. Bending down over the sculpture of Abel, the Nosferatu vigorously rubbed together the thumb and forefinger of his right hand. He used his left hand to steady his weight against Abel's chest, and then stabbed his fingers toward Abel's left eye. Vegel instinctively flinched in expectation of plaster debris raining from the point of impact, but instead Rolph's fingers plunged and disappeared into the pupilless orb as if it were deep, inky water.

Rolph squirmed and turned about, his wrist spinning back and forth in wild gyrations as if the Nosferatu were attempting to grasp something elusive within the sculpture's eye or head. Rolph's hand and arm were suddenly seized with an almost violent rigidity, and he looked up to smile a pained grin at Vegel.

Vegel then followed the Nosferatu's gaze back to the bronze clock, and though Vegel turned back to watch Abel's head and the Kindred fingers extended within it, Rolph's attention remained focused on the clock. It was counting down toward 11:59 PM. As the seconds ticked away, Rolph remained frozen. Until he looked back up at Vegel.

"Ready?" asked the Nosferatu.

"Ready."

With the slimy, sucking sound of a wet plunger releasing its vacuum, Rolph slowly withdrew his hand from the sculpture. Luminosity as if from a 1000-watt darklight blinded Vegel, but he was still able to see the shadow of something oblong and pulsating clamped between the Nosferatu's thumb and forefinger.

As if he held something dangerous or hot or precious—or perhaps all three—Rolph carefully extended the object toward Vegel and slowly lowered it onto the Setite's outstretched palm. Dollops of coagulated goo dripped off the object and onto Vegel's palm before the cold, moist object itself settled into his hand.

Vegel closed his hand and felt the spongy but smooth and surprisingly heavy object, and that blocked some of the flooding light, though his hand was not large enough to surround the Eye completely. His vision partially restored, Vegel looked anxiously about, but he found that none of these astounding events had yet drawn the attention of others. While he stood bathed in the unearthly light of an ancient Kindred's eyeball, the other Kindred continued their debates of petty politics. It made Vegel laugh.

This mirth was short-lived, for Rolph tugged Vegel by the sleeve and then pushed him toward red emergency-exit door. "Go, and don't worry about the alarm," said the Nosferatu, whose skin gained an even less appealing pallor in the purplish light.

Vegel didn't hesitate. He did not run headlong toward the door, though, for he wasn't certain if the cloaking Rolph provided extended beyond the Nosferatu's immediate proximity. Still, the door was but a half moment away, and Vegel achieved it without drawing any attention to himself or the potent orb within his grasp.

As the heavy emergency door crept shut behind him and sealed to a sturdy close, Vegel did hear the clanging of an alarm erupt. Before him were alternating flights of stairs going down only. He did not delay. The rataplan of his feet skipping down the metal steps could surely draw no more attention than the fire alarm.

Vegel was relatively athletic and he had the unnatural vigor of all Kindred, so his progress down the stairs was very rapid. He still clutched the Eye in his right hand, and several paces into his descent, the purplish light faded. At the same time, the Eye briefly throbbed more rapidly than before, but then that subsided as well.

After descending four flights of stairs, two floors of the museum, Vegel came to a landing where the yellow tape used to mark police lines was stretched across the frame of what appeared to be an old service access door. More flights of stairs toward ground level beckoned Vegel, but he suspected the Nosferatu's escape route continued through this door. Otherwise Rolph would have removed the tape to avoid just this kind of confusion.

The door was severely rusted and a worn padlock bound it to an old wooden frame. Even if the door resisted efforts to force it open, Vegel felt certain the frame would splinter and allow access. That tactic, of course, would reveal his route if he was being followed, so he decided there must be a less forceful approach to the problem.

And there was. Upon closer examination, Vegel realized that the disintegrating wooden frame was in fact cracked along its entire length. Vegel applied careful and diligent pressure and discovered that the entire structure—door, frame and everything—could swing open as a unit.

It opened just enough to allow the Kindred to squeeze through, though his effort was rewarded with a handful of splinters, a couple of which penetrated his clothes. They might have cut his flesh as well, but Vegel's skin was tougher than any mortal's and it turned aside the toothpick shafts.

Only emergency lights illuminated the area behind the access door. Vegel first made sure there was no immediate danger, then he turned to press the wooden frame back into place. With a quiet pop it settled back into position, and from the other side it must have appeared as unused as Vegel had first imagined it moments ago.

The small area he was within consisted of a catwalk surrounding what was presumably an old elevator shaft. The odor of old grease told Vegel this was not any shaft presently in use.

At one point on the catwalks, ladders offered access to levels both higher and lower that Vegel's present one. The Setite assumed he should continue downward. He quickly secured the Eye alongside his phone inside the breast pocket of his dress coat, and then he swung off the catwalk and slid down the ladder with his feet and hands pressed hard against the outside of the vertical bars.

He dropped the last couple of feet to another catwalk—the ground floor, he guessed—and then performed the same maneuver to reach the basement-level catwalk. The shaft continued down, but the retired elevator was parked in that recess, so Vegel moved toward an access door behind him.

He paused a moment, though, and turned off his cell phone. He couldn't risk its ringer betraying his position. Then he tried the door.

It was locked, so Vegel looked around again. As he did so, he patted his chest to make certain the Eye was still with him, though the gesture was really a doublecheck since the artifact seemed to be growing cold, and the almost painful icy freeze could be felt through his coat and shirt.

It then seemed to Vegel that a hatch on top of the elevator shell was slightly propped open. He stepped to the edge of the catwalk and leapt down four or five feet to land near the hatch. Indeed, it was ajar, so Vegel folded it open.

The emergency lighting in the shaft didn't illuminate the interior of the old elevator very well, but Vegel thought he could see enough to believe the elevator was empty. Cursing this convoluted Nosferatu escape route, Vegel clambered and squeezed through the hatchway and dropped to the floor of the elevator.

Pausing in the silence and darkness for a moment, Vegel couldn't help but recall Rolph's words: *I promise that you will not see him again.*

What was going to happen to his driver? Was his death necessary for some reason, or was he going to be caught in some larger incident? This thought of danger above caused Vegel to worry suddenly about Victoria Ash. The brief impulse to return to her aid was startling in its clarity and strength, but Vegel resisted that calling, though he did strongly hope nothing untoward happened to her or affected even so much as one of her delicate ringlets.

Vegel shook his head vigorously to clear it, startled by his lapse.

There didn't seem to be any way out of the elevator other than the hatch above him, but he quickly tried to pry apart the doors. They glided apart as if well-oiled and maintained, and Vegel suspected such was the case.

Beyond the open doors, Vegel found a well-lit and more modern passageway. He was amazed the Nosferatu would share such a secret entrance to this Elysium with him, but the mere fact that he'd been shown this one meant there must be another, even better, egress elsewhere.

Monday, 21 June 1999, 11:55 PM
The High Museum of Art
Atlanta, Georgia

At least Stella sang the appropriate praises for his sculpture. Leopold respected her opinion, and he knew she had a discerning eye that had been trained through photography, but he didn't trust compliments from someone he regarded as a friend. It was too easy for a friend to like his work, and too hard for a friend to criticize honestly. Leopold could never understand the usefulness of artist retreats or communes. The same person could not be a good critic and a good friend, so both of these endeavors were doomed to failure.

He'd left her still examining his *Abel Condemns Caine*. Some distance away now, he leaned into one of the glass walls that crisscrossed and divided the gallery. He tapped it sharply a few times and ended up admitting to himself that he should accept Stella's compliments. He was just upset about his exchange with the Setite, and that had fouled his mood.

As if he wasn't upset enough! He smacked his forehead against the glass in frustration. Then, in embarrassment, he looked around to see if anyone noticed his petulant display. At first he thought himself safe, but then he noticed a lone figure sitting beneath a large sculpture of a male figure as yet unexamined by Leopold.

The Kindred at the foot of the sculpture had a feral look. His hair was long and matted, and his face wasn't completely human. It was too pointy, like a dog's head maybe. Leopold suspected this was a

Gangrel, which meant he was probably either Javic or the one who lived north of Atlanta who was called Dusty. From the Kindred's haggard appearance, Leopold suspected this was the latter.

Whoever he was, he looked directly at Leopold but gave no indication of greeting or recognition as Leopold stared back. His gaze made Leopold uncomfortable, though, so the Toreador moved to a spot out of view from everyone.

The delay had not stemmed his frustration, and he smacked his head on the glass again. This time he did it so forcefully that his ears rang.

Still no Hannah! He cursed. Why wasn't she here? Apparently he wasn't the only one who had noticed or been surprised, for he'd overheard two other mentions of the Tremere. Surely, though, no one had such pressing business with her as he did.

He wondered if he had misunderstood her, but he clearly recalled her saying the final step of the process would be some simple magic she would use to do something. Analyze the reaction of the blood in his body, he supposed.

What if it had all been a trick? Leopold shivered at the thought. What if he was bound to her by blood now, and she didn't need to be here because she was seeing through his eyes or maybe even controlling some of his actions from her mansion?

It sounded ridiculous to the Toreador, but he'd heard so many unbelievable things in the past couple of years that he was unwilling to throw out any idea, no matter how absurd.

So, if there was to be no Hannah, Leopold thought about what to do next. Maybe he should go to the Tremere chantry and see for himself what delayed or kept her? He didn't think that was a good idea. If she was avoiding him, or if she had other reasons to not be here, then she would probably think little of another visit.

Or maybe he should just confront Victoria? Just ask her directly, "Are you my sire?" But that was stupid.

On the other hand, maybe he could just speak to her. Even if she didn't know anything about his past, Victoria was still his primogen. That hardly made her his senator—someone obligated to represent him and help him—but perhaps she would help. Maybe she knew secrets of Toreador blood that would allow her to guess his sire. The idea of sharing his blood with her was very appealing, though Leopold shook his head at his infantile infatuation with the woman.

Regardless, he would speak to her. She was the hostess, after all, and he had yet to speak to her within the gallery itself.

There was no fanfare. No dramatic thundering-open of doors. No declarations or pronouncements. Nothing but the impressive specimen of a Kindred himself, and Victoria believed she was the only one who noticed him enter. It would have taken a commotion to draw any attention, because all the Kindred on the fourth floor of the High Museum had abandoned the entrance in favor of the recesses of the gallery where they formed into cliques.

Victoria couldn't say what brought her to the entrance. Just a nagging sense that something was about to happen. Maybe it was because Rolph had disappeared for a time, but then suddenly reappeared a moment ago to bid adieu for the evening. The Nosferatu offered no explanation, and the haste of his departure left her no chance to inquire.

The Toreador took a deep breath, for the endgame of the plot she'd put in motion—and was keeping in motion by virtue of her entrance via Heaven—was about to begin. She watched the newcomer enter, and when he looked at her and smiled after briefly surveying the lay of the chamber, she extended her hands in greeting.

He moved like a cat down the couple of steps that descended from the platform where the doors stood. He was upon her in a heartbeat, quickly closing a remarkable distance without visibly rushing. The effect was almost vertiginous, and Victoria felt her head swim. He accepted her hands in his and made a token bow to her with the nod of his head.

Julius was a brute of a man who helped the Brujah justicar administer Camarilla justice. Victoria liked the look of this archon. A large black man, Julius's face was square cut and his hair was long and dreadlocked. His was a handsome and strong face, and Victoria had the odd desire to trace her fingers along the purplish scars on his face. One lined his right cheek and stretched over his eye to his forehead. Another reached from above his left ear to almost the exact midpoint of his square chin.

He was dressed in baggy red pants and a tight-fitting black turtleneck, across which draped an antique bandolier. The twelve small brass cases along the length of the leather belt evidently contained something, for they rattled as the large man walked. Strapped to Julius's back in a cross-pattern were the broadswords for which he was so well known. They were surely not the swords he'd actually swung in the arenas of Rome when he'd fought there nearly two thousand years ago, but both were inscribed with Latin phrases that Victoria could not read.

Even though Victoria severely doubted the veracity of the stories that told of Julius as a gladiator in Roman arenas, there was no doubting that he was clearly a dangerous man. Regardless, Victoria knew if the law of Elysium was to broken tonight, Julius would find his hands amply full in a conflict with Prince Benison.

Victoria was disappointed the Brujah did not wear any symbols of the Black Panthers, an organization Julius supposedly helped in its infancy. It was apparently his work in Chicago in 1968 that had proved to the Brujah elite (of which Julius surely would have been one if he was two thousand years old, or even a thousand) that Julius was interested in taking an active hand in the business of the clan again.

Nevertheless, Victoria licked her lips. A militant black Brujah. Ah, the fireworks tonight might be splendid if Julius did indeed take the opportunity of this evening to pressure the ex-Confederate Prince regarding his harsh actions against the Anarchs of the city.

And Julius might have a Ventrue as an ally as well in the form of Benjamin, who was also rumored to have civil rights concerns. Victoria had done what she could to put these pieces into place, including surreptitiously revealing to the Brujah justicar that Benison allowed unchecked creation and admission to Atlanta society of all kinds of Kindred—except Brujah. General, a Malkavian had been recently admitted. Javic, the Gangrel refugee from Bosnia, was admitted. Clarice and Cyndy were both Embraced in Atlanta and admitted to Kindred society.

And most of all, even during the time when the city was full and recognized citizenship was not granted because he supposedly feared overpopulating the city, Prince Benison had "allowed" his wife to Embrace Benjamin and so a new Ventrue was admitted to the city. Or at least Victoria could claim he'd allowed it. He didn't know about the deed, so he would either have to lie and claim it was done with permission, or he would have to punish Eleanor for her flaunting of the rules and probably his trust too. Either way, his position was weakened.

"Welcome, noble archon, to glorious Atlanta and my own poor party."

Julius twisted his lips. "I speak and act bluntly, so I won't battle you for humble pie. I apologize if this upsets your Toreador sensibilities, Victoria; but your party looks very nice, although my opinion of Atlanta is distinctly less than yours."

Victoria smiled and said, "It sure takes you a lot of words to speak bluntly. Are you certain you were not an author of Latin epics instead of the creator of great stories within the confines of the arena?"

Julius grunted, "Your flowery speech rubbed off on me, is all."

"I'm certain the Prince will remind you," Victoria began, "so let me do it first, that this is Elysium and no weapons are allowed herein."

Julius just shook his head. "This noble archon keeps his weapons. Disagreements can be taken to my master."

Victoria asked, "And is the disagreement between Benison and Thelonious going to be taken to Pascek as well?"

"Perhaps," said Julius. A sly twinkle lit his eye, and he continued, "If matters progress that far."

The Toreador shook her head with well-acted sadness, "It seems as though matters have already progressed too far. Benison's pronouncement regarding the clanless Kindred pre-dates my arrival, so this is not a new subject. It seems the Camarilla elders have let this progress for some time and for some distance."

Julius said, "The Prince stretched his authority when he demanded that all clanless Kindred formally join a clan."

"Stretched but didn't exceed…"

"Perhaps," said Julius. "Although the stretching itself then gives credence to the position the Anarchs took, which was a refusal to submit to such heavy-handed demands."

"And so it has persisted for over a year. Why intervene now?"

Julius looked Victoria in the eye and said, "Surface-to-air missiles get attention."

Victoria looked at Julius to gauge this response. "But the missiles were fired by the Brujah, or the Anarchs, if you wish to be less specific."

Julius smiled. "True. My information tells me, though, that Thelonious acquired those missiles via a contact secretly arranged by the Prince."

"That does change things," admitted Victoria. Inwardly, Victoria cursed. Eleanor had been right. Julius did have the goods on her, or at least he seemed to. The Toreador had been hoping for the last hour that the Ventrue's words were mere groundless mischievousness. However, Julius didn't give even a subtle hint that he was aware that the suggestion for Benison to provide those weapons to the Anarchs had come from Victoria herself. By means of an unsigned letter, of course, but despite her precautions against discovery—including not writing it herself, of course—perhaps Eleanor had traced it back to Victoria.

"You object to this intervention in Atlanta?"

"Certainly not," Victoria assured the archon. She smiled her warmest and added, "It's time for Atlanta to move into a new era, I believe."

Julius chuckled, "You do, eh?"

Victoria said nothing more on these matters, and changed the subject. "May I introduce you around?"

"No," Julius said flatly.

"Ah, now I see what you mean about plain-speaking. Styling yourself a bit after Lear's Earl of Kent, perhaps."

As Victoria spoke, she saw her ghoul Samuel enter through the doors of Hell. He noticed her immediately, and he saw she did likewise, so he attempted to look relaxed. However, the Toreador saw that Samuel was anxious to speak with her. Not an emergency, perhaps, but something troubled the ghoul.

Meanwhile, Julius just looked at her blankly, clearly not understanding her Shakespearean reference. In a moment he said, "Whatever. Just forget that I'm here. I'm going to make myself at home for a moment over by that demon," he thumbed his hand toward Feuchére's *Satan*, "and then introduce myself to some people. I'll see Prince Benison later, I imagine."

Victoria said, "As you wish, noble archon. *Satan* is a fine work that could understandably occupy a great deal of time. One might even get lost in its examination, causing oversights of etiquette for which no blame could truly be placed."

Julius chuckled softly. "You're a bright girl, Victoria." Then he walked into the empty alcove, his bandolier rattling ominously, where he momentarily made a show of investigating the sculpture before looking back up at Victoria and smiling again. Then he lifted his hand and made a motion of tipping a glass to his lips. He waved her on.

Victoria did walk away, relieved that even when he gave his "bright girl" comment, Julius did not suggest any knowledge of Victoria's underhanded ploys. She waved her hand at Samuel and the ghoul descended the steps and approached his mistress.

Meanwhile, Victoria redirected the second server she saw to deliver a flute of blood to the archon. The first server was not the sharpest of the servants on hand, so she waited for a better candidate. She supposed the servant could deliver a drink, but she would need one to receive instructions about when and how he should make note of the Brujah's presence.

Benison would go wild with anger when he learned the archon was present and had not introduced himself. It was a slight of courtesy upon which he might seize to press the Brujah, but Julius was clearly calculating the results, probably hoping that in his anger Benison would make a larger blunder.

Julius's gamble seemed to Victoria a fine one. It also made her a little nervous, because she planned to put herself in the position of instigating the fight. She had all the right tools at hand, but now Julius was doing this work for her. That worried Victoria because now it didn't matter whether she'd stepped through Heaven or Hell, for her plan was going to be executed without her prompting.

She calmed herself immediately. Perhaps she was rationalizing her control of the situation, but she convinced herself that if she'd entered through Hell and therefore been on a path to scrap or at least delay her plans, then she could have interfered with Julius's intentions by alerting Benison immediately so no slight would be given.

She was still in control of her own destiny.

Samuel softly cleared his throat behind Victoria, and the Toreador turned.

"What is it?"

Samuel said, "A chauffeur in the garage says he must immediately speak to his master, a Kindred of the Setite clan named Vegel."

"He's here," said Victoria. "What's the matter? Has there been trouble downstairs?"

Samuel shook his head. "No, everything is proceeding smoothly, milady. The driver said there was a phone call for Vegel, and the caller is his partner, Hesha."

"Hesha?" Victoria pursed her lips and nodded her head with interest. "Very well, wait outside those doors and I'll send Vegel to you. It will take only a moment to find him."

Samuel glanced around the glass maze of the gallery, and seemed somewhat dubious of this claim, but he dared not question Victoria. "Of course, milady." He bowed slightly and retreated beyond the doors through which he'd entered.

No one else was near, so Victoria withdrew to her cubicle again. She used her opera glasses to scan the gallery for Vegel.

And she could not find him.

She did take a moment to check on Julius, and found him leaning against *Satan* and sipping on a flute of blood.

Victoria assumed Vegel was still somewhere in the gallery since his chauffeur was still downstairs. So she looked again. Failing again, she left her cubicle and walked the gallery for a few moments. She found all of the other Kindred she knew to be present, but no Vegel.

Then she suddenly stopped. What kind of game was being played here? She grew a bit angry. This matter of the phone call and chauffeur was clearly a distraction of some sort. Vegel knew Victoria would be intrigued by a call from Hesha, and so he fed her the bit of misinformation and reeled her right in. But to what end?

Victoria decided she would call the bluff and eliminate the worry about this new matter in the back of her mind. The Toreador stalked toward the gallery's exit and opened the doors of Hell. She was proving to herself that she wasn't superstitious by using these doors, instead of Heaven through which she entered. That game was done; others were now at hand.

Samuel was leaning against a wall down the hall-way toward the elevators. When he saw Victoria, he immediately straightened and stood ready.

She strode toward him, her sandalled feet smacking on the tiled floor. Her face was resolute yet still beautiful.

"All right, let's see if Hesha was really on the phone."

Samuel looked confused, but as usual, there were no questions asked. As the pair stepped into the elevator, he said, "The chauffeur is waiting in the Auxiliary Chamber."

Victoria briefly acknowledged that and stared intently at the closing doors.

Tuesday, 22 June 1999, 12:08 AM
The High Museum of Art
Atlanta, Georgia

The metal-lined corridor was lit with recessed fluorescents. Once he realized that the tunnel extended for a significant distance, Vegel broke into a run. His hurry was partly inspired by the damned cold of the Eye in his pocket.

After a solid minute of running, Vegel achieved the end of the passage. A steel ladder stretched up to a hatch in the ceiling. The Setite had noted no other doors or exits of any kind elsewhere along the length of the tunnel, so he presumed this was the next stage of his escape.

He climbed the stairs, twisted a handle and with his legs securely braced, stood and pressed the door up and open.

All the lights instantly extinguished as soon as the door broke the seal of the floor. Vegel was suddenly and disorientingly flooded in darkness. He craned his neck to look back down what he thought was the direction of the long tunnel in search of even the smallest light source, but there was none.

Hoping this was simply a safety measure to provide cover for those emerging as he was, Vegel steadied himself and then pressed the door open farther so he could crawl out. It was pitch black wherever he'd arrived, so he crouched near the door hoping his eyes would adjust. Even the faintest flicker of light would be enough!

Vegel considered revealing the Eye, but since he couldn't control the amount of the light or whether or not it shed light at all, he thought it too risky. In any event, he kept one hand cupped under the door that was now on the floor beside him. On one hand, he thought some lights might return if he closed it, but on the other he imagined it might also lock behind him and seal him Set knew where.

He remained so for another moment before deciding that the Nosferatu route had been excellent and safe thus far, and since he'd put his trust in Rolph this much already, why not accept the situation completely?

He removed his hand and allowed the door to drop shut. It did indeed lock, for it clicked into place and then he heard a vacuum sealer suck it firmly shut.

But a light flickered on, so Vegel felt his courage was rewarded.

The Setite found he was in a small enclosed area with a dramatically slanted ceiling that was only a hand's space above his head where he crouched. Considering the narrow width of the room, and the angle of the ceiling, Vegel realized this small area must be tucked beneath a staircase or escalator.

He desperately wanted to remove the Eye from his coat pocket and examine it for a moment, but this arranged escape route might not yet be complete, though he was certainly a good distance from the museum. Any delay now might mean the difference between safety and destruction, both for himself and the Eye, so he refused to tarry. Besides, the Eye's freezing cold was subsiding, so there was no excuse even to shift it to another pocket.

Pausing to mentally gather himself, Vegel felt refreshed as he approached the sole apparent door in the place. A sudden rumbling, like a minor earthquake tremor made him pause, but the brief squeal of tires eased his mind. He thought it likely he was in parking garage, so those noises did not worry him. There was nothing to indicate that those in the car pursued him.

Still, he opened the door carefully. He appeared to be on the ground floor of an enclosed stairwell. Gum and paint and bits of trash were littered everywhere, and the faint odor of urine was evident as well.

Vegel slipped through the doorway and walked quietly toward another door, this one presumably leading to the garage proper, or perhaps to the street. A small window on the top half of the door revealed the latter. Vegel looked up the stairwell for a moment, but saw no one, so he returned to the exit door and pressed his face against the window to create the greatest angle of view possible. Outside was a narrow side street. Small stores and restaurants of the variety that claim more residents than tourists lined the street, and all of them seemed closed. Vegel could see a street sign to his left, but it was oriented so that he couldn't read it. More importantly, the street was empty of people and traffic in both directions and on both sides.

It looked like the escape route ended here, for Vegel could not detect any clues regarding where he might go next. No police tape. No pictures of eyes. Nothing.

He withdrew the cell phone from his pocket and considered using it, but immediately discarded the idea as foolish and dangerous. If Rolph was correct, then the chauffeur was dead already, and a phone call might only alert his killers to the sophisticated tracking equipment in the limo. If his car was now in the hands of others who sough to wrest the Eye from him, then they might utilize that equipment to track his location by means of the locator in his phone.

The locator was normally to find Vegel in the event something untoward happened to him, but it was useless now. So Vegel dropped the device into a trash can bracketed to the handrailing at the base of the steps. He then shifted some grubby fast food wrappers so they hid the device from plain view.

He felt his best bet was to head straight to the airport. Not Hartsfield International, where he would be sought immediately, but the DeKalb-Peachtree Airport, a small air field north of downtown where an emergency plane was maintained. If he could be airborne within an hour, then he could be in Baltimore by daybreak. Baltimore was the site of Hesha's primary East Coast United States facilities.

He just needed to get to a major street other than Peachtree Street, on which the High Museum was located, so he might catch a cab. Too bad the streets of Atlanta were not filthy-littered with the yellows like Manhattan. Getaways were so much easier there.

Vegel creaked the windowed door open and stealthily stepped onto the street. He hung close to parking deck's wall as he made his way toward the street sign.

Without warning, he was suddenly ambushed from above.

There was a fluttering of a cape or cloak in the air, and then a heavy weight crashed onto Vegel's shoulders. Fortunately, the Setite was well-trained, and while another might have been crushed or pinned to the ground by this assault, Vegel reacted instantly and instinctively. He buckled his knees and allowed himself to fall backwards, but instead of hitting the ground squarely, he turned his momentum into a roll.

A fraction of a second after the attack, a heavily cloaked figure was on the ground and Vegel was balanced and ready on his feet.

But before Vegel could throw a kick at his prone assailant, there was a stentorian growl from above. The ferocious force and fury of the raging sound was accompanied by the twittering of laughter, also from above. Stepping back to create some space between his visible foe and himself, Vegel looked up.

To his horror, he saw three Kindred. At the center of the group was a hulking brute, and he was flanked by a pair of what appeared to be emaciated and badly burned corpses. But these corpses were the source of the laughter. There was no doubt of the source of the roar.

Vegel's fourth foe slowly rose to his feet. He was the most normal-looking of the bunch, though he was clearly also Kindred. This one smiled devilishly at Vegel and then revealed his humanity was long gone as well. With a hiss, the monster threw his arms wide and his fingers seemed to unfurl until they were sloppy strands of flesh several feet long. The beast laughed then as his jaw unhinged and his mouth opened cavernously wide.

There was no concern for the Masquerade here, Vegel realized. There was no mistaking these animals for anything but Sabbat.

And Vegel knew there was no mistaking himself for anything but dead.

Vegel shouted, "Come on then, you bastards! I'll take one of you with me. Which one wishes to accompany me to the hellish pits of Set?"

The Sabbat in front of Vegel uttered something, but the inhuman sound that issued from his freakish mouth was unintelligible.

Vegel began to back away when he saw the two spidery Sabbat begin their descent down the walls of the parking deck. The powerful-looking beast was throwing a leg over a railing in preparation to leap, though Vegel couldn't tell if his intent was to leap onto the ground or onto him.

Vegel was furious at Rolph's treachery. This indeed had been some "escape route." All that foolishness about Bombay and old debts! Hesha would have debts to repay now. Vegel took some solace in Hesha's well-known propensity to mete out revenge for the death of his agents.

The strong-lunged Sabbat above was now jumping, and though Vegel had by now backpedaled a good fifty feet from the spot of the first ambush, the monster's powerful legs propelled it far through the air...and behind Vegel.

The Setite was now trapped. One large Sabbat behind him and a trio of freaks before him.

One of the corpse-like twins said, "So good of you to come to us."

The long-fingered Sabbat advanced steadily with the other two a half step to the side and rear. He waved his arms menacingly and the fingers wriggled like serpents ready for a victim to crush.

Vegel did not appreciate the irony of that eventuality.

More immediate, though, was the brute behind him who was leaping again. This time, a standing broad jump carried him dozens of feet right at Vegel, who managed to twist away and escape the Sabbat's massive arms. The Setite hit the ground rolling and this took him off the edge of the curb and into a puddle in the street.

He quickly leapt to his feet and made to dash away, but the lithe twins were far quicker than he. Somersaulting and bounding like talented gymnasts, they intercepted Vegel and, when Vegel pulled up short of them, he was entangled from behind by long fingers that bound one of his arms to his side.

Vegel had to wrestle and resist for a moment in order to keep his left arm from becoming entangled as well. He made things difficult enough for the Sabbat that he bought himself the second he needed to draw a short knife from an ankle sheath. A viscous green ichor dripped from the blade, which Vegel twirled in small circles like a honey wand to keep as much of the liquid as possible on the blade. When out of the corner of his eye he saw the large Sabbat closing in on him, Vegel slashed the blade through the air. The Sabbat was not close enough to strike, but a significant quantity of the poison whipped off the dagger and splattered over his eyes and nose.

A murderous roar erupted as the Sabbat clawed in agony at his eyes. His powerful stomping sent hairline cracks rippling through the pavement of the street.

Pulling his left arm free of the other Sabbat one more time, Vegel plunged the blade through the beast's right hand. The dagger dug into Vegel's side as well, but any poison still on the blade wouldn't harm him, and freedom was worth a small wound.

His captor shrieked in pain and quickly released Vegel, who also released the dagger so it remained lodged in the Sabbat's hand, impaling it through the palm. The foe now retreated as well in order to remove the blade painfully. As he did so, though, the poison caught up with him. It was difficult to harm vampires with poison, but the variety on the Setite's blade affected the bloodstream, which was nearly as important to a Kindred as to a mortal. He and his large comrade created a chorus of painful cries.

Vegel had been unable to maintain his balance when flung down by the Sabbat, but as he scrambled to his feet he said to the spidery twins, "Which of you is next?"

And they hesitated.

Vegel flicked a forked tongue at them and the cowards were startled enough to take a few steps back.

Amazed that the disturbance had not drawn a witness, Vegel prepared again to flee, but he was caught in the back by a wild swing from the behemoth Sabbat. Vegel was flung bodily forward and hit the street with tremendous force. He tried to push himself up, but the gymnasts were on him faster. They peppered him with solid but not significant blows that nevertheless made it difficult to recover his senses.

Then he was lifted from the ground by the half-blinded brute. The powerful Sabbat had him by the collar, but spun him around so the two of them were face to face. The skin around the monster's eyes was badly burned from the poison and one of the eyes was scalded black, but the other stared at Vegel through twisted flesh.

Grunting and groaning all the while, the beast smiled as he pressed Vegel into a bear hug. Like saplings in a storm, Vegel's ribs were crushed one by one and it was the Setite's turn to scream. The monster's strength was incredible.

Vegel felt his limbs crumpling under the pressure exerted by the powerfully muscled arms. More devastatingly, Vegel felt his precious blood streaming from every orifice. The blood that welled up into his mouth caused him to gargle and choke, in the process of which he sprayed blood in the face of his adversary.

Feeling his strength almost expired, Vegel tried a final Setite trick. Would he be fast enough to escape the two small and quick Sabbat? But it was his only hope, so those of his limbs that were not already crushed beyond recognition popped out of their joints, and he suddenly slipped from his blood-matted evening clothes like a snake shedding old skin.

Completely naked and badly mangled, Vegel slid between the brute's legs, over the unconscious figure of the long-fingered Sabbat, and with a lightning-fast burst of speed he slithered into the parking garage, under the flag gate and into the thick of several parked cars. As he shot along the ground, he used his last few ounces of blood to build hurried clots in his wounds. There was no way he could completely seal the massive wounds, but if he could just stop the blood flow for a moment then he wouldn't leave a red-smeared pathway to lead the Sabbat right to him.

Behind him, he heard the nearly blind Sabbat roar first in triumph and then in surprise as he discovered the clothes in his grasp were bodiless. The clothes were then shredded and strewn about the street.

One of the two lackeys pursued Vegel into the parking deck, but from his hiding spot curled beneath an old BMW, the Setite realized his escape had not been clearly seen. The lackeys ran in a few circles, looking here and there, but quickly returned to the street to look there too.

Various objects intervened, but from his hiding spot, Vegel could see the Sabbat in the street. The blinded Sabbat who'd nearly killed him was raging with anger. When the second of the smaller Sabbat also reported an inability to find Vegel, the larger Sabbat became livid and literally hopped with anger. To soothe his hurt, he lashed out at the bearer of bad tidings and ripped at the vampire's neck with his teeth so savagely that he practically tore its head off. The powerful Sabbat then paused for a moment to refresh himself by sucking dry his smaller victim. Then he tossed the desiccated heap to the side of the street.

In a deep voice he said to the other spidery-thin Sabbat, "Get rid of *that*, then carry Jorge back upstairs. Now!"

The other Sabbat hastened to obey, but Vegel's vision began to blur and he thought it best to put his head down for a moment....

Tuesday, 22 June 1999, 12:33 AM
The High Museum of Art
Atlanta, Georgia


Victoria put her conversation with Hesha behind her and hurried back into the gallery to check on Prince Benison and Julius. Unless something more came up, Victoria would have to let the ghouls handle the Vegel matter. She needed to concentrate her attention on Julius and Benison.

About twenty minutes had passed since she'd left to deal with the Vegel matter, and that was time enough to irritate Benison when Julius's presence was revealed. As Victoria walked past the alcove near the entrance, she saw the Brujah was still within its glass walls.

Julius was imbibing another flute of blood. He seemed relaxed, poised, and confident. Victoria imagined he always expressed those characteristics, and didn't wish to consider a situation that would lay low one such as this.

She then returned to the party so she would be on hand when the action began. The party continued pleasantly, though Victoria was a bit ruder than usual as she tried to remain free of entangling conversations, particularly one with Leopold that had the makings of too much soul-searching. Now that Julius was here, she had no time for any more such foolishness this evening.

After perhaps fifteen minutes, she returned to the cubicle of glass to check on Julius. She stifled laughter when she found him speaking to Cyndy, who was pressing herself obscenely against the large man's body. Victoria could read the Brujah's lips, and the sweet nothings and empty promises he whispered to the stupid Toreador stripper suggested to Victoria that the wily Brujah was using his powers to make a loyal friend and ally out of Cyndy. With that revelation, Victoria took back some of her disgust at Cyndy, for she surely did not possess the means to resist the powers Julius directed at her.

Some time later, Cyndy came strolling to the back of the chamber where most of the Kindred had congregated. She flashed Victoria a self-satisfied smile that made the Elder Toreador shake her head. She realized the little bitch thought she knew something Victoria did not.

Victoria watched Cyndy for a several moments more, but the saucy wench did nothing. Therefore, Victoria slipped away again. Clarice and Stella were conversing near the cubicle, so Victoria was unable to gain its interior unseen. So she walked a bit further to find a relatively secure location for her next viewing. She risked being seen, but she was on the far end of the gallery and could use the magnifying properties of the glasses. Her watch showed that it was a bit before one o'clock. She turned her opera glasses toward *Satan*, but there was no one in the alcove.

"What do you see, Victoria?" The deep voice issued from directly beside her, and Victoria jumped in surprise.

Julius practically hovered over her, looking expectantly for an answer.

Realizing how much depended on it, the Toreador recovered quickly, though, and she said, "Just looking for ways to reward myself for keeping silent about your attendance, noble archon."

"Indeed." The archon stepped away.

There was a roar from a gallery on the other side of a wall of glass. Prince Benison's voice wavered and screeched like a mute man learning speech again. "How dare he insult my hospitality?"

Julius stopped when he heard the curses that followed. He turned to face Victoria.

"I suppose neither of us is as tricky as we imagine."

Victoria agreed with that. "I'd wager, though, that both our imaginations are quite exceptional, so perhaps half as good as we think we are will be quite satisfactory."

Julius nodded grimly. "I like your style, Victoria." He took a few steps and turned once more. "Don't miss the excitement."

As Victoria hustled the opposite way so she did not arrive beside the Brujah, she noted that Julius adjusted his bandolier and did a test draw with one of his swords. Or at least she assumed he drew, for the blade was in his hand so quickly that Victoria inferred the draw only when he slowly replaced the weapon. She was quick too, but that…well, that was uncanny.

Tuesday, 22 June 1999, 1:02 AM
The High Museum of Art
Atlanta, Georgia

Leopold decided that Hannah simply wasn't going attend the party. If Stella was right earlier when she suggested there would be some representative of the Tremere clan present in the early hours of the event, then it looked like no Tremere at all would show this evening at all.

So the young Toreador decided he would leave. Just as he was mounting the steps to the door, however, he heard the Prince's exclamations. As he paused and turned to see what this new excitement was about, Leopold found himself the target of a distant Prince's gesture.

Prince Benison, with a flushed Cyndy forcibly held to his side by one great hand and one of the aproned servants clasped around the neck and pushed before him with the other hand, led a phalanx of Kindred that streamed from the rear of the gallery toward Leopold. For an instant, Leopold panicked. What could he have done?

Benison shouted, "Where is he, Toreador? Do you see the bastard up there?"

It took a moment for Leopold to realize the Prince was speaking to him and not to Cyndy.

Leopold shouted, "W-who...w-wh-what?" It was only the second time Leopold had ever addressed the Prince, and his voice cracked from the stress of doing so now.

"The motherfucking asshole Black Panther son-of-bitch Brujah archon, that's who, you miserable piece of trash!"

Leopold shriveled under the weight of the abuse, but he looked around. Before Leopold could answer, the Prince unleashed another litany of vulgarities that lasted until he drew even with the alcove where Leopold had spoken with Stella some hours earlier.

Cyndy pointed therein and said, "He was in here."

"When?" the Prince demanded, looking accusingly at both Cyndy and the servant.

Realizing he'd been forgotten, Leopold drifted down the steps and joined the crowd behind Benison. Stella quickly made her way to his side and pressed his hand into hers. It immediately calmed Leopold.

"Twenty minutes ago, Prince," gasped Cyndy.

Benison threw the Toreador and the servant to the floor. The tray the servant had so ably kept balanced while being hauled to this spot clattered to the floor as well. Champagne glasses and blood sprayed across the white tiles.

"And you?" Benison demanded of the servant.

"I served his first drink well over a half hour ago," he stammered.

"Damn it all to HELL," the Prince shouted, grossly emphasizing the last word as he stamped his foot on the floor. "Then where is he now?"

"Behind you, Prince," came a clear, deep voice.

The crowd parted and a corridor outlined by Kindred separated the Malkavian Prince and the Brujah archon.

Julius innocently asked, "Have I offended you in some way?"

Benison smiled a toothy grin. "To the contrary, archon. You've made me very happy. Elysium be damned, I will punish your insufferable attitude."

The rattle of metal rang in the large chamber as Julius drew a sword. "I guess there will be a follow-up story about those terrorists who holed up at that steel mill. Odd that terrorists would hide in a museum, don't you think, Benison?"

Benison was livid with anger, but even his bright red eyes could not light the sudden darkness that washed through the room.

Tuesday, 22 June 1999, 1:04 AM
The High Museum of Art
Atlanta, Georgia

The falling darkness blotted more than just Victoria's sight; it also strangely muffled her hearing so the cries of alarm issuing from the assembled Camarilla Kindred were oddly drawn-out and warped. Tenebrous, almost animate shrouds draped her soul in a sheath of bitterness, regret and disappointment. Her pawns were arrayed before her just as she had planned. The work of months and the ambition of decades was within her grasp, and in the dying light and sound she somehow knew her dream died as well.

Perhaps it would be reborn, for an after-image of her orchestration burned on her dulled retina like a phoenix. Julius and Benison faced one another, Julius drawing one of his swords to impale the crazed Malkavian willing to sacrifice his Elysium and his life merely because a Brujah insulted him.

Though she hadn't seen it as the scene had unfolded, in this mental replay of the scene Victoria saw Thelonious and Benjamin slipping through the crowd toward Eleanor's back. The Ventrue bitch would have been squashed if the two also chose to ignore Elysium, although she'd likely take one of them with her. Victoria expected she would choose her treacherous childe Benjamin, which meant that when the dust settled, the only candidates for Prince would be Victoria and Thelonious. And it wouldn't do for a Brujah archon to stroll into Atlanta and leave with a Brujah Prince in place, now would it?

She didn't scream, but Victoria's anger echoed

in her own mind. She had been so damn close!

The Toreador felt the darkness outside her mind press harder upon her, and her dream images slipped away. It was an almost palpable thing, and with a start she realized the probable source of the danger just as a deep and resonant voice called out. The sound was distorted, but Victoria was thinking the word too, so she understood it despite the warble of its tone.

"LA-SOooM-brA!"

She felt the inky mass of darkness begin to press its way into her orifices, and the mindless, horrific, plasmic mass did not discriminate. Despite her years and experience, despite her own great powers, Victoria panicked. She fell to the ground and rolled as if the pitch encasing and invading her were fire that could be extinguished.

But it did not relent.

However, it did slowly part.

After it did and she saw the horrors the light of the gallery revealed, Victoria prayed that the darkness might return and she be granted a quick and painless Final Death under cover of the senses-dulling cloud.

From Prince to Final Death in a heartbeat.

Even so, hers was not among the screams that sounded then, and the wails and jeers were from offender and victim alike. Victoria shivered and she felt the blood within her—and fortunately there was a lot of it, for she had drunk heavily tonight—coalesce into a heavy bolus that made her stomach seem to sag.

The darkness rippled into pieces, and amid the patchwork maze those fragments made, Victoria witnessed every bizarre malformation of nature she could imagine. Surely there were more ways the body of a Kindred could be made gruesome, but the reality of the examples before her made other possibilities unthinkable. Scabrous, burned, bloated, emaciated, twisted, rubbery, fibrous, gelatinous...and on and on the adjectives whistled through Victoria's overwhelmed mind.

"Sabbat!" Julius shouted. Victoria recognized his voice, and though there was no indication of fear in it, there was desperation.

Victoria too knew they were doomed. The grotesque monsters could only be the result of Tzimisce fleshcrafting, and the darkness was surely Lasombra-created, so the assault was indeed a joint effort by that diabolical group responsible for much of the evil and brutality among the Kindred, the Sabbat.

How and why they had gathered for such an assault was beyond Victoria's reasoning. But then, much about the chaotic Sabbat was beyond her. The "why" wasn't so mysterious, she supposed, if they had managed to organize themselves beyond the "how." However, the "why" still applied to many questions. *Why now? Why Atlanta? Why, why, why?*

Victoria shot a look at Julius. The Brujah archon still looked powerful and dangerous, but no longer unstoppable. Tendrils formed of darkness groped like living things from the oozing puddles of the Lasombra *stuff* that seeped across the floor. The monstrous Sabbat danced and whirled at the periphery of the trapped Camarilla Kindred.

One did stray too close, and Julius's sword bit into it, but the creature was so full of the terror it fed upon in lieu of blood that the blow might have given it courage, not dampened its resolve to feast upon its prey.

All the Kindred Victoria knew—Benjamin, Eleanor, Thelonious, Javic, Cyndy, Leopold and more—immediately forgot their individual plots and grievances and banded together for survival. Victoria saw the defining moment of this more important bond when Julius and Benison locked eyes, and the Brujah whipped the second sword from his back and extended it pommel first toward the Prince, who was supposedly a superior swordsman as well.

Shattering windows sounded above the cacophony of terror. Fist-sized orbs the color of flesh hurtled into the midst of the Camarilla, and as if the panic and disorientation had not been enough before, hell truly broke loose when the flesh grenades burst and spread a film of bloody ichor across the assembled host.

Then the demons pounced upon them. A big-shouldered but pinheaded monstrosity raced toward Victoria. Its arms were as shriveled as its head, so, despite the monster's size, Victoria was able to fend off the groping attacks. Then a bloated and pendulous organ that marked the beast as once having been a man rose like a third arm to club the Toreador. With such a weapon bearing down upon her, Victoria finally screamed. It struck her in the right thigh, and the force of the blow lifted her completely off the floor and deposited her in an unruly heap at the feet of the beast.

Suddenly, a sword flashed in front of Victoria and lopped the throbbing extremity from the monster. Its keening wail was so high-pitched that it sounded above the other ruckus and shattered some of the glass panes nearest Victoria. A large, taloned hand whistled over Victoria's prone body and so Julius, the Toreador's momentary benefactor, was drawn into a different fray.

The beast whose legs straddled Victoria continued its wail as blood and other juices gushed from the grievous wound. The flood of liquid did not allow Victoria to gain purchase on the floor, so she slipped and writhed about without escaping until the monster, its face still twisted in agony, recovered enough to seek revenge. Its arms and head were frail, but its torso and legs were mammoth, and when it leapt onto the prone Toreador, the great weight of its body crushed her hard to the floor.

She thought she heard her leg crack, but there was pain throughout her entire body, so there was no way she could localize any individual injury. The creature's thin arms began to beat her head and Victoria did what she could to fend off the blows, but they rained upon her so quickly the battering began to cloud and disorganize her thoughts.

So few of her powers were of any use now. In a final, desperate move, she called out for aid. Not with her voice, but her vampiric powers. And in an instant, Leopold was there. The young Toreador was not the strongest or most competent of fighters—and in her dimly lit thoughts Victoria wondered why she would call him when she might have summoned anyone—but he did the job.

A booted foot kicked at the head of the Sabbat obscenity once and twice and then, as the beast attempted to right its massive bulk with its tiny arms, a third time. The source of the crack Victoria heard this time was clearly discernible—Leopold's kick broke the fiend's slender neck. The Sabbat's body, at least temporarily denied life, slumped back onto Victoria, its weight crushing her again.

Leopold dropped to his knees beside Victoria and before saying or doing anything more he froze, looking deeply into her eyes. She was surprised, for there was no fear in the eyes, only questions.

Suddenly his eyes bulged in pain, and he was gone.

Covered as she was in slimy goo, Victoria managed to wriggle free of the wrecked heap upon her. She spared a glance only to see what had become of Leopold. A tenebrous tendril as thick as his leg was knotted about the sculptor's waist and it spun about like a bucking stallion, smashing Leopold time after time after time into the tiled floor of the museum.

Victoria felt a fleeting sense of pity, but she stood and ran. Her leg must have indeed been cracked or broken, for she immediately fell back to the floor, awash in pain. So she called upon the power of the blood within her to quickly knit that wound, and she called upon the lessons of her teachers to imbue her body with the potential for great speed. She stood and bolted without surveying the battlefield further.

The Toreador was a blur broken only by hesitations to circumvent an enemy or navigate a body-strewn wasteland in which she nearly stumbled over a black man's shattered body. It could have been either Thelonious or Benjamin.

In the space of a few heartbeats, Victoria was safely ensconced in the cubicle of glass from which she'd spied earlier. She fumbled at her pocket and withdrew the opera glasses, but she couldn't bring herself to look out. Not yet.

There was a single moment of clarity amidst the chaos of darkness, blood and ruin. It was refreshed in Leopold's mind during each split-second interval of the thunderous pounding his body sustained.

Victoria's eyes.

Left side smashed against the floor.

She had needed him.

Head battered another body, and a cry of pain issued from the other.

She had called him.

Left arm dangled by threads of flesh after he was smeared along the floor.

He knew it had been a sort of magic she used to call him. Was it magic available only to a sire? A calling that only went to a childe?

Legs jammed straight onto the floor, and both limbs buckled under the pressure and twisted in unintended directions.

He knew he had saved her. He knew he hadn't needed to respond to the call, but she had wanted him and he couldn't refuse.

Ribs crushed when a tremendous pressure constricted his chest and back.

Let not his last moment on this earth have been spent denying his mother. His love. He had saved her.

Limp body set free, floating through the air. Glass shattering, shards imbedding in his skin or spinning free. A four-story flight down toward a terrible impact on flagstones and concrete.

The Eye!

Vegel woke with a start. He'd left it behind when he slipped from his clothing. He chided himself for a fool, but then calmed, realizing he would likely be dead, truly dead, if he'd not used that trick to escape.

Damn those Nosferatu! What game were they playing? Using a Setite deliveryman to carry the Eye of Hazimel from a Camarilla party to a Sabbat ambush. Even on the surface the plan was so convoluted that only a Kindred could conceive it and probably only a Nosferatu could execute it.

As he sat silently for a moment, though, Vegel remembered the big Sabbat's last words before the Setite blacked out. He'd said to clean up the corpse and get the third Sabbat, the long-fingered one, back upstairs. Nothing about the Eye. No "search these tattered clothes for the Eye." No "the Eye is not here, so find the Setite." Nothing about the Eye.

Vegel was thoroughly confused now, but he admitted he was hardly himself. Probably delirious from lack of blood and nearly dead from his injuries, Vegel couldn't expect the best from himself right now.

The only way to learn more was to crawl back to the street and see what he could discover. And he'd better start crawling soon, for he might have escaped the Sabbat, but there was no escaping the sun. Vegel hoped he could find how to reopen that Nosferatu trapdoor. He didn't relish returning to his enemy's abode, but it was only the light-proof place within the limits of his meager strength.

There was no time like the present. Vegel crawled from the cover of the BMW toward the street. Moving caused him to take better heed of the damage he'd suffered. His rib cage was shattered. His left arm and shoulder were completely crushed. His right thigh was probably broken and the left nearly so. Countless other smaller injuries and bruises covered him, but these other wounds were the ones that would kill him unless he could very soon make it to safety.

He managed to attain the exit of the parking lot. Fortunately, there was still no one on duty. From this vantage he could clearly see the area where the struggle had taken place. His shredded clothes were still strewn about the street, and Vegel's eyes managed to focus just enough to spot the garment that was most likely his dress jacket.

The street was also clear, so Vegel inched his way toward his jacket. The drop off the curb was painful, and various puddles covered him with water and mud, but he eventually made it to the jacket.

Rolling onto his demolished left side so he could use his right hand, Vegel sorted through the fragments of the coat until he felt the silky fabric of the inside liner. He pulled that piece from the pile and found that both inside pockets were still intact. He patted the left pocket and was astounded to discover the Eye was still there.

The shock was almost enough to cause him to black out again.

He went rigid with fear when he heard something above him. It came from the second level of the parking deck—the spot from which the Sabbat had launched their ambush. Vegel couldn't make out the words, but he was certain he'd heard a deep, resonant voice like the one belonging to the brutish Sabbat.

He quickly clamped the strip of jacket containing the Eye in his mouth and crawled back toward the parking garage. His progress was tediously slow. Vegel knew his strength was ebbing.

The Setite heard more voices above him, but either they were muffled or he was too weak to hear clearly. Concentrating hard, Vegel did finally make out the words "time to go." Nothing in the tone of the voices told him he'd been spotted again, but the Sabbat were bound to see him as they left.

A few more inches and Vegel reached the curb, where he propped his head up on this concrete pillow.

He knew his choices were very limited. Die by Sabbat, or die by exposure. Even if he could reach cover, Vegel doubted he would survive until the next night, especially if his cover was the Nosferatu tunnel. And if he opted to retrieve his beeper, who knew who or what might arrive to retrieve him.

*My god,* he thought, *what Hesha would do to claim this Eye.* He only wished he knew how to summon power from it. Perhaps with its help he could survive. But that was a fruitless avenue of thinking.

Then he realized the only thing he could do. The only thing he *should* do. He would be a loyal servant to the end, and that loyalty would be rewarded with Hesha's vengeance on these Sabbat, as well as upon Rolph and his Nosferatu masters.

Vegel pulled the bloody cloth from his mouth and reached into the pocket for the Eye. The Eye began to throb again as he pulled it out. And now he was finally able to have a look at it.

It was a grotesque, black and fibrous thing. Slightly larger than an eye should be and covered with a film of perpetually moist ichor, it also appeared to be covered with a casing of skin. Apparently, the eye had its own eyelid, and the fleshy black lids would not part, at least not for Vegel's one-handed efforts.

Feeling the last vestiges of energy and life leaking from his body, Vegel did not hesitate. He set the Eye of Hazimel carefully down on the strip of jacket, and with his good right hand he gouged into his own eye socket, squeezed the fragile orb within and tore it loose. He tossed it aside and with his remaining eye watched the little mass roll away, picking up dirt and debris as it skittered across the pavement.

He then retrieved the Eye of Hazimel. He laughed, for even if the Sabbat found him now they would never find the Eye.

Rotating the Eye so the lid was oriented outward, Vegel slid it into his skull. With a soft squish it seemed to settle into place, and with a surprise that jolted his dying frame, Vegel felt *something* boring back into his head. Suddenly, he could feel the Eye, its heavy lid and reverberations of power from within.

Vegel opened his Eye, and his strength began to fade forever.

## Tuesday, 22 June 1999, 1:37 AM EST
## The bowels of the earth

His laughter shook the stone walls of the tomb, so that in his delight he caused mild tremors on the lighted surface of the world. It was no matter. No one suspected he was here. In fact, no one had reason to believe he still existed at all.

But now he was whole.

What pleasure it would give him to play childish games again....

A thousand million billion thoughts raced through Victoria's mind. She could be wrong, but she guessed herself not so much in shock as completely and utterly baffled.

She struggled to find a means to put the pieces together. Were the Nosferatu involved? Rolph had left early. The only other early departure was Vegel, but she'd seen the Setite's chauffeur when she returned to the garage with Samuel. If that was supposed to be a distraction, then why one that called attention to Vegel's absence?

Additionally, if forced to guess, she would say that Hesha was surprised by his henchman's absence too. Victoria couldn't read people nearly as well over the phone as in person, and Setites in general were slippery liars, so it was very possible that Hesha was part of the deception. If it even was Hesha that had been on the other end of that line. The Toreador knew to take nothing for granted, especially on a night when a Sabbat attack had decimated the Kindred of her city.

The questions about the Sabbat themselves were limitless, and it only confused Victoria more to give them room to whirl in her conscious thought, so she kept them pushed back.

Some of her questions clearly had no importance any longer. Did Eleanor know Victoria was responsible for the tip to Benison about the missiles? Had she told Julius? Just as with everything regarding the last two years of Victoria's life, those questions were now meaningless.

Because Victoria had no doubt that absolutely every Camarilla Kindred attending her Summer Solstice Ball had been destroyed by the Sabbat. Perhaps one or two more besides herself had escaped, but she couldn't imagine it. She'd managed to escape only because of the trapdoor she'd installed in the floor of her cubicle of glass.

After she had gained the cover of that cubicle, it had taken her a moment to overcome the shock—there had been shock then—and begin to make life-saving decisions. The trapdoor led to a maintenance area between the third and fourth floor, and the less than four-foot height meant Victoria crawled to safety.

She heard the screams and threats and war cries above her, and more than once she crawled through a puddle of blood. She imagined she heard Julius's taunts, and she stretched her fantasies to imagine him victorious, but the odds were too great. Besides, the sounds of struggle ended too quickly. Not even one with Julius's speed could vanquish so many foes so quickly. Perhaps he and Benison together, but the Toreador knew such thoughts were mere fancy.

If she doubted the totality of the Sabbat victory at that moment, then any residual hopes were quashed when she reached the parking garage. She had hoped to find her ghouls unaware of the death above them. They would throw her into her Rolls Royce and race to one of her South Georgia havens—though maybe it would be better to go north—before the dawn arrived.

But they were decapitated and gutted. The same for the driver in the limo, which she now knew to be Vegel's vehicle. Like her Rolls, the limo appeared to have a light-sealed compartment where a sleeping Kindred might hide, but Victoria didn't dare remain so close to the Sabbat horde. The wheels on the cars were all slashed, but she suspected the perpetrators would return for whatever booty these cars might hold. She couldn't imagine a band of that size staying together for longer than it took to annihilate the Camarilla, anyway. No doubt they would be fighting each other for whatever baubles might be found on their victims.

And that's where Victoria was now. Looking inside Vegel's limo for anything of use, she decided there would be one less item for the Sabbat to consider confiscating, because she took the cell phone. Her own phone was wired into the Rolls, so this portable one suited her present need. Besides, she knew the number the chauffeur dialed to reach Hesha, and she would use it if necessary. If it really *was* Hesha and he really *didn't* know why Vegel was missing, then perhaps he would help her. For a price, of course, but any price was worth her life. Well, almost any price.

Then Victoria hurried out of the parking garage to the small street behind the museum. She wanted to find a covered position that allowed a view of the top floor of the building, but satisfying her curiosity wasn't worth the risk of exposure.

The noise seemed to come from a long way off, but the echoing ding of the elevator doors sent shivers down Victoria's spine. She immediately ducked behind a low concrete wall and looked back at the extreme interior of the garage. A gang of oddly shaped shadows emerged from the recesses of the elevator.

She forced herself to remain calm. Panicking now would only bring them upon her more quickly. But when a pair of dark red eyes seemed to flash from the darkness directly toward the spot where Victoria crouched, the Toreador lost her resolve. Summoning every bit of inhuman speed she could muster, the Toreador ran for her life.

Though her powers and her blood meant she rocketed along the street at a speed unknown to the greatest human sprinters, the pursuit seemed possessed of the same uncanny prowess, and Victoria numbered the moments of her life by the steps she took.

Tuesday, 22 June 1999, 2:09 AM
A dark street
Atlanta, Georgia

His tongue lapped at a thick, viscous liquid nearly dried on some hard, rough surface.

And that was all that was important.

Time passed and that solitary act, which had his survival at its core, remained the sole element of his environment even to nudge his conscious thought.

Restlessly, relentlessly, he continued his work. On his hands and knees like a animal, he voraciously sucked, devouring even the finest dew-like film of the liquid.

He was so dehydrated that he generated no saliva to aid his tongue's grisly congress with the ground. And because the liquid was so thick, it was difficult to swallow. But he continued to nuzzle at it, grinding his nose and mouth into the narrowest cavities because he smelled more of it. Where his entire face could not reach, his filthy tongue might, and it pressed into tiny hollows where perhaps a pin's head of the liquid was trapped.

But every drop was sacred.

More than that, every drop meant his life.

Despite his best efforts, though, he could find little of the liquid. A deep-rooted instinct told him there should be more. It was a pre-Kindred instinct. Even pre-Kine. Something from his primordial past before his kind had gained balance on two legs.

He heeded that instinct and mindlessly groped about for more, his tongue pressing beneath every small object it encountered, groping for every available congealed drop.

This kept on for an indefinite period of time.

What was time when life was on the tip of the tongue?

In the end, he found little, but he found enough. The pain and need subsided. Gradually, the Beast subsided, and gradually Leopold's senses returned.

*Blood!*

It was his first thought.

It was the liquid that gave him thought at all.

Then it became clear that he was squatting on the ground near the edge of a paved road. His situation was clear, but his mind was still cloudy, his thoughts suspended in the humid porridge of the summer night in Atlanta. So he was not startled to find himself thus.

As his senses continued to clear, Leopold rocked back onto his butt and sat with the high curb bracing the small of his back. He massaged his head, and as sensation and taste returned, he violently spat and then raked his tongue with angry, impatient fingers. The sand and grit from his mouth was tinged with a touch of lightly red moisture. He shook the debris off and then absently sucked at his damp fingers.

As he recovered further, he became aware of his ridiculous behavior. He plucked a gum wrapper, with tooth-dented putty still within it, from his head. When the gum remained, he furiously tore out a chunk of his hair.

There was also a lollipop plastered to his cheek. The small purple nub of the candy was stuck to him and the short white stick dangled down. His palms were greasy with the leaked oil of an earlier car, and his elbows and knees were thick with reddish-black filth.

*Blood!*

He leapt upright and looked at the dried outline of the nearly drained puddle that had occupied him a moment ago.

He felt confused again. Vertigo claimed him and he stumbled back to the pavement.

Vertigo he did remember, because suddenly he remembered the crashing of glass and a long fall. And pain. Though he must have called upon his blood to heal the worst of his injuries, Leopold's ribs were still tender, and perhaps still broken.

He rubbed his mouth, suddenly aware that something was inside it. Something he was sucking on, rolling it smoothly about his mouth with his scratched and painful tongue to calm himself as a child absently seeks a pacifier. He assumed it was a tooth, perhaps jarred by his first, long fall and now sprung loose when he tripped. But it was too soft.

He stopped swishing it about, and looking at the ground where he had recently found himself lapping like a starving dog, Leopold gained a strange premonition about his mouthful, and he was worried to reveal the contents to himself.

But he did so. He spat quickly before conscious thought could catch him and stay his hand. The roundish object sank softly into his hand and he clutched his fingers about it. It no longer seemed solid to him, and instead felt fragile and flaccid, like an egg yolk.

He slowly uncoiled his fingers and revealed an oval item a good bit larger than a marble. It was sticky now and he realized a good deal of the grit in his mouth must have come from this before it was washed clean by his tongue.

He shivered, but still refused to admit to himself what it obviously was. The white of it puckered like gooseflesh when he pulled a finger from it, a motion he carefully repeated over and over again as he maneuvered it around in his fingers until the pupil bore a gaze upon him. An eyeball.

He flung it aside, and he nervously watched as it jumped and then skittered and then wavered to a stop, once again covered with filth as it must have been before his animalistic needs bade him claim it.

Leopold shook his head. He could well imagine the frenzy of action that must have driven him here from the High Museum. The Sabbat attack. Victoria's summoning. The shattered glass. And he recalled the resounding thud that must have been the ground punishing his body. And now the instinct that had saved his life: blood for replenishment.

Which he ignobly found on this street. But how?

He dared not turn his head to look up and down the street. Presumably up, to his right, for a slight incline rose that way, and the blood he'd consumed must have washed downhill from something.

Something? Come to think of it, the blood had seemed to invigorate him rather quickly. But he could not place the flavor. Not human, his usual game. Nor was it any domesticated pet animal. Something far tastier than any of that lot!

A sudden desire to know the delicacy on which he gorged overwhelmed him, and Leopold looked right and up the slight rise. The shadows were heavy, for the battered lamp lights battled the thick air of a growing humidity, but Leopold could make out the form of what without question was a man. Presumably a dead one.

Shattering glass.

It was not the first corpse of the night. Arrayed before his eyes, from a split-second memory of the scene he'd escaped as he plummeted forty or fifty feet from the fourth floor of the High Museum of Art, were the tattered corpses of a dozen Kindred.

What had happened!?

He looked left, where he could see the top of the High Museum. He could see no evidence of the attack within. It was probably over by now anyway.

The carnage was a jumble in his head and he knew he would have to think hard to piece together any coherent interpretation of the assault. From the many snapshots and sound-bites that whirled through his head Leopold did clearly remember a couple things, like several figures savagely dragging Prince Benison to the ground and someone shouting "Lasombra!"

If he was correctly recalling either of those events, and Lord help him if both were accurate, then it meant that Atlanta was changing hands. Maybe it was simply one of the primogen making a bid to replace Benison, but clearly everyone attending that party was meant to be killed. That he was alive was a miracle. To remain alive would require another, and the blood he'd found so easily was a delicious start.

But what of Victoria? Or Stella? He moaned and looked at the High again. Despair was evident in his face as he considered the loss of his few friends, and probably the answers to his past as well. All gone.

With the exception of Hannah, perhaps. That idea helped him refocus his thoughts on himself. Right now it didn't matter what had happened at the party. The only important thing was that he reach his haven safely. And maybe later he could venture toward the Tremere chantry.

He glanced right again. He could use more blood, and he still wondered about the source of his meal.

Leopold loped up the shallow rise. He reached the prone figure in a moment, and concluded from the quantity of spilled and dried blood that it was indeed a corpse.

It was a man, and he was naked. The figure's bare back was turned toward Leopold, and the head propped up on the curb, the legs slightly bent and tucked into the body. The corpse's left arm—the one on top—stretched away from the body, while the right was folded under its head so the right hand clutched at the face.

No wounds were evident, yet blood had clearly gushed from somewhere.

Perhaps there was nothing left to drink. Now in control of his faculties. Leopold doubted he could stomach copying his earlier feeding methods. He decided to investigate more closely. He at least had to know if it was this poor fool's eye upon which he'd sucked.

Leopold slowly circled the corpse.

Disoriented and weak though he was, and even though the corpse was bereft of the suit and tie on it earlier, Leopold recognized the dead Kindred instantly. It was the Setite, Vegel.

Leopold was a little shocked, and he wondered how the Setite had managed his escape from the attack. The Toreador's fascination was too complete to turn away, though, and he crouched to gain a better view of the dead Kindred's face. Even from a new angle, Vegel's lifeless hand shrouded his face, as if

Final Death had struck and the Setite thereafter rubbed his lids shut with a post-mortem sense of decency.

Bile was already rising in Leopold's throat. Was it Vegel's eye he had sucked?

Carefully, Leopold prepared to knock that hand away to reveal the Setite's face. When he was ready, he moved quickly and with the precise motion of a sculptor chipping off an unwanted bit of marble.

The revealed face was so terrifyingly inhuman that Leopold's legs melted from beneath him and he swooned toward the ground. The right eye was intact and strained desperately wide. The left eye was chilling, almost surreal in its obscenity. It too was blankly staring wide-eyed into the distance, but Leopold gained the unnerving impression that it was looking at him too.

The gruesome orb suddenly seemed less an eye to Leopold than a malignant, perhaps malevolent, tumor fitted with a pupil and cornea. And like a painting of an old spinster in a haunted house, the eye's baleful glare seemed to follow Leopold no matter how he repositioned himself.

Leopold shivered, but he looked at the eye more closely. Someone more superstitious than himself would have crossed themselves or whatever they thought might protect them against the evil eye.

The luminous white of the eye was crisscrossed with deep and brilliant striations of blood. It was perhaps surgically grafted to Vegel, because it protruded slightly more than an eye should and there was patchwork flesh about its edges where it seemed to overlap the flesh of the Setite's face. In any event, Leopold was certain he had not been so engrossed by his work during their earlier meeting Vegel that he had over-looked something so obvious and disgusting.

It did indeed seem something a gypsy woman might brandish to curse those who wronged her.

Perhaps the eye had been implanted in Vegel. But how could such a procedure be done so quickly? Leopold admitted to himself, though, that he didn't really have a good idea of the time. Who knew how long he'd wandered the streets between his fall from the High Museum and devouring the blood from this street?

Leopold felt little sympathy for Vegel. Perhaps if the Kindred had shown a bit more interest in his work…Besides, he expected to hear news of many other deaths, and the loss of this Setite would weigh little on his mind.

Then the Toreador went slackjawed. *That* was why the blood tasted so different, so rejuvenating: it was Kindred blood! Leopold knew stories of what some others of his kind called Diablerie—Kindred feeding on Kindred—but he'd not understood the temptation. Now he did. Even the sweetest of blood from the juiciest mortal would not compare to the smooth liquor from this cold-blooded Kindred.

Of course, Leopold had also heard that Diablerists had another motivation as well: power. To devour the blood—*to the last drop!*—of a Kindred of an earlier generation meant moving closer to Caine yourself. Evidently something of the power of the blood was retained, absorbed by the tissues of the body perhaps, even if the liquid was later lost or expended.

This idea gave Leopold pause. It also encouraged him to a turn a more critical eye to the dead Setite.

Dead or alive, Vegel held no favor in Leopold's

eye, but the corpse of the Kindred now enlivened the artist's eye within the Toreador. The pale yellow of the lamplight obliquely struck the Setite's body and created ribbons of shadow that highlighted and accentuated what was after all a rather fine and muscular figure.

What was it he had been trying to tell Vegel as the Setite turned away from him for more important business? Leopold remembered his words. *These harder substances still don't respond well for me. Perhaps I should try something more malleable…*

*Like wood*, he'd added.

*Or flesh*, Leopold mused now.

At that moment, Vegel ceased to be a once-living, or even unliving, being in Leopold's thoughts, and the Toreador instead viewed the corpse as the spectacular sculpture it could be. Limbs splayed but powerful-looking. A pool of blood but no heinous wounds. An expression that stared at and through the viewer. And that eye as a centerpiece. What a remarkable work it could be!

Leopold glanced furtively about, suddenly worried that someone might be noting how much time he spent with a corpse. But more than that, he realized that he coveted this eye. If it had been planted within Vegel's skull, then it could be removed as well. It would serve as his Muse, the centerpiece of some great work. And Leopold knew with a chilling clarity that such a work would be a masterpiece, something so much more than the technical achievements of his past.

With a savage determination born partially of fear and partially of greed, Leopold attacked the Setite's head, shivering as he plunged two fingers of each hand deep along the sides of the hideous eye-ball.

The texture of the eye was at once revolting and fascinating. Spongy, yet somehow inelastic, the eye ultimately delighted his sculptor's sense.

Extraction was surprisingly easy. Granted, the Toreador had never gouged out an eye before, but he'd expected some variety of fibrous or at least fleshy cord to connect the back of the eye to the brain or somewhere. But there was none. It slid out like a quick-growing weed that has had no time to gain purchase below the ground. Indeed, the few slender bluish veins that trailed from the back of the eye did branch like fragile roots.

It was done so quickly that Leopold was surprised to find himself still crouching, but now with the oversized orb nearly filling his palm. As he rolled it over in his hand, fleshy lids began to close over the eye's pupil. Leopold was startled, and he watched in fascination as first the deeply bloodshot perimeter of the eyeball was covered, and then, gradually but methodically, the lighter, almost apricot color around the dark pupil was extinguished as well.

Leopold was distracted by a slender rivulet of blood that welled within the shallow depression and promptly flowed from the Setite's now vacant left eye socket. The Toreador peered briefly into the recesses of the shadowed hollow, but could see nothing other than darkness and the blackness of blood softly welling within.

And without another thought, Leopold crouched close to the Setite's skull and his tongue probed the eye socket. The thick liquid was pure, unblemished by the dirt and trash of the street. It was a sweet treat to Leopold and he worked his tongue deep, lapping at the scraps of flesh in the rear of the socket.

Once the depression was dry, Leopold sat and licked his lips. Then he ran his coarse and abused tongue across his prodigious canines. He still needed blood!

Desperately, Leopold folded himself around Vegel like an airless parachute and promptly sank his teeth into the Kindred's pale neck. A trickle of blood eventually grew to a pool that oozed into his mouth, and the Toreador drank a deep draught of the ambrosia.

Leopold closed his eyes and let the silken elixir drain through his lips and down his throat. When the supply grew meager, he applied some suction, and eventually he found himself inhaling with tremendous force for the benefit of mere drops. But these drops were the most exhilarating of all. Each one set his mouth ablaze.

Finally, Vegel was so completely drained that his body lost all density and collapsed under its own weight. The beautifully poised sculpture drooped into a jumble of spare body parts that intersected at impossible angles.

Only then did Leopold back away, his tongue stretching to inconceivable lengths to catch the drops that lingered on his lips or that slid toward his chin. He gazed at the collapsed and desiccated Setite and could not dispute the tingling sensation of confidence and energy that radiated throughout his body.

He knew it was true. Much of what he had heard about Diablerie must be true. He had no doubt that Vegel belonged—had belonged—to an earlier generation, and now he, Leopold, had absorbed some of that might for himself.

That plus the palpable sensation of power that emanated from the eye he grasped. The Toreador knew he had been near death earlier that night, but now he felt reborn. Potently reborn. He yearned to direct this newfound prowess onto his art. Yet at the same time he felt deep within that a greater destiny awaited him. Yes, some miraculous masterpiece was on the fringes of his consciousness. With the depths of resolve and creativity he knew he could apply toward that still unknown endeavor, Leopold did not doubt that he would change the world.

**Tuesday, 22 June 1999, 3:12 AM**
**Manhattan, New York City**

There was no single voice. Or single purpose. Or even single sentience. Instead, an amalgamation of impulses, needs, instincts.

Of course, one being's instinct was another's careless assumption. Animals have mysterious means of finding water. Men merely turn their faucets. Kindred merely find men.

However, the assumptions made now were not careless ones. Instead, they were infinitely complex. So intertwined that conscious thought was too weak to separate the strands.

It took something greater, and the collective of impulses, needs and instincts was far greater indeed. It was also a dark intelligence that could only be deemed malevolent, if indeed there was anything in existence that could gauge such an unknown.

Its response was precise and sufficient, put into motion as casually as a sleeper swats a mosquito. Then slumber resumed.

But the tiniest stone cast into water spreads ripples.

A half-dozen workers were preparing to reopen subway tunnel 147, when hundreds of swarming rats flooded into the tunnel and left nothing of the workers but picked-clean bones.

# About the author

Stewart Wieck is the co-creator of the **World of Darkness**, designer of the original **Mage: The Ascension** Storytelling Game, and co-plotter of the Clan Novel series. Writing as Stewart von Allmen, he is also the author of the award-nominated **Saint Vitus Dances Eternity: A Sarajevo Ghost Story** (1996) and **Conspicuous Consumption** (1995).

# The Vampire Clan Novel Series .......................

**Clan Novel: Toreador**
These artists are the most sophisticated of the Kindred.

**Clan Novel: Tzimisce**
Fleshcrafters, experts of the arcane, and the most cruel of Sabbat vampires.

**Clan Novel: Gangrel**
Feral shapeshifters distanced from the society of the Kindred.

**Clan Novel: Setite**
The much-loathed serpentine masters of moral and spiritual corruption.

**Clan Novel: Ventrue**
The most political of vampires, they lead the Camarilla.

**Clan Novel: Lasombra**
The leaders of the Sabbat and the most Machiavellian of all Kindred.

**Clan Novel: Ravnos**
These devilish gypsies are not welcomed by the Camarilla, nor tolerated by the Sabbat.

**Clan Novel: Assamite**
The most feared clan, for they are assassins of both vampires and mortals.

**Clan Novel: Malkavian**
Thought insane by other Kindred, they know that within madness lies wisdom.

**Clan Novel: Brujah**
Street-punks and rebels, they are aggressive and vengeful in defense of their beliefs.

**Clan Novel: Giovanni**
Still a respected part of the mortal world, this mercantile clan is also home to necromancers.

**Clan Novel: Tremere**
The most magical of the clans and the most tightly organized.

**Clan Novel: Nosferatu**
Horrific to behold, these sneaks know more secrets than the other clans—secrets that will only be revealed in this, the last of the **Vampire Clan Novels**.

# ............................continues.

**Clan Novel: Toreador** is a tale that's been told, but don't expect this is the last you've seen of either Leopold or Victoria. Their story, as well as those of other important characters in the **World of Darkness**, continues in twelve more Clan Novels.

Astute readers of this series will begin to put clues together as the series progresses, but everyone will note that the end date of each book is later than the end date of the prior book. In such a fashion, the series chronologically continues in **Clan Novel: Tzimisce** and then **Clan Novel: Gangrel**. Excerpts of these two exciting novels are on the following pages. And even after those two novels, the story is only one-fifth told. Layer upon layer…

CLAN NOVEL: TZIMISCE
ISBN 1-56504-802-4
WW# 11101
$5.99 U.S.

CLAN NOVEL: GANGREL
ISBN 1-56504-803-2
WW# 11102
$5.99 U.S.

Three sharp knocks. At the sound, Sascha Vykos checked her pacing and looked up with more than a slight hint of annoyance. She carefully refolded the letter. It vanished into an inside pocket of the immaculate Chanel suit.

The door opened just far enough to allow Ravenna to slip through. He did not shut the door behind him, but put his back against it, as if to keep it from opening farther.

"I am sorry, Vykos. There is a...*gentleman* here who insists he must see you without delay." The ghoul managed to maintain just the proper tone of distaste, but his anxiety was obvious.

Vykos smiled at his discomfort. "And what is this gentleman's name?"

A look close to terror flitted across the ghoul's carefully controlled features. "My lady! I did not...one does not... What I mean to say is..."

It was apparent Vykos was not going to help him out of his predicament. Ravenna's voice fell to a conspiratorial whisper.

"He is an Assa..."

There was a sharp crack and Ravenna fell to the floor.

"*Assassin* is such an uncouth word," said the visitor, stepping over the inert body of the ghoul. "A thousand blessings upon you and your house. You may account this the first."

Vykos held her ground and studied the stranger.

His motions were like dripping honey—fluid, tantalizing. His form was almost entirely concealed in a draping robe of unbleached linen. *An unusual garment for an "assassin,"* Vykos thought.

She had come to think that there must be some sort of unspoken dress code among these hired predators. All seemed to favor close-fitting garments that would not interfere with the necessities of combat or flight. But she had already mentally run through four or five ways her visitor's flowing garment might be turned to his disadvantage, should it come to close fighting. It was quite likely, however, that those folds concealed a number of lethal ranged weapons which might render such speculation moot.

It was also her understanding that dressing entirely in black was something of a badge of office among practitioners of this second-oldest profession. Her visitor's garment would shine even in dim moonlight, frustrating all efforts at stealth. Surely not even an amateur would make such a mistake. No, it stood to reason that her guest was utterly unconcerned with concealing his approach. His words, his actions, even his dress spoke of a healthy confidence in his own prowess. Vykos found this slightly irritating.

"Was that strictly necessary?" Vykos's tone betrayed only a businesslike displeasure—enough to make clear that she would not account the ghoul's death a service rendered.

Her guest turned up the palms of his hands and bowed his head slightly. His hands were long and delicate—the hands of a pianist, an artist, a surgeon. Their languid grace spoke of a barely suppressed energy. They fluttered gently like the wings of a delicate bird.

by eric griffin

Vykos's eyes never left those hands.

"You might at least return him to the front room so that we might not have to look at him as we talk," Vykos continued. "I find it hard to believe that you are always so casual about disposal of bodies and the like. And bring in another chair as you come. My servants have hardly had a chance to unpack yet."

An ice-white smile stole across the visitor's chiseled ebony features. "I am not in the habit of concealing my handiwork. Unless, of course, you count the removal of witnesses. And you need not concern yourself for my comfort. I will stand. We are quite alone? You spoke of servants."

"Yes, we are *now*. I have, of course, sent my most valued associates away for the evening. Some of my guests have a reputation for being somewhat…excitable."

The stranger's voice became low and menacing. "And you do not fear for your safety? There are many in this city who would see you come to harm."

"Tonight, I am the safest person in all of Atlanta." Vykos purposefully turned her back to him and crossed to the cluttered desk. "Your masters are not so careless as to dispatch an agent to kill me when we still have unfulfilled business. Very unprofessional. Nor could they allow me to come to harm from a third party when suspicion would be sure to fall squarely upon themselves."

Vykos turned upon him and pressed on before he could interrupt. "No, I do not fear you, although you bring death into my house. Tonight, you are my guardian angel, my knight-protector. You will fight and even die to prevent me from coming to harm before you can conclude our business. Is it not so?"

"Tonight," again the Assamite flashed a predatory smile, "I am your insurance policy. But for tonight only, Lady."

From beneath his robes, he produced a burlap sack. With a sweep of his free arm, he cleared the clutter from the center of the desk and deposited his parcel with a thud.

*Dramatic bastards*, thought Vykos. But there was no choice but to play along at this point. She couldn't very well bring this business to completion otherwise. With a sigh of resignation, she opened the sack.

She recognized the familiar features immediately, from the reconnaissance photos. It was Hannah, the Tremere chantry leader. More precisely, it was her head.

Hannah's hands had also been severed and were folded neatly beneath her chin. *Nice touch*, Vykos thought. Just the right blend of superstition and tradition. She was well aware that the Assamites' hatred of the warlocks was as ancient as that of her own clan.

Of course, she did not give him the satisfaction of expressing that admiration aloud.

"She's dead, all right."

The Assamite tried his best not to look crestfallen.

Before he could respond however, she continued, with perhaps a hint of malice, "Are you certain it's her?"

His pride pricked, he seemed about to make a retort. Then he checked visibly and composed himself. "Ah, now I see you are having a small jest at my expense. Surely you are more than casually acquainted with…the deceased." The Assamite's tone was soft and formal, like that of a funeral director—couching an indelicate concept in the gentlest terms possible.

"I have never seen her before," Vykos answered coolly, pronouncing each word separately and distinctly. "And if I understand you correctly, I did not even arrive in this country until after her death."

"Have no concern on that account. All has been carried out in exactly the manner you have specified. As to the matter of the witch's identity, there can be no doubt. If you will allow me…"

The Assamite absently knotted a fist in the hair of the severed head to steady it as he slid one of the lily-white hands from beneath its chin. He turned it over, palm up on the desk.

"The witch's magic is still in her hands. The knife cannot sever it, the scythe cannot gather it in." He recited the words with reverence, as if quoting some ancient scripture.

He caressed the hand gently, like a lover.

Under his touch, the network of delicate lines that crisscrossed the palm darkened, deepened. As he continued to brush the hand with his fingertips, the lines seemed to writhe and then curl up at the edges as if shrinking back from a flame. As Vykos watched, the snaking lines knotted themselves into a series of complex and subtly unsettling sigils. The Assamite drew back with a satisfied smile. The glyphs continued to twist and to slide gratingly across one another. "Do you know these signs?"

Vykos said nothing, but her eyes never left the dance of arcane symbols.

"It is not given to me to interpret the sigils," the Assamite continued. "But an adept could give them each their proper names. Each sign is a unique magical signature—a lingering reminder of some foul enchantment that occupied the witch's final days. Do you have need of such knowledge?"

Still staring at the hand, Vykos shook her head slowly. Then, as if coming back from a great distance, she replied, "No. No, it doesn't matter now. With Hannah dead, the entire chantry will be…"

She changed gears suddenly, without pause. "But where are my manners? I must not bore you with details of such trifling and personal difficulties. Really, you are much too indulgent of me. Now, what were you telling me about indisputable proof of Hannah's identity?"

With a slight upward curl of his hand, the Assamite gestured towards the sigils.

"A fascinating exercise," Vykos countered, "and let us assume for the moment that I believe unquestioningly your account of what I have just seen." She held up a hand to forestall any protestations.

"But this still tells me only that the hand belonged to a Tremere witch. It does not tell me that it belonged specifically to Hannah.

"Appearances," Vykos intoned, "can be fatally deceiving."

She sat down at the desk. As she spoke, her hands absently brushed aside a few wayward strands of Hannah's hair that had drifted down over the pallid face. She ran both of her hands slowly downward, stroking the unresponsive flesh of cheek and throat.

When she again addressed her guest, her gaze never lifted from the death mask before her. "I have seen her, of course, but only in photographs." Her fingertips came together at the nape of the neck. "Do you think her beautiful?"

The question seemed to take her guest by surprise. He snorted dismissively before regaining his composure. "Lady, these considerations, they have no place in my work."

Vykos smiled. Her thumbs swung up, tenderly smoothing closed the eyelids.

"No, of course not." Her voice was soft, her eyes lowered. Her thumbs lingered upon Hannah's sealed eyes, pressing slightly as if to ensure they did not flutter open again. "But I was not asking a professional opinion. You surely had ample opportunity to see her, to study her. Would you say that she was beautiful?"

The assassin wheeled away from her and muttered a few syllables in a harsh and foreign tongue. "You will, perhaps, forgive me if I say that you are the most exasperating of clients. Of course I observed the movements of the witch. How could I not do so? There is room for neither error, nor hesitation, nor mercy when dealing with her kind. She is there before you now. Judge for yourself whether she is beautiful!"

Vykos, apparently unmoved by his outburst, regarded the unmoving face before her with a critical eye. After some deliberation, she opened a desk drawer, extracted a silver hairbrush, and began to brush Hannah's long hair.

"Yes, but you saw her in the full flush of the blood—when she was yet 'alive'—when there was still movement and gesture, expression, emotion. These are the things that the photographs—and this little keepsake—cannot tell me."

He paced the room briskly and was a long while

before answering. "Yes, I saw the witch living. I was, as you well know, the last person who might make such a claim." His gaze fixed on some imaginary point in the middle distance as if seeing, not for the first time, people and things that were no more.

"I felt the arch of her back as my hand closed around her waist. I saw the delicate throb in the line of her throat as the flowing hair pulled taut. I saw the lips part to form words of power that they would never complete. Yes, she was as beautiful in dying as she is in death."

Vykos smiled and continued her brushing, counting softly under her breath.

Her guest stirred uncomfortably but did not resume his pacing.

An uneasy silence ensued, filled only by the regular stroke of the brush. As if suddenly struck by a thought, Vykos looked up and fixed her gaze upon him. From beneath half-closed lids, she asked, "What, then, shall I call you, my sentimental assassin? You have not yet told me your name."

He cocked his head to one side and regarded her for a moment as if to determine whether she really expected an answer or if she were simply goading him further. There was a peculiar undertone to her question. Something subvocal, almost feline, certainly dangerous. It belied the innocent allure of her gaze. Without volition, he slipped into a more defensive stance.

"Nor am I likely to. You may call me Parmenides."

"Ah, a philosopher then. I had nearly mistaken you for a poet." She continued to muse aloud. "You do not appear to be a Greek and you surely are not so wizened as to have walked among the luminaries of the School of Athens. You are then something of a classicist, a scholar…a romantic."

He almost visibly shrank from this last epithet and began to protest.

"No. Say nothing more of it. The conclusion follows inevitably from the premises. But have no fear, your secret shall remain safe with me." She picked up her brush and resumed her task, apparently forgetting him entirely.

He stared at her in open disbelief, but she seemed completely absorbed. Under her unrelenting brush, Hannah's long hair came away in great tangled clumps. Soon the surface of the desk was covered, but still she did not pause.

"My lady, I believe we yet have business to discuss."

Vykos still did not look up from her labor. The brush began to scrape gratingly across the exposed stretches of scalp now visible through the remaining patches of hair. The sound seemed to play directly upon the nerves without first traversing the intermediary of the ear.

The flesh began to blacken and bruise. After a long while, Vykos said absently, "You were endeavoring to prove that this is, indeed, Hannah, the Tremere witch and the leader of the Atlanta chantry. The more I subject this specimen to scrutiny, however, the less resemblance I see between the two."

She set down her brush and pushed her chair back to study the results of her efforts. She nodded, satisfied.

"There is a certain…luster missing." Vykos pinched the cheeks gently as if to bring up the color in them, but seemed disappointed at the result. "A certain defiance no longer apparent in this delicate line of jaw." She illustrated with a slow caress of the index finger.

"And the eyes. Even in the photographs one could see that the witch's eyes were set deep—as if shrinking from the things she had witnessed in the dark hours. These eyes bulge noticeably, and without any of the fire that is the legacy of the Tremere's deviltry."

Vykos ground her thumbs into the sockets as if to set things aright. Parmenides made a noise of disapproval or disgust and turned away. "Enough. You know these signs for what they are, my Lady. They are the marks of the grave, of the Final Death, nothing more. If you continue along these lines, however, you will certainly mar the remains beyond all recognition."

Vykos pushed back her chair and stood. Her voice was conciliatory. "Now you have gotten your feelings hurt again. Come here my young romantic, my *philosophe*. If you tell me that this is the witch, I will accept your pledge." There was a scraping noise as she rotated the head on the desk to face him.

"Look upon her. Do you not find her beautiful?"

Almost against his will, he looked. The flowing auburn hair was gone entirely. The flesh of face and scalp was darkened to a uniform blackness. The line of jaw was set proudly, powerful and masculine. The cheeks had lost their feminine roundness and drawn taut so that a hint of the skull was discernable beneath. The eyes had become wary—small, dark, recessed.

None of these individual changes, however, made the slightest impression upon the stunned

Parmenides. He had fallen victim, instantly and completely, to the sum of these alarming alterations. The face that stared back at him was unmistakably his own.

Vykos's voice, when it broke in upon him, came from directly behind him and very close. He could feel her breath upon his neck and ear. "…The reason I do not place my trust in photographs. Images may be altered."

He felt her lips upon his throat, and let his eyes fall closed.

by eric griffin

Ramona perched on the top rail of the fire escape and watched Zhavon sleeping peacefully. The first nights after the attack, the girl had tossed and called out, trying to escape whatever hoodlums haunted her dreams.

*There's worse out there*, Ramona silently warned her.

From several blocks away, car tires screeched. Ramona cringed and waited for the crash, which never came. Almost as a second thought, she glanced back and made sure that the noise hadn't awakened Zhavon. The girl still slept quietly. Over the past few weeks of watching, Ramona had developed an uncanny sense of when the sleeper would awake—the slight turn of the head and stretching of the neck just before the telltale fluttering eyes. Ramona was sure that, aside from the night of the attack, Zhavon had never seen her, and even that night was easily explained away as hysteria or trauma. Even so, there were times when Zhavon was awake, times when Ramona knew beyond a doubt that she was out of sight, that the dark-skinned girl seemed to know that someone—or something—was watching her.

*I remember that feeling*, Ramona thought.

She was distracted for a moment by the sound of movement from the shadows below, but there was nothing there.

*You're jumpy tonight, girl.* Probably because of that biker last night, she decided—the thought of which reminded her that she shouldn't leave Jen alone so much. Darnell didn't spend any more time with her than he had to, and what if the biker did come back?

But Ramona's gaze drifted back to the sleeping Zhavon. Ramona understood Jen's fears, and even shared a few, but, with Zhavon, a strange affinity ran more deeply. The mortal girl looked so peaceful lying there beneath the sheet. When she was awake, however, she possessed a certain defiance, a naïveté coupled with a wrong-headed sense of invulnerability.

*I remember that feeling too*, thought Ramona. She had once felt almost exactly that way. Now she knew better. She knew better than to think everything would turn out all right. She knew better than to expect nothing too bad to happen to her. Zhavon, though, continued sleeping, oblivious to the worst fears the night had to offer.

After a few minutes, Ramona realized that she'd been staring at the mortal—and that's what normal people passed for these days: mortal, meat, blood. Above the line of the white sheet, Zhavon's hand rested limply on her chest, and above her hand was her bare neck. Ramona imagined that she could see the pulse of the jugular—or could she really? The surrounding sounds of the city faded away beneath the thump-thump, thump-thump of a single human heart, beneath the intermittent swish of blood forced through arteries and veins.

Ramona was halfway through the window—licking her lips—before she caught herself. She retreated back to the fire escape and shook her head forcefully.

"Damn, I *hate* that!" Ramona growled under her breath as she sat and hugged her knees to her chest.

by gherbod fleming

Losing control like that, even momentarily, brought memories of the change flooding back, of the first night she'd tasted blood at her lips and lost herself to the undeniable hunger.

Sitting there, Ramona wanted to look over the window sill at Zhavon, but was afraid to let herself.

*What if it happens again? What if I can't stop? Why'd I even bother to save her?* Ramona wondered, though she knew that ripping those two men apart had been less an act of heroism, and more the predatory impulse of a hunter whose prey was being stolen away.

*Hell, if those bastards hadn't stepped in the way*, she fully realized for the first time, *I might've killed Zhavon myself.*

The instinct for the hunt had taken over, as it had so many times. Who was to say when it would happen again? Ramona knew better than to think it wouldn't. For all her newly found powers, it was another way she was helpless.

Angry with herself and seeking distraction, Ramona pointedly did not look at Zhavon, but instead tugged at her own shoes. They'd been bothering her for some time, and she was in no mood, at the moment, to take crap from inanimate objects. She yanked at the tongues of her leather sneakers as if they were the source of all her problems, and when she pulled her feet free, the cause of her physical discomfort was readily apparent.

The shoes were fine. But Ramona stared in horror at her feet. From the heel to the ball of each foot was mashed together and only about half as long as it should've been. Her gnarled toes, however, were abnormally elongated. They stretched almost like tiny fingers, tipped with thick, curved nails.

*Claws*, Ramona thought, aghast.

She'd watched before as her fingers transformed into razor-sharp claws, but that had only happened when she'd been angry or upset, and it hadn't lasted long. She continued to stare at what couldn't be her feet and waited for the illusion to fade, or, at the worst, for them to change back.

But they *were* her feet, and they didn't change to suit her.

*Oh my God.*

Ramona tentatively reached out and was actually surprised that she felt the sensation in her foot of her own fingertips brushing across wrinkled and twisted skin.

"You gave in to the Beast," said a voice from below.

Ramona jumped to her deformed feet. A level below her on the fire escape stood, not the Puerto Rican man from the downstairs apartment she'd expected to see, but instead, a complete stranger.

The hair on the back of her neck shot up straight.

The stranger neither retreated nor advanced. He stood there with a blank, unfriendly expression. Dark sunglasses and his long, tangled hair partially obscured his face. The shades of the torn, wrinkled clothes he wore blended almost perfectly into the night-time cityscape.

Ramona's initial shock quickly gave way to a low growl that rose up from her gut, but the stranger raised a finger to his lips. "Shh." He nodded toward Zhavon's window.

He was right, Ramona knew. She didn't want to risk waking Zhavon. Even so, Ramona bristled. Who was he to tell her what to do? She swallowed the growl, but her anger demanded an outlet, and before realizing that she was going to, she leapt down the steps at the stranger.

He seemed less surprised by her actions than she did. With one fluid motion, he placed a hand on the top rail and vaulted off the fire escape.

As Ramona's knees uncoiled from the impact of her landing, she sprang after him without the slightest pause. Her shift in momentum carried her over the rail, and she landed crouched and ready to attack in the alley only feet away from the stranger.

"Hold still, you bastard," she growled, now that she was safely away from the window.

The stranger cocked his head as if he heard a distant sound and then gazed up toward Zhavon's window. "Who will you leave unwatched?" he asked.

The question froze Ramona. *He knows about her*, she thought with alarm, and in the instant she followed his gaze to the window, he was gone. Ramona stood alone in the deserted alley.

The stranger was gone, but his scent lingered— a faint yet distinctive smell that Ramona had noticed other times, but never before had she been able to connect the odor to its source. At once, she began in the direction her nose told her the stranger had gone, but she stopped after only a few steps.

*Who will you leave unwatched?* His words of just moments before came back to her.

She glanced again up at the window. Was there a threat to Zhavon?

*Who will you leave unwatched?*

He obviously knew about the girl, although not even Ramona understood what drew her here almost every night. *The smell*. Ramona forced herself to think. Her instincts had swung instantly from aggression toward the stranger to protectiveness of Zhavon, but Ramona needed to think. She'd noticed the smell last night at the garage. Did that mean he also knew about Jen and Darnell and their resting place?

*I'll be back,* the biker had said—like a bad rerun of a Schwarzenegger flick. Was this stranger part of the Sabbat as well?

Ramona glanced up at the window again.

*Or is he luring me away so he can come back?* she wondered.

Like so many nights over the past few weeks, she found herself torn between staying and watching over the sleeping mortal, and going to those of her own kind. Without consciously resolving the dilemma, Ramona found herself following the scent, and though it soon faded away to nothing, the first steps had set her on a path to the George Washington Bridge.

After half a mile, Ramona realized that she'd left her shoes behind on the fire escape, but she had dithered long enough. Besides, her malformed feet moved easily over the pavement. Neither gravel nor broken glass pained her tough, leathery soles, and the rhythmic tap of claws on asphalt lulled her into a loping trance.

*Who will you leave unwatched?*

The blocks and miles fell away behind her until she was crossing the bridge, passing a car that swerved away from the shadow flashing, only for an instant, through the driver's peripheral vision. Then the bridge, too, was receding in the distance. Ramona passed the spot where she'd faced the biker the night before. She pressed onward frantically, urged ahead

by gherbod fleming

by the great dread building within her. What if she was too late reaching her friends? What if she'd made the wrong decision, and something terrible happened to Zhavon?

As the garage came into view, Ramona felt, not relief, but an instant of inexplicable terror. All seemed dark and quiet from without.

*Normal quiet or too quiet?*

The question had scarcely flashed through her mind before she was at the door. She ripped it open. The chain on the handle shattered as the links were met with force they couldn't resist. The clinking of the chain fragments scattering across the parking lot was lost in the explosion of the metal door slamming open against the aluminum wall of the building. Ramona charged in, ready to attack.

Darnell jumped up from where he'd sat and spun to face her. Ramona caught only a brief glimpse of Jen as she scuttled down into the nearest pit.

"Mother…!" Darnell started to yell, but his curse trailed off as recognition slowly replaced shock on his face. "What the *hell* you doin'?"

Ramona quickly scanned the darkened interior of the building. "Has he been here?" she blurted out.

"What…? Who?" Darnell, already angry and more than a little embarrassed at having been caught off-guard, was not calmed by Ramona's near-frantic manner.

*The biker*, she started to say but then realized that wasn't who she was most worried about. *The stranger.* "Anyone."

"Nobody but your crazy ass breakin' down the damn door!" Darnell said.

A light flickered to life in the pit where Jen had